BIRTHRIGHT

Visit us at www.boldstrokesbooks.com

By the Author

All Things Rise

The Time Before Now

The Ground Beneath

Whiskey Sunrise

Valley of Fire

Birthright

The Adventures of Nash Wiley

Death By Cocktail Straw

One More Reason To Leave Orlando

Smothered and Covered

Privacy Glass

Writing as Paige Braddock:

Jane's World The Case of the Mail Order Bride

BIRTHRIGHT

by
Missouri Vaun

2017

BIRTHRIGHT

ISBN 13: 978-1-62639-485-8

THIS TRADE PAPERBACK ORIGINAL IS PUBLISHED BY
BOLD STROKES BOOKS, INC.
P.O. BOX 249
VALLEY FALLS, NY 12185

FIRST EDITION: FEBRUARY 2017

CREDITS
EDITOR: CINDY CRESAP
PRODUCTION DESIGN: SUSAN RAMUNDO
ILLUSTRATION BY PAIGE BRADDOCK
COVER DESIGN BY SHERI (GRAPHICARTIST2020@HOTMAIL.COM)

Acknowledgments

Birthright was a story that I originally imagined back in 1994. A list of names, places, sketches of the main characters, and mythology of their world sat in a "suitcase of ideas" for years. Finally, Aiden gets to share her story with you.

I don't read a lot of fantasy books, so that wasn't the origin for this tale. This story idea came from, oddly, a history of Christianity class I was taking at the time at Emory University. I couldn't help wondering what faith practice was in place in northern Europe before the Romans took over and rewrote the religion of the druids. Even though that's where the idea germinated, *Birthright* is not a story of religion. The characters in this story took it in a different direction although elements of faith present themselves throughout Aiden's journey.

This is my sixth novel even though it was the first story I wanted to write. I'm glad I waited because I've learned so much from my editor, Cindy. And this narrative is better for it. Thanks also to Radclyffe, Sandy, Sheri, and Ruth for all of your continued support.

A special thank you to Jenny, who pushed me to expand the "faith" content in the book and also to create a map of the four kingdoms.

D. Jackson Leigh, I don't ever want to publish a book that you don't read first. You're the best.

Alena, thank you for talking through scenes while the book was in progress and reading rough bits of it along the way. I really appreciate all the notes from you and from Vanessa.

Aiden is a character I've wanted to write for a long time. *Birthright* is a story I've wanted to tell for a long time. I hope you enjoy reading it as much as I did writing it.

Dedication

For Evelyn

CHAPTER ONE

A iden looked down at the swirled patterns of dust on her boots. The scuffed toes of the soft brown leather pierced the edge of light cast on the ground from the pub's entryway. A battered wooden sign squeaked on metal hooks above her head as it swung back and forth in the ocean breeze. *The Thirsty Boar* was painted on the sign in faded letters. Laughter, singing, and a discordance of other noise spilled out the open door of the pub into the cool damp night air.

A fat orange striped cat, perched on a wide windowsill, watched Aiden with a bored expression.

As Aiden weighed whether to enter the pub, two thick-waisted men tumbled through the opening, leaning heavily on one another. She stepped aside before they caught her up in their stumbling exit.

Aiden's hunger won the brief internal argument, and she stepped inside. Aiden scanned the room for a moment from the door. A plump maiden slapped the hand of a groping fellow as she passed by his table, but then quickly fell into his arms laughing. A chair fell backward with a loud bang, knocking its occupant to the floor. Two of his chums helped him back to his feet.

The noise, the patrons, the scene of general debauchery was in stark contrast to anywhere she'd ever been. Different was good.

Aiden hadn't set huge goals for herself when she left the monastery, except to get away and wait for fate to guide her. She figured she'd start with small objectives, work on attaining one and then another until they rippled out from one another like a stone dropped into a pond. She'd start small, a pint of ale and a hot meal.

Rough wooden tables and benches filled the room. Each one packed with men and women eating, drinking ale, and celebrating. Celebrating what? Life? Aiden tried to study the room without staring. She wasn't sure her curiosity would be welcomed.

She tried to seem nonchalant as she passed through the crowd toward a bar with stools at the far end of the large open space. Only two seats were unoccupied. Aiden settled herself on one of the stools and checked out those seated closest to her.

On her right, a man and a woman with their heads pressed together spoke in hushed tones. To her left stood two men with broadswords at their belts. They were obviously men-at-arms; maybe they were charged with guarding the harbor of Eveshom. One of them nodded a greeting, and Aiden mimicked him, nodding back. He'd probably noticed the sword at her belt and assumed some kinship of a common trade.

"What can I get you?" A barmaid wiped ineffectively at the well-aged boards in front of Aiden, boards worn smooth from a thousand hands.

"Can I get some food and ale?"

The young woman nodded and disappeared. Aiden had only just arrived in this port city; the trek on foot from the monastery had taken two full days. She looked down at her clothing and began to compare herself to others in the room. She was dressed in trousers and boots that rose almost to her knees. Her loose collared shirt had been white when she'd begun her journey, and even now, with smudges of soot and dirt, it still stood out amongst the clothing of the locals. Most of the other revelers looked like they were wearing work clothing, the sort of things a person would wear to the field, except for the two swordsmen nearest her.

The room was drab and earthy, but the heavy smell of beer and sweat mingled with something savory. She swiveled on her stool, following the delicious scent coming from a wooden bowl of stew that had just arrived. A moment later, the barmaid delivered an earthen mug of ale.

Aiden's mouth watered. She dropped the leather satchel off her shoulder to the floor near her seat. The bag contained all her worldly possessions. She wanted to keep it close, but her shoulder ached from the weight of it.

"How much?" Aiden held two coins out in her open palm.

The maiden took one. "I haven't seen you before." It was a statement that implied a question.

"I'm just passing through." Aiden tasted the stew. It was delicious. She realized how hungry she was.

"I'm Faye." Faye leaned onto the bar. The dress she wore was low-cut at the neck and gathered at the waist. Laces up the front pulled the fabric tight along her hourglass figure. Faye's distracting cleavage was brazenly displayed, and Aiden didn't really try to hide the fact that she'd noticed.

"I'm Aiden." She'd almost finished the food already, one heaping spoonful at a time.

"Here, I'll get you more." Faye took the dish and returned with a second helping.

"Thank you." Faye was pretty and nice. A friendly conversation after two days alone was a welcome change.

"So, will you be here long?"

"What?" Aiden looked up again from her dinner. It was hard to hear her in the noisy pub.

"You said you're just passing through. Will you be here long?"

"Oh, I hadn't really decided."

"Eveshom is small, but it's a nice place. There are great views of the sea from the cliffs."

"Yeah, I noticed that as I walked into the village."

"Would you like another drink?"

Before Aiden could respond, Faye had taken her mug and refilled it. Aiden had never been much for drinking ale, and given how empty her stomach was, she had the woozy feeling that the beer was going straight to her head. As an orphan raised by monks, she'd had to share their ascetic lifestyle. No drinking, except the rare glass of wine during special ceremonies.

The orphanage run by the Brethren of Fire, warrior monks, had previously housed only boys. And so Aiden had been raised as a boy among boys. This meant that women were a bit of a mystery to her. She was twenty-one and ready to discover life outside the walled community. Other orphans reaching their twenty-first year had decided to stay and follow the warrior's path, or remain in the settlement near the monastery, preferring the comfort of the familiar. Aiden was restless to see the world, and for her, the world began at the edge of the sea. She felt drawn to the ocean for some unknown reason. Some sense of destiny pulled her toward the coast.

The trail she'd followed down from the mountains had emptied onto an open, grassy knoll along a cliff. Moonlight lit the white caps of the surf, but beyond the breakers, the blackness of the sea extended to oblivion. Aiden had stood there for a long time and peered west, but could see no end to it. The horizon was lost as the dark waters blended into the night sky. For a moment, the immensity of the churning dark water had made her dizzy.

The arrival of the second pint brought her back to the present.

Aiden tried to hand Faye another coin for the second serving of food and drink, but Faye shook her head. "No charge." She smiled at Aiden and gave her a lingering gaze that made Aiden's stomach feel funny. Faye leaned against the high wooden boards that separated them, watching Aiden finish the second bowl of stew.

It wasn't long before Faye relocated to the open spot near Aiden on the other side of the bar. She brushed away a loose clump of Aiden's hair that had fallen into her eyes. The intimate gesture caused Aiden's cheeks to flame with heat. Faye's breasts pressed against Aiden's arm as she leaned forward to whisper in her ear. "Are you shy?"

Faye was girlishly full-figured, her face had rounded soft features, and her eyes were sparkling green. Her auburn hair was gathered in a loose braid. Her proximity and the scent of her pale skin was making Aiden's head swim. Or was that the beer? Possibly, it was an intoxicating combination of both.

"You're pretty." Faye blushed and giggled at the simple compliment. Aiden laughed and took another long swig of ale. Aiden didn't know much about how to compliment a woman, but Faye's reaction seemed to signal she was heading in the right direction.

Faye edged closer. She partially stood between Aiden's legs, and the folds of her skirt rustled against Aiden's thigh. Aiden shifted on the stool so that they faced each other. She offered Faye a sip of her ale and Faye took it.

"Your eyes are beautiful." Faye leaned closer.

"Are they?" Aiden felt her face heat up from Faye's concentrated scrutiny.

"I didn't know it was possible for eyes to be that blue."

Faye leaned forward and kissed Aiden on the cheek. The movement allowed Faye to lean against Aiden's inner thigh. Aiden decided that flirtation was her new favorite pastime. She made a silent vow to spend as much time as was necessary to perfect it.

She was smitten with Faye's charms, especially the ones from the waist up, and had stopped paying attention to the other patrons altogether.

"What's this now?" A booming male voice came from behind. Faye was facing the direction of the voice. She frowned and moved away from Aiden.

"Nothing that concerns you, Gabe." Faye sounded as if she were scolding a child.

Aiden swiveled on her stool to investigate. Gabe was not a child. He was a big fellow with a sword in a sheath at his side. It was hard to tell from his attire what his station in life might be. He had several days' growth of beard and looked as if maybe he'd been traveling also. His clothes were rough-textured and dusty.

"Gabe, join us for a beer. I'm buying!" She swiveled back to face Faye and motioned with her arm for him to join them at the bar. Warmed by the ale and Faye's interest, Aiden was feeling euphoric and friendly.

"That's not a good idea." Faye's hushed words were urgent. She placed her hands on Aiden's arms.

"Faye, I'm gone two days and you've taken up with this pup?" Gabe shoved Aiden's shoulder, which caused her to fall into Faye, her face enticingly close to the scooped neckline of Faye's bodice.

"Sorry," Aiden mumbled to Faye. She wasn't sure what Gabe meant, but being called a pup didn't sound like a compliment. "Listen, no one here is a pup. And there's no reason to get upset."

"Upset? You dress like a man, but you talk like a woman. Stand up!" Gabe stepped closer, but Faye moved between them.

"Now listen, Gabe. Sit down and I'll bring you a drink." Faye put her hand on his chest, obviously not afraid to stand up to him. Maybe Aiden should make a quick, gracious exit. She was ready to admit she'd already gotten in over her head in the flirtation department. She stood.

"Where are you going?" Gabe tried to reach around Faye and grab Aiden's arm.

"I'm leaving. It's suddenly very crowded in here." Aiden raised her open palms in Gabe's direction. "Faye, would you like to join me?" She extended a hand to Faye.

"You disrespect me by showing attention to my woman, and now you think you will just leave? And invite her to go with you?" Gabe's voice grew louder with each question. He pulled his sword free, and benches skidded across the floor as those nearest him gave him space. The room was still noisy, but many standing nearby stopped their conversations to watch what might happen next.

"I'm not your woman, Gabe."

"You. Quiet." He pointed at Faye and glared.

"Gabe, don't—" Faye reached for his arm, but he shoved her aside so hard that she fell against the edge of a nearby table.

Aiden stepped back and pulled her sword free. Her head was swimming a little from the drinks, but she still thought she could take Gabe. He looked as if he'd be slow and heavy on his feet. He had more body mass, but she felt sure she had skill and agility on her side. And she was of a mind to teach him a lesson about how to treat women.

Aiden excelled with the broadsword. Wielding the weight of the long steel blade from the time she was a teen had strengthened her shoulders and arms. Those not schooled to notice details would certainly have assumed her to be a young man with her broad shoulders and narrow hips and waist.

She circled Gabe, moving away from the bar so that she'd have a wider range of motion in the event that she needed it. The tavern quieted, all eyes on them. If Aiden had hoped to have a quiet meal and find shelter without being noticed, that hope had been dashed like waves against the nearby rocky shore.

Gabe widened his stance, bent his knees, and raised his sword.

Aiden prepared for his first advance. He lunged and she easily deflected the strike. She stepped sideways, putting more space between them with the intent to make Gabe take the offensive. She needed a better idea of his skill with the sword.

He struck next from a high position. She redirected his downward strike, the force of it taking a chunk out of a nearby plank table. Patrons scattered farther away, opening a larger space as Gabe and Aiden slowly circled each other.

Aiden lost sight of Faye in the crowd, and as she searched those standing nearest for her, Gabe swung in Aiden's direction. She averted the first strike despite being distracted. The drink she'd consumed had slowed her reflexes, and she fumbled her attempt to block his second lunge. White-hot pain shot down her arm, and she took a step back. The edge of his blade sliced through her shirt just below her left shoulder. It was a glancing cut and not very deep, but crimson soaked her shirtsleeve. She'd obviously underestimated him. He might be slow on his feet, but he was tall and had a wide reach. Time to stop playing around and take the offensive.

Aiden raised her broadsword to strike, but before she could complete the motion, a searing pain radiated from the back of her head. She felt herself topple forward as everything went black.

CHAPTER TWO

A iden blinked, unsure where she was. Her head was foggy and throbbing. She sensed that her body was in motion, but when she tried to move her legs, she couldn't find her footing, her ankles boneless and wobbly.

Cobblestones passed beneath her face. Damp rock walls moved past on either side, lit intermittently by the flame of a lantern. She realized she was being dragged. She tried again to get her feet to work properly, but she couldn't. Strong hands held each of her arms as two men dragged her through a stone doorway and tossed her onto the floor.

She struggled to her feet and lunged toward the door. One of the men grabbed her by the shirtfront and shoved. She staggered backward, almost falling again, and the door closed before she could reach it. She heard the unmistakable sound of a heavy bolt sliding into place.

Moonlight filtered into the sunken room through a single high window. She touched the back of her pounding head, and when she looked at her fingers they were red. She felt sick from the ale and the blow to her skull. The room was tilting. She dropped to one knee and tried to settle her stomach. After a moment, she slumped back onto a large pile of loose hay and closed her eyes, willing the room to stop spinning.

❖

Aiden wasn't sure how long she'd been lying in the straw, maybe an hour, maybe two, when she heard muffled voices and then the door opened. Faye entered the cell first. She was carrying a pail of water, and behind her trailed a tall, thin elderly man.

"I'm so sorry. I never meant for this to happen." Faye knelt beside Aiden and handed her a small tin cup of water. "Here, drink this."

Aiden sat up. The first sip made her cough. Her throat felt sore and dry. As she took a few more sips, Faye pressed a damp cloth to the back of her head.

"Where am I?"

"You're in the Eveshom jail." Faye dunked the cloth in water and again pressed it against Aiden's throbbing head.

"What happened?" Aiden asked.

"I hit you over the head with a flask. I didn't want you to get hurt."

"Getting hit on the head hurts."

Faye muffled a laugh. "I know. I'm sorry. I was afraid Gabe would do more damage than that. When his temper flares he tends to take things too far."

"Is he your intended?" Aiden brushed at her clothing. Strands of hay clung to her shirt, and she pulled a few dry twigs from her hair.

"He'd like to be."

"If I were you, I'd rethink that."

"I've brought the doctor. Let him have a look at your arm."

Aiden's head had been pounding so painfully she'd forgotten about the gash on her arm. She looked down at the blood-soaked sleeve as if the arm belonged to someone else.

"Well, this is a fine mess." The gray-haired man carried a leather pouch and a long narrow box with a wooden handle. Various instruments were visible in the open box. All of them looked as if they'd inflict more pain than they'd cure. The elderly man's clothing hung loosely off his shoulders, and his heavy overshirt draped to mid thigh. He had a neutral expression on his weathered face.

"This needs stitches." He spoke to Aiden as he tugged at the torn sleeve for a better look at her arm. As he pulled the shirt away from the cut, he furrowed his brow. "What's this?"

He'd opened her shirt enough at the collar to see the back of her left shoulder.

"I have a birthmark." Aiden couldn't read the expression on his face, but he stared at her intently, frowning, as if he doubted her response. "It's a birthmark." She said it again. She sounded less certain the second time, but she wasn't sure why. Something about his scrutiny made her uncomfortable, like she was a child under a disapproving parent's gaze.

Faye leaned over with the lantern in her hand for a closer view. "It doesn't look like a birthmark."

"It's not." The old man rummaged in his small box of torture devices and pulled out a needle that looked far too large.

"It's a birthmark." Aiden sat between them looking back and forth. She felt confused and outnumbered despite the fact that their attentions seemed to carry no particular malice. However, the old man regarded her somewhat suspiciously now.

Why was she in jail? How soon could she leave? "I don't understand what's going on here." Aiden looked toward Faye for an answer, but it was the doctor who responded.

"I suppose you're not very bright if you picked a fight with Gabe."

"I didn't—" Aiden's denial was cut short.

"It wasn't like that exactly. I'm partly to blame." Faye looked at the doctor.

"What's your name, stranger?" asked the doctor.

"Aiden."

"Well, Aiden, you were lucky. The cut is clean, but it will need a few stitches." He directed Faye to hold the cloth away from the wound. "Clean this up a bit, Faye, while I ready the needle."

"Why am I being held here? That was a fair fight and Gabe started it." Aiden's foggy brain was beginning to clear, and she wanted some answers.

"Obviously, you're a threat to yourself and local bar maidens."

The old man was joking, but Aiden didn't find any humor in her situation. She was pretty certain there was none.

"I'm sure they just want to keep you here for the night. For your own safety." Faye gently wiped dried blood away from the gash on Aiden's arm.

"I can take care of myself." As she uttered the words, she felt around in the straw near where she was seated. "My sword? Where's my sword…and my satchel?"

"You can't have a sword in here. I'm sure it's with the guard." He dismissed her questions. He pinched the cut together with one hand while he held the large needle in the other hand. "This might hurt."

CHAPTER THREE

Kathryn sat at the end of the long formal table. The chancellor, a gray-haired man dressed in dark clothing, hovered nearby. Dispatches were separated into small haphazard stacks in front of her while she signed the two documents in front of her.

She waited for a moment for the ink to dry and then handed the papers to the chancellor.

"Thank you, Your Highness." He bowed respectfully and left Kathryn alone in the immense dining chamber.

She had to rely on her father's cabinet of advisors for many decisions, and this sometimes troubled her. The chancellor seemed above reproach, but which of the Eldermen could she truly trust? She'd probably be foolish and naïve not to assume that Balak had spies everywhere.

Balak Roth, the ruler of the neighboring kingdom of Belstaff, was ruthless and unpredictable even among his inner circle. Stories circulated about how even Balak's friends were wary of him. He was the sort of man to laugh with you one moment, then run a sword through you the next.

The deeper she sank into the matters of state the more she realized how much her father had sheltered her. She wished he'd explained more fully, but they'd both assumed they'd have more time to make the transition of power. His death had come too quickly.

Kathryn pushed the closest stack of papers away and slouched back in her chair. She was fighting to hold on to optimism, but the affairs of the crown began to occupy the ever-widening space between herself and happiness. She worried that she would be forced to sacrifice the vision she'd had for her own life for the sake of the citizens of Olmstead under her care. Her people depended on her in her father's absence.

"Frost just returned." Rowan entered the large dining hall. Her thick dark hair fell in loose waves past her shoulders, and she wore a dress of midnight blue that touched the floor. Rowan was Kathryn's first cousin, born four years ahead of Kathryn to her father's sister. As children, they'd been very close, always together with family for holidays, anniversaries, and birthdays, all the events that mark the passing of time and the transition to womanhood. Rowan lost her parents to illness halfway through her sixteenth year. It was then that she came to Olmstead to live in the royal house full-time. Now, at twenty-eight, she was one of Kathryn's most trusted friends and confidants.

"Who's with her?" Frost, the commander of Olmstead's imperial guard, had been called away two days earlier by scouts who'd reported a skirmish near the southern border of Olmstead, the region that adjoined Balak's kingdom of Belstaff.

Kathryn followed Rowan out of the great hall and into the courtyard. She spotted Frost just as she dismounted. She looked road weary, her face and clothing soiled and her boots muddy. As she crossed the courtyard, Kathryn could see blood on the front of her uniform and a cut on her face across her cheekbone. Frost turned when Kathryn called out to her.

"Your Highness." She dipped her head in deference to Kathryn. Frost Sylven was a formidable figure—tall and well muscled, with barely discernible feminine curves beneath the royal blue wool of the uniform that signaled her position as one of Olmstead's elite warriors.

"You were away longer than I anticipated." Kathryn tried to give Frost a moment. She'd just arrived and exhaustion was evident on her face, but Kathryn was anxious for a report.

"The scouts were correct. Three farms in the boundary lands have been ransacked and burned." Frost's shoulders slumped a little. "We were too late to offer assistance to the first two homesteads, and I'm afraid the two guards who were with me will not be returning. They fell in the skirmish at the third farm."

"No survivors from any of the homesteads?" Kathryn placed her fingers over her mouth waiting for the answer.

"None."

"This is terrible news."

"I also intercepted this from one of the raiders." Frost held a paper up to Kathryn. The wax seal had been broken, but the crest was obvious. The document was from Balak Roth or a ranking member of his court at Windsheer Castle. "The seal was broken when I found it on him. He'd obviously received the message and was en route, but decided to pillage a few farms along the way."

"What does it say?" asked Kathryn.

"You should read it."

Rowan stepped closer and read the paper over her shoulder.

"Possible heir to Belstaff found. Wounded. Roth family crest on shoulder. Held in guarded cell at Eveshom. Reward. Alive or dead."

Kathryn turned the paper over in her hand to examine the red wax seal bearing the Roth mark, a crescent moon and three stars. A small jolt of elation shot through her body at the possibilities this message implied.

Frost shifted her stance and looked at Kathryn. "I need fresh horses and supplies, then I would like to take a small detail to Eveshom right away to investigate this claim."

"No." Kathryn's response was quick.

"But, Your Highness, this lead might not—"

"I need you here, Frost. Rowan and I will go, but I can't afford to pull any of our guards away from protecting Olmstead. Not with Balak actively testing our borders. We can't risk assigning troops for this errand. It might turn out to be a dead end." Others had claimed to be the heir and had turned out to be imposters. The lore of the missing heir was longstanding, but she held out hope that maybe it wasn't a myth.

Frost didn't speak but looked at Rowan as if she hoped Rowan would talk Kathryn out of the idea.

"Don't look at Rowan. The decision is mine to make." Kathryn tried to evoke authority without condescension. Kathryn didn't want to challenge Frost, but at the same time, she was the reigning queen. Frost needed to learn to follow her directives without question.

"Yes, Your Highness, I meant no disrespect. But I've taken an oath to defend you as well as the kingdom."

"I'll ask Gareth to ride with us. If we dress as commoners we'll attract little or no attention on the journey." Kathryn felt the need to take action. She'd spent too many days already on the defensive.

She hugged herself, but not from the early morning chill in the air. She longed for the comfort and security of her father's arms. He'd left this life barely a year earlier, and Balak's aggressive ambitions for her lands had been a constant worry since the king's passing. He obviously already held some sway over the magistrate in Eveshom, otherwise why would they hold someone at his request.

The truth was that Balak would likely have challenged her elderly father's rule at some point, but now, surely he considered Kathryn a weak monarch and one that he could easily overrun. How little Balak knew of her resolve. She would not go down without a fight, a fight to the death if necessary.

Olmstead would be just as safe without her for a few days. She desperately needed to take decisive action in some way. Sitting for hours, holding sessions to decide petty disputes between members of her court and authorizing endless documents was only making her restless. And besides, finding the missing heir of Belstaff would help the people of Belstaff as much as her kingdom of Olmstead. She'd likely have a better chance of finding this missing prince than a group of armed guards. It would be very hard for armed troops wearing imperial uniforms to travel unnoticed or unchallenged. And even if they did succeed, why would the missing heir agree to travel with an armed battalion? He'd feel as if he were under arrest and in all likelihood flee before they found him, that's assuming he was the real heir and not a charlatan just out for financial gain.

"Please speak to Gareth about this and have him ready the horses and supplies. I need to change and pack a few things. We'll be ready to leave within the hour." Kathryn spoke to the groom who'd come to take charge of Frost's horse.

"I'll talk with Gareth myself." Frost left little room for argument, but Kathryn persisted.

"You're exhausted. You should rest." She wanted to touch Frost's arm, but she didn't want to offend the stoic warrior by fussing over her.

"I'm the only one who can brief Gareth on what's happening in the field. The three of you need to be prepared to defend yourself." Frost shifted her stance and regarded Kathryn with an almost parental look. "May I speak frankly?"

Kathryn nodded. "Of course."

"I think this journey is ill-advised, and I'd prefer to send a small group of soldiers instead. And if you won't agree to that then please allow a few swordsmen to accompany you."

"If the queen were to travel, then anyone she passed on the road would expect a detail of guards to be with her." Kathryn spoke of herself in the third person to gently remind Frost of who held command. "The queen would be much safer and much less conspicuous traveling in common clothing with her cousin and a friend."

"There is merit in your logic, Your Highness. I'll speak with Gareth." Frost gave a slight bow to acknowledge Kathryn's authority, but didn't seem happy about Kathryn's decision. She led her horse away toward the stables.

"You're sure about this?" Rowan asked. They walked side-by-side back to the main entrance of the great hall.

"No, but I need to find out. What do your feelings tell you?" Rowan was very intuitive by nature, and Kathryn trusted Rowan's feelings sometimes more than her own.

"I've felt some sort of unease for a few days. As if something or someone was coming."

"Then let's get to Eveshom as quickly as possible."

❖

Kathryn strode toward the stables. Her long cloak caught the breeze as she walked, tugging against the fastener at her shoulder. Rowan was already there fussing with a side bag on her saddle, and Gareth, who held the reins of Kathryn's mount, looked up as she approached. Blaez sniffed the air, his white coat glowing in the early morning sun. She rubbed Blaez's gray velvet nose and greeted Gareth, who Kathryn loved like a brother.

Gareth's close-cropped auburn hair and beard made him look a bit older than his twenty-four years. He'd worked in the stable since he was a child, and was stout through the chest, but not through the middle. He was well muscled and fit.

She and Rowan had both changed into riding trousers and leather boots that covered their calves and were cuffed just below the knee. Kathryn had chosen to also wear a dark green hooded cloak because it would double as a blanket at night if necessary.

The day was already warming even though it was still early. In another hour, she'd end up shucking the cloak, but for now, the warmth of it felt good around her shoulders. And the hood would come in handy if she needed any additional disguise. She was not so self-important as to assume that she'd be recognized by anyone, but she had traveled with her father through Fainsland as far as Eveshom so she'd chosen to be cautious.

Gareth held the stirrup for her after she'd fastened her gear bag to the back of the saddle. Once she was seated atop Blaez, he handed her a crossbow, her weapon of choice. She tethered it at the left fore of her saddle so that she could reach for it quickly if necessary. A quiver of arrows hung by her right knee.

She could see the questions in Gareth's eyes, but—ever aware of her station—she knew he would hold them for a more private time. The three of them settled atop their horses and faced Frost and the two stable boys who'd assisted with the saddles and gear. Blaez sidestepped and shook his head, his silver mane shifting from side to side. Her anxious feelings were undoubtedly causing his unease.

"Speed of the goddess to you, Your Highness." Frost lightly grasped the cheek strap of Blaez's bridle to settle him and looked up to meet Kathryn's gaze.

"Thank you, Commander Frost." Kathryn looked to Rowan and Gareth, and they nodded their readiness to depart. She reached down, and Frost took her hand. "I'm trusting you with the safety of my kingdom, Frost."

"I will not let you down." Frost dipped her head.

"Nor I you." Kathryn looked back at her mounted comrades. "Let's ride." She pulled away from Frost and allowed Blaez to set the pace as they passed beneath the stone arch of the main gates of Starford Keep. A fourth horse traveled with them, a large chestnut mare that, for the moment, carried extra gear. She would also carry Belstaff's heir back to Olmstead if they actually managed to find him.

The dampness of the early morning air hovered close to the ground like a low fog. The thigh-high lush grass, wet with dew, lined the road as they crossed the grassy field that surrounded the castle. Within moments, they'd left the exposed open ground for the cover of the dense forest that surrounded her small walled village fortress.

Chapter Four

Aiden placed both hands against the cool, rough wall and tilted her gaze toward the high window. Stars against a black sky were all that she could see. Nightfall again. Frustration hung around her neck like a millstone. How many days had she been left to languish in this cell? Three? Or was it four?

Faye had been kind enough to bring the doctor and food on the first day. Since then, food and water had been delivered by one of the guards. Other than that, Aiden had seen no one, and she was no closer to getting an answer about her release. The guards never spoke or responded when she pelted them with questions.

She balled her hands into fists as she paced back and forth across the hay-strewn floor. When she got near the bucket in the corner where she was forced to relieve herself, she frowned and returned to the far side of the room. The small space was beginning to close in on her.

"Hey! I want to speak to the magistrate!" Aiden yelled through the small barred opening of the heavy door. No one answered. She pressed her ear to the opening and listened for any sounds. She heard nothing.

Getting more frustrated by the hour, she sank to the floor, propped up on a pile of straw. She rested her elbows on her knees and covered her face with her hands. Faye had brought enough water for Aiden to wash her face and hands the first day, but she hadn't been able to truly bathe since. She was miserable, and she had the body odor to match her mood. She studied her hands, turning them over in the dim moonlight. They appeared otherworldly, pale and ghostly.

She rested her head back against the wall and willed herself to relax, to breathe. She was never skilled at meditation. This had been one of the daily rituals at the monastery, and one she had never mastered. She was easily distracted; she'd fidget and long to be outdoors. She heard her mentor's voice in her head as if he were in the room with her. Brother Francis would sit next to her on the stone tiles of the chapel. They'd kneel facing the ornate emblem of a blazing sun that bore a woman's face. The face of the goddess.

The creation myth, a poem of incantation was first sung by the goddess Amarigrin, and it began with *I am the ray of the sun*.

In the beginning, there was nothing but walled heat from the sun. Until the goddess sang her melody of creation from the place of unknowing, from the place where all things originated. Only then did the night fold over the stars. The land greened and curved as gravity bent the terrain. And then, in the head of mankind, she created the fire of thought.

Although no one knew exactly where the melody first rose, the myth was believed to point toward the mountain region that extended east to west bordering the great forest of Taiga. This was where the monks who kept the old stories, the old beliefs, gathered. Monasteries were constructed every hundred miles through the range, each with its reigning element. The monastery where Aiden had been raised, where the warrior monks trained, represented fire, the Brotherhood of Fire.

Aiden was never sure she belonged with the Brotherhood of Fire. For some unexplained reason, she'd always been drawn to wind. The sky at the horizon, the air of open spaces, the winds of change.

The lines of the ancient creation poem filled her mind. Aiden took a deep breath, closed her eyes, and repeated them silently as a meditation:

I am the ray of the sun
I am the wind that blows across the sea
I am the wave of the ocean
I am the fairest of flowers
I am a salmon in the pool

I am an idiot. She'd clearly learned nothing. Her training hadn't prepared her for the real world. How could she be so stupid?

All she'd been after was a pint of ale and a warm meal. If only she'd had some gruff bartender instead of Faye serve her food she'd have never gotten in this situation in the first place. Look where flirtation had gotten her. Things had been so promising until Gabe showed up all grumpy and territorial. She released a long sigh and tried to think of something else to occupy her mind.

When she'd been lonely as a child, in the monastery's orphanage, she'd sometimes lain awake at night and entertained herself by imagining adventures. She had envisioned herself as a knight, sword drawn, slaying mythical dragons or rescuing maidens. Or she had imagined herself a pirate sailing with a crew to foreign lands.

There were always young women in her fantasy adventures, damsels in need of rescue, romance, or whatever. That's usually where the fantasy would hit a dead end because Aiden didn't really know what came after the initial spark of romance. She'd never even personally experienced true romance. There'd been one young girl in the village near the monastery that Aiden saw every Saturday during the summer at the village marketplace around the central square. Their relationship never got past hello or a question about the price of an apple.

She'd been optimistic while Faye was flirting with her that she might finally find out what happened after hello, but instead, Gabe happened. And now she wondered if women might be more troublesome than she'd realized.

She shifted against the cold of the rough stone against her back, closed her eyes, and tried to mentally transport herself into one of her imagined adventures, an adventure without maidens.

CHAPTER FIVE

Kathryn watched the sparks rise as Gareth stirred the campfire, then turned her focus back to the map of the four kingdoms. Taiga to the north of the Arranth Mountains, Olmstead to the east, Belstaff to the south bordering the Abbasson Sea, and Fainsland to the west along the Oran Sea. And the Great Salt Desert in the middle, the site of an ancient inland sea long evaporated.

They were well into the kingdom of Fainsland, just south of the Theirry Foothills. They'd ridden the entire day after spending two days crossing the salt flats by wind ship. They'd almost had to set up camp in the dark, and still they were a day's ride from Eveshom. But if all went well, they'd arrive with the cover of darkness and extract the potential heir with no resistance. She folded and stowed the map.

Was she being overly confident? Gareth thought so. He'd pointed out more than once that there might be others who'd received the message from Balak about the missing heir. He agreed with Frost that they should have brought soldiers with them, so why had he consented to come with her? He was watching her now with intensity as if he were trying to read her thoughts.

"What?" she asked.

"What do you mean, what?" Gareth threw one more stick of wood on the fire and leaned back into a reclined position.

"You want to say something. I can see it on your face. Just say it." Kathryn was amused that he ever tried to hide anything from her. His face was an open book.

"I think this is a wild goose chase."

"By all means, don't hold back your true opinion."

"The notion that there is some missing heir to the Belstaff throne is a myth. You can't convince me that if an heir truly existed Balak or someone else wouldn't have located them by now."

It was true. The stories of a missing heir had almost become folklore at this point. Yet for some reason Kathryn still clung to the hope that there was some truth at the root of the myth. She had been just a toddler when the King of Belstaff was killed in battle. As the stories were told, his queen was with child at the time, but no official announcement was ever made about a royal birth. Maybe the queen had feared Balak would harm the child. Knowing what she now knew of Balak that seemed plausible. Some believed the queen died in childbirth and the unborn heir with her. Some believed that that infant survived and was taken into hiding. But where?

There was some merit to what Gareth said. After all these years it did seem that if the legend were true, the heir would have surfaced by now.

Any royal born would carry the mark of their family crest as proof of kinship. A few imposters had tried to pass themselves off as the missing heir, but their ruse was uncovered when it was revealed that the ink used for the tattoo had no gold in it. Only the royals could afford ink infused with equal parts of twenty-four-karat gold.

"This may very well turn out to be another hoax, but even if there's a slim chance that the heir is real, I have to know."

"Have you thought about what will happen when we get to Eveshom?"

"Yes. I mean, I can't possibly anticipate everything, but yes, I've thought about it." Kathryn wasn't sure exactly what he was getting at.

Rowan was watching the exchange between them from across the fire pit.

"What if this prince turns out to be someone you don't expect?"

"Why do you both assume the heir is male?" asked Rowan.

That was an interesting observation. There wasn't any particular reason to assume the heir was male. "I'm not sure. In my head I just picture a prince." But Kathryn wanted to get back to Gareth's original question. "Explain what you meant."

"I meant, what if this prince, this heir, turns out to be a complete jerk? What if this heir turns out to be worse than Balak? I mean, they're related. Right? What if bringing the heir back to Olmstead turns out to be a bad idea?"

"Leave it to you to imagine the worst, Gareth." Rowan spoke up from across the flame.

"I'm a realist." Gareth sipped from a flask and offered it to Kathryn. She declined. "I just want Kathryn to be prepared if this guy turns out to be a disappointment."

"I'm prepared for that."

"I hope so, because I might turn out to be psychic."

Rowan chuckled. "That would be special indeed."

"Hey, I have my moments." Gareth leaned back on his elbow and grinned, the light from the fire catching the white of his teeth in the darkness. He was a handsome man. It was too bad he couldn't seem to settle down with anyone, and Kathryn could never feel for him the way he'd wished she had.

Kathryn relaxed under her cloak, using her gear bag as a pillow. She watched the embers of the fire and thought about what Gareth had said. It was true that she was optimistic about this missing heir, hopeful even. If he turned out to be even half of what she hoped he'd be, then she was willing to commit troops, supplies, and advisors, whatever it took to see him assume his rightful place on the throne of Belstaff. Whoever he was, he couldn't possibly be worse than Balak.

But the entire endeavor was just a big gamble.

If this missing heir turned out to be worse than Balak or even as bad as Balak, then she'd be crushed. She'd try to hide it from the others, but she would feel defeated. Somewhere in the deepest recesses of wishful thinking she'd allowed herself to imagine some union with this heir, either through marriage or treaties of alliance. She'd consider it for the sake of Olmstead. Then her lands would be protected.

If marriage was the only option, could she go through with it? She wasn't sure. She'd always dreamed she'd marry for love and nothing less. But as the threat of invasion loomed, she was willing to consider every option.

She closed her eyes and tried to redirect her thoughts. She willed herself to call up memories of happier times, her birthday the year her father had given her Blaez. She'd just turned twenty-one and her whole life lay ahead of her. Kathryn knew her father had a tendency to spoil her, and she'd let him. She mourned the loss of those carefree days.

CHAPTER SIX

Ascuffling sound from outside the cell made Aiden jump. She'd heard nothing for hours and couldn't see what might be going on outside her cell door now. She stood in the center of the room, straining to identify the noises, hopeful but also a bit scared. Muffled voices were followed by a loud banging sound, like metal striking metal. Not good. Aiden stepped farther away from the door, tensing at the sound of footfalls. Was she their target? She didn't even have a weapon to defend herself.

The bolt slid noisily sideways, and the heavy door swung open. A woman stood backlit in the doorway. She was stunning, despite the fact she raised a crossbow and looked as if she wanted to skewer Aiden. She tossed back the hood of the cloak that fell just past her knees to reveal long golden hair gathered into a clasp just above the collar of her shirt. Two others, a woman with dark hair and a bearded man, slipped around the woman and into the room. The man's sword was drawn as if he expected Aiden to fight him. She raised her open palms to show them she was unarmed.

She returned her attention to the blonde standing in the doorway. The look on her face telegraphed fierce determination, but everything else about her was soft and feminine.

"Take off your shirt and turn around." The blonde commanded.

"What?" Aiden's throat was dry, and it made her voice sound lower than normal. The woman issuing orders had girlish hips visible within the draped cloak and the trousers she wore cinched at her slender waist with a wide belt. A snug-fitting bodice of dark leather was laced tightly over a light colored blouse, which was open at the neck to reveal a hint of cleavage.

"The lady asked you to take your shirt off. Do it." The man, standing to her left, raised his sword and brought the blade close to Aiden's throat.

Aiden lifted the loose, slightly tattered shirt over her head. She stood bare-chested before them. The only light in the room came from the moonlit high window and the small lantern the dark-haired woman held aloft to illuminate the chamber.

Kathryn lowered the crossbow and stared. "You're a woman." Even in the low light and despite the boyish physique, she could see that the person standing shirtless in front of her was female.

"Thank you for noticing." The prisoner frowned and held her shirt up to cover her small breasts.

"I need to see your shoulder." Kathryn stepped closer, but allowed Gareth to keep his sword trained on the captive. Kathryn wanted to see the mark for herself. She motioned for Rowan to bring the light near. She was after truth, not rumor.

"She has the mark," Kathryn said unnecessarily as both Gareth and Rowan stared, too. The flecks of gold imbedded in her skin sparkled in the lantern light.

"It's a birthmark. Can I put my shirt on now?"

Kathryn was surprised. This person appeared to have no idea who she was. How was that possible? "I'm sorry. Yes, you can."

"Who are you people?"

"I'm Kathryn. This is Gareth and Rowan." Kathryn pointed to each of them as she said their names. "And you are?"

"Aiden."

"Aiden." Kathryn echoed her name barely above a whisper. She took a step back.

Kathryn was struck by how beautiful Aiden was. Her face was elegant, her features refined in contrast to her lean, muscled body and broad shoulders. Aiden had dark, unruly hair and blue eyes the color of the sea in full sunlight. Clearly, she'd been in captivity for several days. Her face was smeared with dirt, and bits of straw clung to her clothing and her soiled shirt. Under all the grime, Aiden was a magnificent specimen androgynously regal. And even in her disheveled state, she had a presence about her that fairly pulsed against Kathryn's chest. She took another step back.

"We should go." Gareth checked the chamber hallway, his sword still drawn but now held at his side.

Aiden slipped on her shirt and stared at the three visitors suspiciously.

"Aiden, we've come for you. To aid you in escape." Rowan supplied the answer to Aiden's unspoken question.

"But how did you know I was here? I don't even know you."

"We will explain everything once we leave Eveshom. We need to move before someone discovers we're here." Kathryn stepped out of the room as if she expected Aiden to follow, but Aiden stood frozen.

Kathryn shifted back to the door of the cell. "Are you coming, or would you rather stay here?" There was the slightest hint of impatience, or possibly sarcasm.

Aiden shook her head. "No, I definitely don't want to stay here."

Chapter Seven

Aiden stepped over the unconscious guard, and spotted her things in a small side chamber as they headed down the dim hallway. She retrieved her satchel, but her sword was missing.

"What's wrong?" Rowan joined her in the small room.

"My sword. It's not here." She checked inside the bag for the small leather purse of coins. That was gone too.

"There's no time to search for it now. We must leave." Rowan pulled at Aiden's arm, and they fell in step behind Gareth and Kathryn as they headed toward the chamber's exit.

Aiden knew she was blindly following three people she knew nothing about, but she didn't know what else to do. She had no memory of the path she'd taken to the cell, so she had no idea how to find her way out. Plus, she'd rather take her chances with these people than spend one more night locked away. She'd begun to think no one would ever come for her.

She shouldered her gear, but before they'd gone too far, Rowan stopped in front of her. Gareth and Kathryn were a bit ahead and Aiden heard voices. She felt useless and unprotected without her sword.

She strained to see who was blocking their escape. They had only traveled along one narrow corridor that led from the chamber and taken one turn since they left her cell. But for the first time in days, Aiden felt the slight brush of a breeze. Fresh air.

She strained to see why they'd stopped moving.

"Stand aside." Katherine spoke to three men who'd blocked their path in the narrow, poorly lit corridor.

"Not likely, girl," a man gruffly responded.

Kathryn raised her crossbow, but the man closest to her lunged and struck the bow with a sideways blow of his sword. The arrow misfired against the wall. She recovered quickly and struck him across the face with the butt of her weapon.

Gareth challenged one of the men, the steel of their broadswords echoing loudly off the rock walls. Rowan pulled a small dagger free from her belt. Damn, Aiden had no weapons with which to join in the fray.

A third man grabbed for Rowan, and Aiden landed a solid punch to his jaw that made him stumble into the wall. Well, no weapon but her fists. Rowan was quick to follow by kicking him in the crotch. He dropped to his knees, and Aiden grabbed him by the collar. She hesitated. She'd received training with the sword and hand-to-hand fighting techniques, but at the monastery it had all been abstract, hypothetical, nonlethal. This was different.

She stared into the man's eyes. What was she looking for? Some sign of tangible malice. Aiden paused too long. He began to regain his strength and struggle to his feet, so she banged his head against the rock wall. Once, twice, and then a third time for good measure. Giving in to the urge to do the man bodily harm uncorked some deeply buried anger, and once she'd tapped into the fury, it had surged to the surface as she lashed out. The side of the man's head oozed blood. He sank to the floor and didn't move.

"Working out some frustrations?" Rowan's question carried a note of humor.

"I...I...something like that."

Rowan offered her dagger to Aiden. "Here, given what I just witnessed, I think you might be better with this than me."

Aiden nodded. Finally, she was getting a bit of her anger out for having been held without explanation and against her will. Payback was improving her mood.

"Stay behind me." She motioned for Rowan to step back. Kathryn was struggling. Without a sword, she was at a disadvantage.

The crossbow wasn't an effective weapon in such a tight space, and the blow to the man's jaw had only slowed him for a moment. He lunged at Kathryn, but Aiden struck downward with her short blade, catching the cross guard of the man's sword near the handle and giving Kathryn a chance to step beyond his reach.

Kathryn loaded another arrow and fired.

Gareth's opponent swung his sword ineffectively as Gareth sunk his blade into the man's chest and twisted before the man fell to the ground.

Aiden faced off with Kathryn's attacker. She managed to block another strike and then, with the blades locked together near the cross guard again, she pressed his back to the wall. He slipped free somehow, reversing their position. His blade was dangerously close to finding purchase in Aiden's shoulder when she heard the unmistakable thwack of the crossbow firing. He slumped to his knees, an arrow protruding from the center of his back. Kathryn stood across from Aiden, her discharged crossbow still raised.

The man groaned loudly, fell sideways, and then there was no noise except the sounds of the breathless survivors. Gareth's shirt was bloodied, but he looked as if he was uninjured so Aiden reasoned the blood was not his.

"Let's go before someone else discovers we're here." Gareth wiped his sword and slid it into the sheath at his belt.

The hour was obviously late. No one was about. They kept to the shadows, away from the moonlight as they worked their way through the slender alleyways of the village toward the main gate.

Once past the large stone archway, Kathryn stopped. She stepped into the shadows of the gatehouse wall. "We have horses tied just at the tree line there." She pointed south. Aiden nodded.

One by one, they slipped through the gate to cross the open ground for the trees. Four horses waited for their arrival, just as Kathryn had said.

Aiden was itching to put distance between herself and Eveshom. So much for her first solo journey to the sea. Everything had gone horribly wrong. She was hungry, tired, and probably looked like she'd been sleeping underground for a month. She stood silently and waited for the others to choose their mounts.

Gareth handed her the reins to a large chestnut mare. "Her name is Sunset."

"Thank you." Aiden didn't really know what else to say. A group of total strangers had fought to free her, but she had no idea why. She didn't know whether to feel grateful, anxious, or suspicious.

Aiden decided she would feel nothing for the moment.

Just before they entered the heavy woods to head east, Aiden looked back toward the moon reflected on the surface of the nighttime sea. Once again, lines from the primordial poem came to her:

> *Who tells the ages of the moon, if not I?*
> *Who shows the place where the sun goes to rest, if not I?*

She paused, rotating to gaze back at the churning dark water. She had many questions. She hoped answers would come with the sunrise. Until then, she was glad to be free. She faced into the light wind and breathed in the crisp night air.

CHAPTER EIGHT

They rode until they could no longer hear the distant crash of the sea against the rocky coast. Aiden was so weary that dizziness threatened her balance, as if she'd been drinking too much ale again. Finally, her companions stopped and dismounted.

"Let's camp here for the night." Kathryn freed a bedroll that had been lashed to the back of her saddle, and Aiden pulled on a worn leather overshirt against the chill. It was too late to make a fire so they just spread blankets in a clearing near the trail. A wool blanket Aiden had brought with her from the monastery was still tethered to the outside of her satchel, but she was angry about losing her sword. Without it, she felt exposed, vulnerable.

She had a million questions she was too tired to ask. As she spread out her bedroll, she watched Kathryn from a few feet away. The others deferred to her, but she appeared too young to be in a position of power. Aiden studied her delicate profile in the moonlight. The golden strands of her hair were luminous in the moonlight. She stood with her blanket in her hand as she watched Kathryn, but quickly averted her eyes when Kathryn glanced her way.

She busied herself spreading her blanket as if she hadn't just been staring unabashedly at Kathryn. She felt Kathryn's eyes on her now and tried not to acknowledge the attention. She stretched out on the ground, wrapped tight in her blanket, facing in Kathryn's direction. Kathryn's eyes were closed so Aiden had the luxury of studying her once again from several feet away. Gareth and Rowan were also nearby, but Aiden was drawn to Kathryn. Exhaustion finally claimed her, and she drifted into a deep sleep.

❖

Aiden jerked awake. She sat up and tried to focus on her surroundings. She was on her blanket on the ground. She looked about. The others were sleeping around her. Would she always wake up among strangers? She took a deep breath and rubbed her eyes with the palms of her hands, then rose quietly to go relieve herself.

As she walked away from their camp, she thought of her mother, the woman who had given her life but abandoned her. These thoughts often came to her in the latest hours of the night.

Had her mother cared for Aiden but been forced to relinquish her child? The monks at the monastery who raised her would only say that Aiden had no family and nothing more. No matter how many times Aiden asked, there were never any answers. The men of faith would only say she came to them alone as an infant. Eventually, she stopped asking.

It was a strange thing to be alone in the world, to have no story, to have no legacy, only the life you made for yourself. And yet she'd always had the sense she was destined for something, something bigger, something yet unknown. Maybe every orphan had those same feelings.

She'd been well treated by the monks, clothed, fed, educated, and taught to defend herself, but still she'd always felt isolated. She'd lived among them but was not one of them. It was not just her gender that marked her as separate but some other thing she didn't have a name for, a feeling, a sensation of hidden destiny perhaps.

The night surrounded her like a dark cloak so she stepped carefully, eyes on the ground for fear she'd stumble in the darkness. She froze when a rustling noise sounded just ahead.

The dampness of the earth seeped through her trousers, just above her leather boots, as she dropped to one knee and strained to see the cause of the noise. Clouds cleared, and moonlight revealed a great horned owl several feet away.

Aiden sat awestruck and watched as the owl hunched over whatever prey he'd captured. When he swiveled his head slowly to give her a fierce look, she decided to give him his space.

Just as Aiden stood and began to move around his position, the predator took flight, his wingspan equal to the height of a man. The owl turned to face her, almost hovering as he made several powerful strokes with his massive wings. The white of his inner feathers glowed in the moonlight. His piercing yellow eyes bored into hers before he disappeared up the hillside into the night with a series of mighty wing strokes against the damp night air.

Surely this was an omen.

Aiden stood quietly, reflecting on the teachings of the monks. The owl's energy was supposed to be at its peak in the blackness of night. The owl had the ability to discern the shadows. This creature was also believed to be a guardian of the underworld, and protector of the dead. She'd doubted the myths about animal guides, but maybe they were true.

Was the great bird trying to tell her that her mother was dead?

Aiden stilled as a cool draft swept past her, and she spun in both directions. She saw no one. She was alone.

CHAPTER NINE

The next morning, Kathryn woke first. She'd slept soundly, although now she realized her shoulder ached from its weird position on the hard ground. She shifted a little and watched Aiden sleep. What a surprise to discover that the heir to the Belstaff throne was a woman. She didn't yet have a sense of what Aiden was like, but she'd seen enough to know she was intrigued.

Nearby, Rowan stirred and moaned softly. She stretched and yawned. "I hate sleeping on the ground." She sat up and rubbed her back. "Why do I always end up with a rock under my blanket?"

"I'll get some wood. I think I need coffee before I can face this day." Gareth yawned also and slowly got to his feet.

Aiden began to stir. Her sleep-tousled hair was adorable. Kathryn smiled at Aiden before she could stop herself.

"Good morning." Aiden sounded a bit hoarse. No doubt she'd had a rough few days in the Eveshom jail. Aiden sat up and rummaged around in her satchel. She pulled out a shirt and trousers. "I think I'll walk back down to the stream we crossed and wash up a bit."

"We'll make coffee and eat something before we break camp." Kathryn held a kettle as Gareth worked to create a spark to start a fire.

Aiden nodded and then turned to walk down the slope toward the stream.

Kathryn watched her retreating figure, lost in thought.

"She's gorgeous isn't she?" Kathryn hadn't realized that Rowan was standing next to her until she spoke.

"What?"

"Aiden is gorgeous."

"I guess. I hadn't really noticed." Kathryn could never hide things from Rowan, but she was determined to try. She could tell by the grin on Rowan's face that she hadn't succeeded.

"I don't think she's anything special." Gareth added more kindling to the fire and then brushed dry leaves onto the blaze.

"She's not exactly your type, Gareth." Rowan reached for the kettle in Kathryn's hand. "I'll go fetch some water."

"Oh, I'll get it." Kathryn pulled the kettle she'd been holding closer to her chest.

"I thought as much." Rowan crossed her arms. Kathryn smiled back at her over her shoulder as she followed the path Aiden had taken.

Kathryn paused in some thick laurel shrubs and watched Aiden from a small distance. Aiden's shirt was off as she knelt beside the stream and doused her hair a couple of times to rinse out the soap. The shock of the cold water caused her to catch her breath. She swept her fingers through her hair as she tossed her head back. She jumped when she saw Kathryn.

"Sorry, I didn't mean to surprise you." Rivulets of water ran down Aiden's neck, chest, and shoulders as she stood up. "I was, um, getting some water for coffee."

"I thought maybe you just wanted to catch me with my shirt off again." Aiden smiled and Kathryn's stomach fluttered. Her cheeks felt hot, and she feared she was blushing.

"Sorry about that too." Kathryn wouldn't have asked Aiden to take her shirt off in the first place if she'd known she was a woman. As she stood in front of Aiden now, she marveled that she could have ever mistaken Aiden for male. True, her body was toned and lean and her breasts were small, but she it was also subtly feminine. Beautiful.

"I didn't mind." Aiden spoke softly, barely above a whisper.

Kathryn was standing close but still she wasn't sure she'd heard Aiden. "What?"

"I didn't mind taking my shirt off for you."

Kathryn met Aiden's gaze with equal intensity. After a few seconds, Kathryn cleared her throat and looked away. "You're wet."

"Sorry, what?"

"You're wet, from the stream." Kathryn reached for a small towel draped over a nearby shrub and handed it to Aiden. She wiped her face, arms, and chest. She kept the towel in front of her chest.

"You're also hurt." Kathryn noticed an angry cut on Aiden's upper arm.

"It's nothing. A doctor stitched it up for me." Aiden dabbed her arm lightly and then gave Kathryn a searching look. "Can I ask you what it looks like? The birthmark?"

"You've never seen it?"

"I grew up in a monastery. No mirrors."

"A monastery?" Kathryn hadn't even gotten a chance to ask where Aiden had been hiding the past two decades. If she'd been sequestered in a monastery then that might explain why she'd just surfaced and why no one knew where she was.

"The monastery is in the Theirry Foothills north of Eveshom. I was taken there as an infant. They have ideas about things like any clothing that might be considered adornment and they had a thing about mirrors."

"Ah yes, the insidious threat of vanity." Kathryn smiled. Aiden probably had no idea how good-looking she was.

"Something like that."

Kathryn stepped around Aiden so that she could see the back of her shoulder. She hesitated but then began to slowly trace the outline of the design with her fingertip. Aiden's skin was cool and damp from the stream. "This part is a crescent moon."

Chills spread down Aiden's arm and across her shoulder from Kathryn's touch. She let the towel she was holding slowly drop to her side and closed her eyes, savoring the soft contact.

"And here is one star, and another here, and one more. Three stars." She lightly touched each spot.

Aiden turned to face her. They were so close. Aiden wanted to touch Kathryn, but she was afraid. She'd never met anyone like

Kathryn. She had no idea how to build a bridge between them, but every cell in her body craved connection. Kathryn's lips were parted, and she moved closer.

"Oh!" Aiden gasped. Kathryn was still holding the kettle between them, next to her chest, and when she leaned into Aiden the cold metal touched bare skin. The possibility of the moment had been lost as quickly as it had materialized.

"I'm so sorry...I...I forgot I was going to get water." Kathryn backed away from Aiden. "I should let you finish getting dressed." She blushed and looked down at the kettle. She turned and hurriedly filled the pot with water.

Aiden pulled on her shirt, droplets of water from her dripping hair dampening it in spots. She smiled at Kathryn. She wanted to recapture the closeness they'd just shared, but Kathryn had withdrawn.

"You really have no idea who you are, do you?" Kathryn wasn't accusatory; she seemed genuinely curious.

"Of course I know who I am." But she knew that wasn't what Kathryn really meant. A person without a place in the world, without ancestry, was no one.

"You don't know what the mark on your shoulder indicates?"

"No." Aiden was reluctant to admit it, but she had no idea what it meant.

"It's the Roth family crest."

"The Roth family?"

"Come with me. I want to show you something."

Aiden rolled her soiled clothing into a bundle and followed Kathryn back to their camp. Washing her clothes would have to wait for another time.

CHAPTER TEN

Kathryn handed the kettle to Rowan, who filled it with coffee and set it on the fire to boil. Some bread and cured meat was spread on a cloth near the small blaze.

"I was just about to come look for you." Gareth reached for a piece of the dried venison and then reclined as he pulled a bite free.

Kathryn gave him a look that she hoped would deflect more questions.

"Aiden, you must be hungry. Please eat something." Rowan motioned for Aiden to share their food.

"Thank you." Aiden reached for the food before taking a seat on her bedroll.

Kathryn searched through her bag for the parchment and then returned to the group. "Aiden, this is what I wanted you to see." She took a seat on the ground near Aiden and handed her the folded paper.

"What is this?" Aiden turned the document over in her hand.

"Read it." Kathryn took a piece of bread and tore small pieces of it off as she watched Aiden read the note.

"Is this supposed to mean something to me?" Aiden frowned and looked up at Kathryn.

Rowan spoke from across the fire. "Aiden, you are the heir."

Aiden laughed. "Right." She reached out to hand the paper back to Kathryn shaking her head. "No, I'm not."

"Look at the broken seal."

Aiden examined the wax seal, the Roth family crest that featured a crescent moon and three stars. She looked confused.

"I don't understand. This note is about some missing heir. And whoever wrote this wants that person dead."

"Your uncle, Balak Roth, authored that message. The captain of my imperial guard took it off the body of a paid mercenary less than a week ago." Kathryn couldn't tell if Aiden believed her, because her expression was hard to read.

"An uncle I've never met wants me dead? Why?"

"Because you are the rightful heir to the Belstaff throne." Kathryn hoped Aiden would accept the truth. She knew it was a lot to absorb. She wasn't sure what her reaction would be if she were in Aiden's shoes. She turned to Rowan for support. Rowan was always better at getting people to listen to hard news than she was. It was her way. She was very empathetic. She just sensed things. She knew how to read a person and tell them what they most needed to hear. Rowan had been sitting silently through the exchange until Kathryn looked at her.

"Aiden, take some time to think about what Kathryn has said to you," Rowan filled a tin cup with coffee. "Here, drink this."

Aiden didn't respond, but stared blankly into the forest. Kathryn wanted to reassure her, to touch her, but she stopped herself, unsure how Aiden would respond.

"Aiden." Rowan closed her hands around Aiden's as Aiden accepted the coffee. "Everything is going to be okay."

Kathryn quietly watched her cousin work her magic. Aiden sipped her coffee and appeared to relax a bit. She glanced sideways at Kathryn. There were questions in her eyes. "What did you mean when you said something earlier about your imperial guard? Who are you?"

"She's the queen of Olmstead." Rowan refilled Aiden's cup as nonchalantly as if she were discussing the weather.

"You're a..."

"A queen. Yes, Kathryn is royal born," Gareth interjected.

Kathryn's cheeks felt hot under Aiden's scrutiny.

"I don't believe this. This is too much." Aiden's words were edged with exasperation.

"Search your thoughts and feelings, Aiden. Carry this with you for a while until you're comfortable with it. We don't have to talk about it right now. You should eat." Rowan handed a strip of venison to her.

The parchment with the broken seal lay on the ground next to her feet. Aiden couldn't stop staring at it as she pulled small strips of the meat free and slowly chewed.

"Is my mother alive? My father? Does this mean I have parents?" Aiden's hopefulness broke Kathryn's heart. She had to look away as Rowan delivered the truth.

"No. I'm so sorry, Aiden. Your uncle is the only Roth family member left."

"The uncle that wants me dead. Perfect." Aiden covered her face with her hands then briskly brushed her fingers through her still damp hair.

Gareth tossed remnants of coffee from his cup and stowed it in his saddlebag. He picked up the rest of his gear and began to make ready for departure.

After a few minutes, Kathryn followed him. She wished there was a way to give Aiden time to absorb all that they'd just told her, but she felt some urgency to get them all back to Olmstead and under the protection of Frost and her imperial guard. She wasn't so naïve to think that there weren't others looking for Aiden. Possibly even the three men that attacked them outside the cell. She would do everything within her power to keep Aiden safe and give her time to come to terms with the birthright she'd just discovered was hers.

Kathryn tied the bedroll to her saddle. She looked back to where Aiden sat packing her things, then to Rowan, who stood nearby adjusting her horse's bridle.

"What do you suppose she's thinking?" Kathryn asked.

"Probably that her entire world has just tilted on its axis."

CHAPTER ELEVEN

Aiden's thoughts traveled to the great owl she'd seen during her brief excursion the previous night. The omen had been true. Her parents were dead. Her mother was dead. She was alone in the world, just like before. Well, at least now she knew for sure.

And what about the other things Kathryn had told her? She'd always had the feeling that something in the outside world awaited her, some greater destiny, but heir to the throne of Belstaff? That was hard to believe.

She stroked Sunset's neck and was just about to put her foot in the stirrup to climb into the saddle when Gareth spoke behind her.

"She put herself at risk for you. I want you to know that." His voice was insistent but hushed. He obviously didn't want the others to hear.

Aiden turned to face him. "Who?"

"Kathryn."

"I didn't ask her to do that. I didn't ask for any of this."

"Well, it happened just the same didn't it?"

Aiden faced him. She wasn't sure what sort of response he was seeking. He was protective of Kathryn, but it wasn't like Aiden asked to be rescued. Twenty-four hours ago, she didn't even know who Kathryn was.

"I just hope you're worth the risk." He launched himself onto his horse in one smooth movement, jerked the reins, and trotted away from where Aiden was standing.

She tried to shake off his remarks, but she wasn't feeling very worthy. She hadn't asked for any of this, and she wasn't sure she deserved it or even wanted it. She'd had plans of her own, and now all of those plans had been knocked off course.

Aiden climbed into the saddle and urged Sunset to follow the others as they threaded through the trees back toward the wagon road they'd been following the previous night.

Aiden trailed the others. She watched them and envied their palpable bond. She'd left any friends she had when she stepped through the arched stone gateway of the monastery. In her teens, she couldn't wait to escape its confines. Now she almost wished to be back there, to center herself and maybe seek guidance from Brother Francis. He was the eldest of the monks and had been her mentor in so many things.

Now it made sense to her that he'd tried to convince her to stay. She hadn't understood why he was so protective, why he'd insisted she not leave the monastery alone. Had he known who she was all along? He'd never said anything to indicate he did, but he must have had some idea. He was so restrictive about her movements, but she'd always assumed that was because she was a girl surrounded by boys.

She was beginning to realize his protectiveness had nothing to do with gender. And she'd ended up sneaking away from the monastery before sunrise, while it was still dark. She'd felt a little guilty about not saying good-bye, but she'd vowed to return and offer her gratitude and a proper good-bye after her journey to the coast.

As she reflected on her time at the monastery, movement caught her attention. Aiden lagged behind the rest of the group, who was moving at a faster pace.

Her mount didn't seem spooked by anything, but Aiden was certain she'd seen something. There it was again, off to the left, a flash of white fur in the shadowed forest. Aiden strained to get a better look. She pulled Sunset to a stop, and the creature stopped too.

Aiden could see it clearly now. The animal made no attempt to hide its presence. The great white wolf studied them, with its head low and eyes laser focused. A ring of thick tufted fur around its broad shoulders stirred in the breeze. Aiden met the wolf's eyes in an intense stare down, and still Sunset gave no indication that she sensed the predator's presence. Why hadn't the mare spooked at the scent of a wolf?

She heard hooves on the path and glanced away quickly to see Rowan riding back in her direction. It was only a split second that she looked away, but the wolf had disappeared. She searched the shadows, but the animal had vanished.

"Is something wrong?"

"You didn't see it?"

"See what?" Rowan scanned the woods that Aiden was facing.

"A white wolf."

"A white wolf?"

"Yes. That's the second time I've seen it. Assuming it's the same animal." Aiden had glimpsed the animal the first night she'd camped away from the monastery, before arriving in Eveshom. She thought she'd imagined it because she only saw it for an instant before it disappeared into the thick forest.

"I would think a white wolf is rather rare."

"So would I," Aiden said softly to herself. She turned and spoke to Rowan. "Sorry, I didn't mean to make you come back to check on me." Aiden was determined not to require more assistance from the three of them than she'd already needed. She wanted to be self-sufficient.

If what Gareth has said was true then they'd done enough for her. The sooner they could all go their separate ways the better for all of them, especially if this Balak fellow really wanted her dead.

Except, there had been that moment at the stream with Kathryn. She'd felt something between them. Something besides the shocking cold of the metal coffee pot against her bare chest. She'd like just a little more time to see what that feeling was about. Just a little more time, then she'd be on her own again and a burden to no one.

"You said you've seen the wolf before?"

Aiden almost forgot what they'd been talking about as the recollected sensations of Kathryn's fingertips on her shoulder filled her head with strange ideas. "Yes, I saw it the first night after leaving the monastery."

"Interesting. Maybe you have a guardian."

"Maybe." Aiden figured it was probably just more bad luck to have a predator for a guardian. What else could go wrong? She scolded herself for even putting the question out to the universe. She was in no position to tempt fate.

Rowan guided her mount to fall in step beside Aiden's.

"Are you and Kathryn sisters?" Aiden eyed Rowan. She wanted to find out a little more about the group's dynamics before they caught up to Kathryn and Gareth.

"First cousins, but Kathryn feels like a sister."

"And Gareth? Are he and Kathryn…"

"A couple?" Rowan finished Aiden's question. "No. Kathryn prefers the company of women. But she and Gareth are very close. He's worked in the castle stables since he was a boy."

They rode in silence for a few minutes before Rowan spoke.

"And you? You really know nothing of your origin?"

Aiden shook her head. "No. I used to ask lots of questions about who my parents were, but there were no answers. I suppose no one knew."

Kathryn glanced over her shoulder. Aiden and Rowan were talking, but she couldn't make out what they were saying. She frowned. If only she could read lips.

Gareth twisted in his saddle to follow Kathryn's gaze back at Rowan and Aiden. "Look at her. She doesn't have a clue of who she is or why she's with us. I don't care if she is the missing heir. I think you're making a mistake taking her back to Olmstead."

"Keep your voice down." Kathryn frowned at him.

He faced forward and made a lame attempt at keeping quiet. "Trouble is going to follow her back to Olmstead. We don't need to give Balak a reason to act against us. And taking her there will definitely cause him to take aim at us."

"He's already acting against us. His men have been raiding the outlying farms for weeks. It won't be long before he strikes closer to the palace."

"Well, I still don't think she's the savior you've hoped for. She can't do this. Balak will end her."

"You're not even giving her a chance. She only just found out who she really is. That's a lot to absorb." Kathryn wasn't sure if Gareth saw something in Aiden that she didn't. Maybe her hopefulness and the allure she felt was clouding her judgment.

"You're attracted to her."

"Is that what you're so angry about?"

"No, I suppose you could do worse. And if you could get her on the throne at Windsheer Castle that wouldn't be the worst thing for us." Gareth looked at her and his tone softened. "I just worry about you. That's all."

Kathryn smiled weakly. "I know."

Finding Aiden had made Kathryn feel hopeful, for the first time in months. And then they'd almost kissed by the stream. Kathryn brushed her fingertips over her lips. It was an *almost kiss* that she couldn't stop thinking about. Or about Aiden's broad shoulders glistening in the early morning sunlight. Aiden's toned arms, her fine hands, her wild hair, and her piercing blue eyes. Kathryn cataloged Aiden's features until heat rose to her cheeks.

CHAPTER TWELVE

They rode for another two hours before taking a break to rest and let the horses graze in a small clearing with tall grass.

Aiden held the cheek strap of Kathryn's horse while she dismounted. His silvery mane stirred in the breeze. "He's a beautiful animal. What's his name?"

"Blaez. It's a word from the old language." Kathryn rubbed her palm over his neck. "It means wolf."

She stood in shocked silence as Kathryn began to riffle through her saddlebag. A white horse named "wolf." That seemed too bizarre, and thinking about it gave Aiden the chills. In a bit of a daze, she moved away to stand near Gareth. She was fairly sure he didn't like her, but he'd offered her his canteen nonetheless. She was taking a long draw, savoring the cool water, when Gareth held up his hand, a strange look on his face.

"Did you hear that?" Gareth rotated away, stepped in front of Aiden, and scanned the tree line.

"Hear wha—" An arrow struck Gareth in the shoulder and he fell backward. She juggled the canteen to catch him, and the two of them fell backward on the ground. Blood spread across his shirt. Another arrow whizzed past her face. "Get down! Everyone get down!"

Kathryn looked back at them, a startled expression on her face. The horses spooked, and Blaez stepped away from Kathryn, leaving her exposed. Kathryn quickly followed Blaez and pulled her crossbow free, then crouched low. Rowan crawled in the high grass toward Gareth.

Aiden stood and pulled Gareth's sword from the scabbard on his saddle. The blade had just cleared the leather when a rider galloped toward her, sword raised. She blocked the blow as he rode past, but he pivoted quickly to come back in her direction.

Aiden saw Kathryn fire at someone who'd just stepped from the cover of the trees surrounding the clearing, probably the archer who'd shot Gareth. She wondered for an instant if Gareth had taken an arrow meant for her. Kathryn's arrow hit its mark. The man fell forward as Kathryn's hands moved in a blur to reload. Aiden readied for the rider's second approach when pounding hooves sounded behind her. Her mind raced. How would she defend against both riders? They already had the advantage of being on horseback. She held the sword in both hands and pivoted.

"Move!" The second rider was clad in men's clothing, but the voice was definitely a woman's. Dumbfounded, Aiden stepped back as the rider pounded past her and dislodged the other rider from his mount with an epic swing across his midsection. His body hit the ground with a thump.

The second rider pulled to an abrupt stop, dismounted, and returned to the fallen attacker. She stood over him, and then with her jaw clenched, she plunged her broadsword into his chest.

Gareth's head was in Rowan's lap. Kathryn lowered her weapon but kept it cocked. This woman, the second rider, had clearly come to their aid, but there was no recognition in Kathryn's eyes to indicate that she knew her.

Aiden lowered her sword and scrutinized the stranger as she wiped her blade and strode toward them. She was at least six feet tall. She was large boned, muscled, and looked very strong. Her tanned complexion spoke of someone who spent a lot of time outdoors, but the straight blond hair that hung past her jaw, just striking her collar, was clean and she appeared freshly bathed. Her clothing was hard to identify. While she carried herself like a warrior, tightly coiled and pulsing with energy, her attire looked like a feeble attempt to hide her true vocation. She wore the drab brown clothing of a merchant or tradesman, a leather vest over a pale shirt and heavy trousers with tall leather boots.

"Are you hurt, Aiden?" The warrior woman strode toward her, a fierce expression on her face.

"She's okay. I'm the one who got shot!" Gareth complained from his reclined position on the ground. The woman barely glanced down as she stepped over him.

"Are you all right, Aiden?" she asked again.

"Who are you?"

"Venn." She slid her broadsword into a leather sheath that hung at her hip. "Venn Lyons."

"How do you know my name?"

"You probably know by now that I'm not the only one looking for you." Venn braced her hands on her hips. She was a few inches taller than Aiden and radiated an intensity that made Aiden want to take a step back. But Aiden wasn't in the mood to be intimidated.

Kathryn, her loaded crossbow loosely in front of her body, moved closer to Aiden.

Venn ignored her, never breaking eye contact with Aiden. "Balak wanted you dead twenty years ago. He's not going to stop until he's ended you and erased the threat to his rule. Trust me. I know him."

"How do you know so much about Balak?" Kathryn asked. "How can we trust you when we don't know you?"

Though the question came from Kathryn, Venn's gaze never wavered from Aiden. It was a bit unnerving. "I was once a member of the royal guard in Belstaff."

"You're from Belstaff?" Aiden's voice rose a notch, and Kathryn half raised her crossbow as though preparing to aim.

"I was delayed or I'd have been at the monastery before you left." Venn shifted her stance, but not her focus on Aiden.

"How did you even know I was leaving, when I hardly knew myself?"

"Brother Francis sent word that you were anxious to depart from the monastery. I expected as much since you just turned twenty-one. I had planned to arrive well before your birthday, but things conspired against me."

"Wait…I've seen you before." Aiden searched her memory. A vague mental image was rising to the surface. She'd seen this woman once at the monastery when she was a teenager. "You were there."

"I've always been there." Venn's expression softened just a little.

"Well, that sounds ominous." Gareth spoke from the ground.

For the first time since she'd arrived, Venn looked down at Gareth and actually acknowledged him. "Maybe we should see to your friend."

Kathryn uncocked her crossbow and walked over to the body of the man Venn had killed. She rummaged through his clothing, and after a moment, removed something from inside his coat. She handed it to Aiden. It was blood-soaked, but the broken seal was unmistakable, another missive from Balak.

Aiden unfolded the paper and read it. The message was the same. Balak wanted her dead. She dropped the paper and walked a few feet away from the group. She scanned the tree line and ran her fingers through her hair. Why couldn't people just leave her alone?

Gareth groaned and she turned back to the group. Kathryn and Rowan helped Gareth sit up and held him while Venn broke off the arrow point that had passed through the soft tissue of his shoulder.

"Hold him steady now," Venn said as she gripped the remaining shaft and pulled it free.

"Aaugh!" Gareth grimaced and cried out as she pulled the rod out of his shoulder.

Rowan was quick with a cloth, putting pressure on the wound.

"Keep pressure on it until we can cauterize it." Venn tossed the bloody shaft into the tall grass.

"I'll get some wood for a fire." Kathryn seemed almost in shock.

"Do you think it's safe to build a fire? Won't we be noticed?" Rowan asked.

"I think we're safe enough." Venn got to her feet. "We should build a fire, see to the wound, and then keep moving."

Aiden was worried about Kathryn and grateful to Gareth. He'd taken an arrow for her even though she wasn't his favorite person. But for the moment, Gareth was under Rowan's attentive care, so she followed after Kathryn, who had disappeared into the surrounding woods.

Kathryn was leaning against a tree with her forehead against her arm and holding her stomach with her other arm. Aiden hesitated. Should she say something or give Kathryn space?

Uncertain if Kathryn was aware she had followed, Aiden spoke softly so that she didn't startle her. "Hey, are you not well?"

Kathryn abruptly moved away from the tree, shook her head, and smoothed her palms against her thighs. The knees of her riding pants were soiled from kneeling beside Gareth. She brushed at loose wisps of hair around her face. "No, I'm fine."

But she didn't seem fine. Her gaze darted about the forest, avoiding eye contact with Aiden. On impulse, Aiden reached out to place her hands on Kathryn's arms. "Gareth is going to be all right."

Kathryn looked down at Aiden's hand on her arm and then looked up at Aiden. Tears gathered along her lashes. Instinctively, Aiden pulled Kathryn into her arms. She made slow circles on Kathryn's back. "Hey, don't cry. Everything is going to be okay." She didn't really know if everything would be okay, but Rowan had said the same thing to her earlier and it helped, whether it was true or not.

She felt Kathryn's arms encircle her waist. The boys in the orphanage hadn't been big on displays of affection, nor had the monks who cared for them, so being held like this by anyone was a new experience for Aiden. She'd reached for Kathryn out of an impulse to comfort her, but as soon as they were in each other's arms she was flooded with emotions she didn't fully understand.

As they held each other, sensations washed over her like successive crashing waves. Affection, need, desire, relief, and an array of protective impulses powerfully coursed through her body. Kathryn shifted in her arms, so that her cheek rested against Aiden's chest. She gave in to temptation and swept her hand gently over Kathryn's silky hair.

Kathryn sniffed. "This feels good."

Such a simple statement, but Kathryn's words made Aiden's insides flutter as if a hundred butterflies had just taken up residence in her stomach.

"We should get some wood for a fire." Kathryn's face was still pressed against Aiden's chest. She gently moved out of Aiden's arms, and Aiden reluctantly released her.

Kathryn wiped at wet paths on her cheek. They didn't speak further. They each collected small pieces of dried wood and then walked back toward the clearing. The horses had been gathered and tied to a stand of small saplings. Rowan sat on the ground beside Gareth who was propped up on blankets watching Venn spark tender for a fire.

Who was Venn? She'd never really answered Aiden's question about how she knew her name or how she knew she was at the monastery. And she'd openly admitted that she'd been part of Belstaff's royal guard. Sure, she'd come to their aid, but why? For all Aiden knew, Venn carried one of Balak's death memos in her pocket even now. If Venn were working for Balak, then she'd just put Kathryn and the others at risk. If she'd had any notions about leaving the group and going her own way, she couldn't do that now. She needed to see Kathryn safely back to Olmstead or she'd never forgive herself.

Aiden dropped the wood at Venn's feet and stepped back from the group. Gareth smiled up at Kathryn as she fussed over him, his eyes never leaving her face. Aiden wouldn't have minded being in his place—Kathryn doting over her—except for the pain awaiting him once Venn's fire was hot enough to cauterize his wound.

CHAPTER THIRTEEN

Kathryn watched Venn kick dirt over the fire with her boot to smother the flame after Gareth's wound had been tended and bandaged. She was grateful to Venn for coming to their aid. Although she felt confident they would have prevailed, the victory might not have come without further injury.

"You know who Aiden is. Do you know who I am also?" Kathryn wanted to pull more information from Venn in hopes of finding out who she really was.

Venn glanced up from her task. "You are Kathryn Warrington, Princess of Olmstead."

"Queen of Olmstead," Kathryn said softly, wishing again that she was still princess, that her father was still waiting at home for her return.

"My condolences." Venn stopped and gave Kathryn her full attention. "Your father was a good man. Kind and thoughtful."

"Thank you."

They were silent for a moment as they studied one another. Gleaning information from Venn was going to be a little like pulling teeth, painful and slow. Maybe Rowan would have better luck.

"We should keep moving." Venn bent to assist Gareth to his feet. Then she and Aiden helped him climb onto his horse using his uninjured arm.

Aiden held the stirrup for Kathryn. She studied Aiden's hand for a moment and then placed her boot in the stirrup and climbed into the saddle. She looked down as Aiden released the stirrup with a brush of her hand against Kathryn's leg, but Aiden's expression was impossible to interpret. Kathryn wanted more than anything for Aiden to see her, to really see her. If only things were different. If only she and Aiden could linger here, in the sun, in the soft grass. It would be such a pleasure to just lounge in the warmth of the sun and talk, to really talk with someone. Someone other than her cousin, Rowan. But there was no time for that now.

She smiled at Aiden once she, too, was mounted and turned Blaez to resume their eastward trek. They'd covered a lot of ground because they'd ridden halfway through the first night without stopping. Barring further incident, they'd breach the boundary of the salt flats by late afternoon. A wind ship would carry them to the border of Olmstead, and then another day's ride would bring them to the palace. She was anxious to be safely within the stone walls of Starford Keep.

Even though Venn was a newcomer to their group, she led the riders. Gareth followed with Aiden riding close behind him. Rowan dropped back alongside Kathryn.

"What do you think of Venn?"

"I'm not sure what to think yet." Kathryn squinted at Venn's back, probably thirty feet ahead of them. "It's hard to get any real information from her. Maybe you can talk with her when we reach the wind ship."

"I find her very intriguing."

Kathryn turned to look at Rowan, surprised by her flirtatious tone. "I see." Rowan rarely if ever showed a romantic interest in someone. "Maybe speaking with her further won't be such a burden for you then."

Rowan laughed. "I'll manage to suffer through."

"How old do you think she is?"

"My best guess? Early forties."

"She's not too old for you?" Kathryn grinned at Rowan to let her know she was joking.

"Experience has its merits, cousin."

❖

Aiden shifted in her saddle. She was tired and achy in odd places. Her previous travels had been mostly on foot or by wagon. She'd never journeyed this far on horseback. She couldn't imagine how Gareth must be feeling, although he hadn't complained.

They had been gradually descending for the better part of the day, the terrain transitioning from the shade of thick conifers to a more open landscape of scrub brush, juniper, and large, loose rock formations. Soon Aiden could see an enormous expanse of white stretched out before her. A great salt basin—white and perfectly flat with no discernible topography—was all that remained of what had once been an ancient inland sea. She'd heard of the Great Salt Desert, but she'd never been this far east.

As they drew closer to the boundary of the barren white expanse, Aiden could see the outline of a large object that appeared to be a ship. She'd never actually seen a wind ship, although she had heard travelers talk of them when they visited the monastery. She was excited to see one up close.

It was exactly as its name described, a wind ship. The enormous wooden craft looked like the square-rigger ships Aiden had seen in port cities to the west, except this ship had a broad flat bottom mounted on a series of axles set close together, with large, solid wooden wheels several feet wide lined up along the axles that were tucked under the flat undercarriage of the craft. The ship had three masts. One main mast and two smaller ones fore and aft, along with what looked like a jib mount at the front.

Aiden wondered who owned the vessel, but before she could finish the thought, a woman appeared near the railing and looked down at them. She walked down the access ramp and strode toward them as they dismounted.

She was tall like Venn. The woman's skin was dark brown, her strikingly beautiful face was framed by a mane of long black hair, and her full feminine curves were draped in a loose-fitting crimson shirt open at the neck to reveal deep cleavage. She wore thigh-hugging pants tucked into knee-high black leather boots. A wide leather belt draped around her waist from which hung a sheath with a dagger. The jeweled handle of the large knife was distractingly ornate.

Aiden stiffened, then took a half step back as the woman walked directly to her, encroaching into Aiden's personal space. Venn remained stoic, apparently not intimidated in the least by this brash woman whom Aiden assumed was the wind ship's captain. The captain cocked her head to the side and surveyed Aiden from head to toe through squinted eyes as if to size her up, before turning to address Kathryn.

"The ship is prepped and ready for departure, Your Highness," she said to Kathryn.

"Nilah, this is Aiden. And this is Venn." Kathryn motioned in Aiden's direction and then in Venn's. "This is Nilah. She and her crew will handle our transport across the salt desert."

Nilah nodded to Aiden before she turned and strode back toward the ship. Several other crew members had gathered near the bow of the ship, and Nilah began issuing orders for them to disembark and assist with loading the gear, horses, and passengers.

Aiden had a sinking feeling in her stomach and turned to walk a few feet away from the group. She began to walk in small circles trying to calm herself.

Up to this point they'd traveled through a territory she was at least somewhat acquainted with. If she'd wanted to leave the group, she was within a few days' walk of familiar territory. Now she was about to cross the desert into a completely unfamiliar land.

Not to mention that the closer they got to Belstaff the sooner she would have to make a decision. She wasn't stupid. She knew Kathryn and the others carried some silent hope that she would help them instigate a coup to unseat Balak, the ruler of a kingdom she felt no kinship for, a place she had no memory of.

Aiden tried inhaling and exhaling deeply to get her heart rate to slow. *What am I doing? I don't want this. I'm not ready for this.*

Kathryn offered Blaez's reins to one of Nilah's ship stewards. The horses were being led into the lower portion of the ship where they'd be shielded from the desert sun in dark stalls, where fresh hay and water awaited them.

As the steward walked away, Kathryn watched Aiden who was several yards from the ship, walking back and forth, shaking her head, and gesturing with her arms as if she was carrying on a conversation with some unseen presence.

Kathryn hesitated but then decided to approach because Aiden appeared to be in some sort of distress. She heard Aiden muttering as she neared but couldn't make out what she was saying.

"Aiden?"

Aiden stopped pacing as Kathryn approached. She had a startled look on her face as if she'd forgotten she wasn't alone.

"Why are you doing this?" Aiden asked.

"What?"

"This." Aiden motioned toward the ship. "Why did you come for me? I didn't ask you to do any of this."

"You'd prefer that I'd left you in that dank cell in Eveshom?"

"Of course not." Aiden shook her head and started to pace again. Dust from the parched earth gathered in puffs around her boots. "I'm just not sure I should get on this boat." She halted her march and looked at Kathryn. "What's going to happen when we get to Olmstead?"

"We will make plans for you to claim your throne as the rightful heir."

"Just like that. You make it sound so easy."

"No, I don't think it will be easy." Kathryn was feeling frustrated by Aiden's apparent reluctance. "When I came to Eveshom I had no idea if I'd actually find you. I had no idea who you'd be if I did find you. But now that I have found you, I'm willing to help you claim your throne."

"You don't even know what kind of person I am. A birthmark doesn't make someone a leader."

"It's not a birthmark."

"Whatever." Aiden ran her fingers through her hair briskly. "That's not the point."

"Then what is the point?" Kathryn stepped closer and put her hand on Aiden's arm. Energy pulsed through her palm; the casual contact sent chills up Kathryn's arm. Aiden stilled and focused on

Kathryn's hand and then turned her focus to Kathryn's face. Those eyes, Kathryn swam in them for a moment.

"The point is that I'm not sure I'm the person you hope that I am." There was a note of sadness in Aiden's words.

"We don't have to know all the answers right in this moment." She squeezed Aiden's arm lightly. "Let's just get to Olmstead where you'll be safe. Okay?"

Aiden didn't say anything. She turned and looked out across the vast nothingness of the simmering plateau.

"Aiden?"

Aiden looked back at her and nodded. "Okay."

"Come with me. We'll get some food. The ship will be ready to leave soon." Kathryn placed her hand on Aiden's back as they walked back toward the ship.

Nilah's crew climbed the rigging at the forward mast.

"Stepping off!" one of the men yelled to his mates as he stepped off the yard footrope, and a large white sail dropped and caught the wind.

Aiden put a hand on the railing as the heavy wooden land craft began to move forward. They had at least four hours of sunlight left, and Kathryn was anxious to cover as much ground between where they were and Olmstead as possible.

The main sail dropped and the wind ship picked up speed.

"Set the sail!" Nilah barked orders from the rudder wheel.

The ship creaked and rocked as it sailed across the vastness of the salt flats. Kathryn leaned against the railing in the shade cast by the broad main sail. She closed her eyes and savored the warm air blowing across her skin. It stirred loose tendrils around her face, and she brushed them off her cheek. The wind ship was moving at a good speed. They would be halfway across by sunset, which settled Kathryn's nerves a bit.

The openness of the desert would allow them to see any who tried to approach their position. It would be easy to spot anyone who followed, and there were no other ships anywhere in sight. She knew the central region was Nilah's domain. By treaty, the Great Salt Desert was neutral territory, sharing its borders with all four kingdoms—Taiga to the north, Fainsland to the west, Olmstead to the east, and Belstaff to the south. She was sure Nilah guarded her desert trade route with vehemence. Kathryn knew she could relax for now, safe under Nilah's watch.

She sensed someone close to her and opened her eyes. Rowan had joined her at the railing. The breeze from the ship's momentum stirred her dark hair. She pulled it back and twisted it a few times to tame it.

"I saw you talking with Aiden earlier. What was that about?"

Kathryn smiled at her question. "You hate not knowing things."

"Don't tease me. You know you'll eventually tell me, so why make me wait?" Rowan playfully bumped her shoulder against Kathryn's.

"I think she was having second thoughts about coming with us."

"Where else would she go?"

Kathryn shrugged. "Anywhere." Kathryn turned to face Rowan. "There have been times when I've thought how great it would be to just disappear."

"I know you have. And I've wished there was some way to take some of the burden from your shoulders."

"Thank you." Kathryn leaned against Rowan's arm then resumed her watch of the horizon. "If I were Aiden, I would be tempted to just walk away and get on with my life."

"I don't think she could. Balak will see to that. Now that he suspects she's alive, her path is no longer her own."

"What do you think of her?"

"I assume we're not talking about her potential abilities as a leader?"

"No." Kathryn laughed.

"You mean, what do I think of her besides the fact that she's incredibly good-looking, which I think I've already mentioned."

"Yeah, besides that."

"I think she's led a sheltered life in many ways. I sense she knows how to take care of herself in a fistfight, or a sword fight, but emotionally…"

"What?"

"I think she doesn't know how to shield her feelings. She's open, authentic, unafraid because she's never experienced hurt or betrayal." Rowan looked at Kathryn, shifting her stance to face her fully. "Earlier, when she spoke with you, she allowed you to see her uncertainty and her self-doubt. Didn't she?"

"Yes, she did."

"That's what I mean. She doesn't know to shield her feelings. I mean, you won't use her vulnerability against her, but there are others who might."

Thinking about someone hurting Aiden in any way made Kathryn's stomach turn. She wanted to change the subject. "What about Venn? Did you find anything else out about our mystery hero?"

Rowan grinned, and there was a mischievous glint in her eyes. "Not yet, but we have at least another twenty-four hours in close quarters on this ship so I plan to make her my personal mission."

Kathryn laughed. "I hope she can handle your undivided attention."

"I have the feeling Venn can handle anything." Rowan touched Kathryn's arm. "One more thing."

"Yes?"

"I get the sense that Aiden has absolutely no experience with women. I can tell that you like her. So if you want something to happen you're going to have to make the first move."

"Thanks." *No pressure.* She once again turned to look out over the barren landscape that surrounded them.

The wooden craft cast a long shadow behind them due to the sinking position of the sun. It would be dusk soon, and they'd have to stop for the night. Sailing a wind ship wasn't the same as sailing a square-rigger at sea. The terrain of the ocean couldn't swallow a ship in an unseen crevice in darkness. She knew the sea held other perils, but sailing at night wasn't one of them.

Her thoughts returned to Aiden, as they'd done often since the first night they'd met. Maybe she should make the first move soon. At the moment, they were on neutral ground. Once they arrived in Olmstead, Kathryn's position might be intimidating for Aiden. Not to mention the fact that the affairs of the kingdom would erase any free time to explore the impulses she was feeling. Maybe tonight was the perfect opportunity to test the waters, despite the fact that they were traveling across the driest spot on the planet.

Aiden leaned against the aft rail and savored the opportunity to watch Kathryn from a slight distance, unobserved.

The sleeves of Kathryn's blouse billowed with the wind. She closed her eyes and leaned into the breeze. With her clothing pressed against her from the forward motion of the ship, Aiden was able to appreciate every subtle curve from her shoulders to her shapely legs.

She wondered what Kathryn's life was like. Probably nothing like hers. Aiden got the impression that Kathryn was always in control of herself and in charge. There was kindness in the way she directed the others, but her strength and position were evident in the way Rowan, Gareth, and Nilah responded to her.

Now she and Rowan were laughing together about something. Then Rowan went below deck and Kathryn turned to face her. For a moment, they held each other with their eyes. At least that's the way it felt to Aiden. Like a physical touch. And after another moment, Kathryn smiled and turned away.

Heat warmed Aiden's cheeks. She wasn't sure if that warmth was from the low-hanging sun or the attraction she was feeling for Kathryn. Aiden leaned back against the railing and watched the desolate landscape speed past.

CHAPTER FOURTEEN

A iden was seated near the center of a long plank table. Dinner in the main galley had been a casual affair. The sails had been lowered and the ship was anchored for the night so the deck was solid and unmoving. Aiden was grateful that the motion had stopped. The constant rocking had proved a bit unsettling for her land loving stomach. When she was younger, one possibility she'd imagined for herself was a life at sea. She'd have to rethink that given this recent discovery of a weak stomach.

She'd eaten in silence, listening to the conversation and banter at either end of the table. The only other person who hadn't joined in the friendly mealtime exchange was Venn, seated across from her. Every now and then she caught Venn watching her, but after a few seconds, Venn would look down as if the food on her plate suddenly held some great interest.

What was her story? Aiden was dying to know more, but she wasn't going to ask. If Venn wanted to connect with her then she'd have to make more of an effort. For some reason, Aiden didn't feel like making it easy for her.

Nilah's crew was friendly enough, and Gareth and Nilah seemed to have some history. Maybe they'd been more than friends at some point. There was certainly a flirtatious air between them. Aiden didn't understand some of the things that they spoke about. The meanings were hidden, like inside jokes. At least Gareth's mood was better and his injured shoulder didn't seem to bother him too much. She figured the vast amounts of wine he was consuming had helped his mood and dulled his pain.

Aiden envied the easy way that Kathryn was with Rowan and how she laughed with the others. Part of her wanted to be included in their circle. But if she were honest, what she really wanted was a chance to be alone with Kathryn. She just wasn't sure how to make that happen, or if it would be a good idea if it did happen. And if she did get Kathryn alone, then what? She'd have no idea what to do next.

Frustrated, she pushed away from the table and quietly left the room for the small quarters she'd been assigned onboard the ship.

Aiden dropped onto the narrow bed mounted to the wall in her room. She folded her hands behind her head and stared at the plank ceiling. She hadn't been lying there long when she heard a soft knock at the door.

She was surprised and secretly elated to see Kathryn.

"I'm sorry to disturb you, but you left dinner rather abruptly. I wanted…well, I just wanted to see that you were all right."

"I'm sorry. I should have said good night. I was…I don't know what to say. Sorry." Aiden knew she was fumbling with her words.

"May I come in?"

Aiden's stomach clenched. Her silent wish had just come true. Now what? "Of course. Please come in." She stepped aside for Kathryn to enter the narrow space. Accommodations on the ship were private, but very small.

Once Kathryn was inside and the door closed, Aiden was at a loss. Should she ask Kathryn to sit? The only place to sit was on the bed, but that didn't seem right. She nervously ran her fingers through her hair and smiled weakly at Kathryn.

Kathryn took a step toward her, and Aiden reflexively took a step back, but there was nowhere to go. Her back was against the wall. She looked down at Kathryn's upturned face as Kathryn moved even closer.

"Is this okay?"

"Yeah." Aiden's voice cracked. Her heart thumped against her breastbone.

She caught her breath when Kathryn's hand rested against her torso. Then Kathryn's hand, warm even through Aiden's shirt, slid around her waist. She lightly pressed her soft lips to Aiden's.

Aiden froze. Her arms were at her sides, her hands open but holding nothing. The heat of Kathryn's mouth against hers settled in her stomach and then dropped lower.

Kathryn's tongue brushed against her lips so she opened them and invited Kathryn to deepen the kiss. Aiden realized she'd been holding her breath and tried to relax into the kiss. Instinctively, she swept her hands up Kathryn's arms and then let one of them rest at the small of Kathryn's back.

"Hmm, that was good," Kathryn whispered against Aiden's mouth.

Aiden opened her eyes to see that Kathryn was smiling.

"Could we do that again?" Aiden asked.

Kathryn's smile widened. Without speaking, she put her hand at the back of Aiden's head, then filled her fingers with Aiden's hair and pulled her into another kiss. Aiden's knees trembled and went weak as Kathryn's body pressed against hers. The sensations she'd felt during their embrace in the woods came rushing back and, along with those feelings, many others. A deep ache began to build at Aiden's core, and she tightened her arms around Kathryn, pulling Kathryn up on her tiptoes.

Breathless, Kathryn broke the kiss. "Will you take your shirt off?"

Aiden smiled against Kathryn's cheek. "You seem to have a thing about taking my shirt off, but since it pleases you so much, I'll do it gladly."

That made Kathryn laugh, and Aiden's stomach muscles twitched when Kathryn's fingertips touched bare skin as she helped tug Aiden's shirttail free.

She wanted to ask Kathryn to take her shirt off too. Luckily, she didn't have to muster the nerve to ask. Her breath quickened as she watched Kathryn loosen the bodice over her shirt, toss it aside, and then pull her blouse over her head. Her breasts were larger than Aiden's, her skin creamy and smooth. Perfection. Aiden moaned as Kathryn's soft breasts pressed against her bare chest.

She filled her fingers with Kathryn's hair and kissed her tenderly.

Kathryn reminded Aiden of the Alpine lakes that dotted the terrain that surrounded the monastery—pristine, their glassy surfaces reflecting the deep blue of a cloudless sky. But from the edge of the pool, you were never sure of their depth or of what hazards might hide beneath the still surface. That's how Kathryn felt to Aiden. And every fiber in her body wanted to dive in, regardless of what dangers might lie beneath the surface. She felt as if she were already underwater anyway, struggling for air, fighting against her arousal to breathe.

Kathryn slid her hand down Aiden's firm arm but drew back quickly when Aiden flinched.

"Sorry. I forgot about the cut on your arm." She studied the dark stitches.

"It's okay." Aiden was breathing hard and her face was flushed.

"I never asked you how that happened." Kathryn traced the skin around the cut with her fingertips, careful to be gentle. "That day at the stream I meant to ask, but then…I forgot." She'd forgotten to ask because they'd almost kissed. It was difficult to remember to ask now because Aiden was feathering kisses down her neck.

"It happened in the pub in Evesham. This guy got angry that I was talking to his girlfriend—"

"This happened because of a woman?" Kathryn jerked back.

Surprise registered on Aiden's face as Kathryn pulled away. "Uh, sort of."

"What do you mean, sort of?"

"I was talking to this woman in the pub, she kissed me, and the guy got mad and pulled a sword on me."

"So you were in the cell in Eveshom because of a fight over a woman?" Kathryn knew she was growing louder with each word, but she was incredulous. Rowan had said Aiden was inexperienced. Brawling over a woman in a bar didn't sound like an innocent to her.

"Yes."

"Was she pretty?"

"Well, yeah, but, wait…are you mad at me?"

"No, I'm not mad at you. You're an adult; you can do whatever you like, with whomever you like." Kathryn hated her childish petulance but was powerless to hold it back. Flustered, she couldn't stay there a moment longer. She began gathering her discarded clothing.

"You say you're not mad, but you seem mad. Are you leaving?"

"I'm going back to my room. This was a mistake. I don't know what I was thinking." She certainly wasn't thinking like a queen. She must appear no better than that barroom tart throwing herself at Aiden like this.

"Kathryn, I don't know what just happened. Can we talk about this?" Aiden reached for Kathryn's arm, but she shrugged away.

Once she was safely inside her chamber, she fell face-first on the narrow bunk and cried. What was wrong with her?

She'd had such an instantaneous and visceral reaction to the thought of Aiden with another woman that she'd made an utter fool of herself. It wasn't as if she hadn't been with other women. Two days ago, she hadn't even known Aiden existed. Why did this upset her so much?

She rolled over and let out a long, shuddering breath.

Because she cared, that's why. She knew she already cared too much. *Dammit.*

CHAPTER FIFTEEN

Aiden stood shirtless in the center of the small space in numb silence. What had just happened? Anger quickly replaced confusion as she tugged on her rumpled shirt. She had one thought on her mind, getting off the ship. She yanked at the door and stormed into the narrow hallway.

A strange energy pulsed through her system. She felt so tangled and wound tight inside that her usual solution of simple physical exertion like splitting wood or climbing a sheer rock face would not come close to relieving the tension squeezing the breath from her. This was deeper. She wanted to punch something. Hard. She felt like bursting into tears. Then she wanted to punch something again.

She didn't fully understand why, but she was fairly certain that her current miserable state was all Kathryn's fault. She burst onto the deck of the ship. A lone sentry walked along the railing beside a gangplank that had been lowered to the ground.

Aiden took a deep breath and feigned nonchalance. She nodded a greeting to the sentry, then strolled down the gangway. Once she was on the ground, she picked up her pace. She didn't care where she was going as long as it was away.

Every so often, she turned to look over her shoulder. She could still see the dim lights of the lanterns along the deck in the utter darkness that surrounded the ship. She figured there was no way to get lost as long as she kept the ship in sight. She marched north in a straight line as fast as she could walk. She was breathing hard from the physical exertion and the dry climate. In hindsight, it might have been prudent to bring a little water along, but her thirst was a welcomed, however small, distraction from her churning thoughts. She halted and bent to brace her hands on her knees to catch her breath.

When she looked up, something glowed faintly before her. The bright orb was blurry at first, then began to take the shape of a wolf.

Aiden's pulse quickened, and she reached for her sword. *Damn.* When she grasped empty air, she was reminded that she didn't have one. She'd borrowed Gareth's during the skirmish in the clearing, but she'd returned it. Aiden dropped to one knee and averted her eyes. She wanted to make herself small and nonthreatening. Direct eye contact with a wolf might be interpreted as an act of aggression. Getting mauled by a wolf would be the perfect end to a terrible day.

Aiden stared at the ground as the animal brushed against her like a cat. The wolf swept the top of its head across Aiden's shoulder. Her heart thumped in her chest so hard she was sure the wolf could hear it and would sense her terror. If eye contact didn't invite attack, then the pungent scent of fear surely would. But the wolf surprised her by nudging her chin as if it wanted Aiden to raise her head, so she did.

The wolf sat down and cocked its head like a playful puppy.

"What do you want?"

The animal stood and started to walk away, then looked back when Aiden didn't immediately follow.

"Okay, I'm coming." Aiden got to her feet. She'd only taken a few steps when the wolf circled back so that the ruff of hair at its neck passed beneath her hand. She sank her fingers into the wolf's thick fur. The moment she did she heard a scream.

Shocked, she released the fur. She stepped away from the wolf and spun in every direction, searching for the source. She could no longer see the lantern lights on the ship. She was surrounded by utter darkness. No stars, no horizon line. Aiden took another step back, suddenly dizzy.

The wolf circled her legs, as if to reassure, to comfort her. She filled her hands with its fur again to steady herself. This time she didn't let go. She squeezed her eyes shut and held tight.

When she opened her eyes again, Aiden found she'd been transported to a great hall built of stone. Torches were mounted at regular intervals along the high rock walls. A maiden rushed past her as if she weren't there. A second woman was running straight at her, and Aiden braced for impact. But the woman, carrying a basin of water, passed through her as though she were ghost. She looked down, where her fingers touched the wolf. The wolf was still with her. She wasn't dead. She could still feel its fur in her hand.

Still, she was moving without walking, following the maidens who'd run past her. Suddenly, without opening any door, Aiden was inside someone's bedchamber, as if she'd simply materialized on the other side of the wall. The furniture in the room was ornate, and the draperies covering the windows and hanging around a tall, framed bed were lush, indicating the occupant must be of some importance.

Someone was leaning over a woman who lay in the bed, and from a nearby bassinet, a baby cried softly.

And then, without moving of her own accord, Aiden was at the side of the bed. She recognized the woman seated at the bedside. It was Venn. Only she was much younger.

Aiden's chest seized; she could barely breathe. She placed her hand over her heart and balled the fabric of her shirt into her fist. She didn't understand how, but she could feel the agony, the grief etched across Venn's handsome face.

The woman lying in the bed extended a pale, slender hand to caress Venn's face, and Aiden felt the warmth of the touch as if it were her cheek.

"Leave us." The bedridden woman dropped her hand to the bed, as though the effort had exhausted her, then spoke to the room. The two women who'd been tending to her nodded and left, and she returned her attention to Venn.

"If you truly love me, you will do this for me."

Venn's voice broke with emotion. "Isla, don't ask this of me." She wiped at tears with her hand. "Please don't ask me to leave you. Not when you need me most."

"I'm…I don't have long." She lifted her hand again, and Venn grasped it and held it against her cheek. "My dear husband is dead, and I'm to follow him. Balak will kill the baby. You know he will. He wants the throne for himself."

"Don't give up, Isla. You have time. This can't be the answer."

"Venn, if you love me, then save my soul." She rotated her head toward the infant in the small crib. "Hide the baby. Protect her. Her birth has not been announced. If you take her away from here, she'll be safe."

"I can't leave you. Don't ask me to."

Aiden felt tears trail down her cheeks. The sadness pulsing off Venn's hunched shoulders was palpable. She took a shuddering breath but couldn't tear her attention away from the scene unfolding in front of her.

"I've named her Aiden."

It was then that Aiden's knees almost buckled. This woman was her mother. She examined the woman closely. Yes, a fair complexion, blue eyes, and dark wavy hair. Isla was her mother. She'd never known her name before.

Venn broke down, her shoulders shaking as she sobbed. She pressed her face against the bedding beside Isla, and Isla tenderly stroked her hair. But it was obvious that Isla was extremely weak. Her hand shook with each feeble movement.

"Will you give me this gift, Venn? Will you save my baby?" Isla's spoke in a hoarse whisper.

Venn nodded, wiping her face with her sleeve. "If this is your wish then I will see it through."

"Thank you." Isla was fading fast. "Take her. Go now before it's too late."

Venn kissed Isla's forehead and then pressed Isla's slender, pale fingers to her lips. "I love you, Isla. With all that I am, I love you."

"I love you."

Venn scooped the infant in her arms, swaddling her in a blanket. She opened the front of her jacket, which Aiden now realized was a red uniform coat of some kind. She tenderly tucked the baby inside.

Venn looked back at Isla one more time before she opened an unmarked door with no visible handle and slipped into a passage concealed in the wall.

Aiden watched her mother draw a few shuddering breaths. She was beautiful and fragile and pale. Aiden shut her eyes tightly. To find her mother and see her last hour in the same moment was almost more than Aiden could bear.

When she opened her eyes again, she was no longer in her mother's room.

It was still dark and she and the wolf were outside somewhere, skimming across an open grassy space. Aiden gripped the wolf's fur. Now they were in a stable. Venn was preparing to leave. The wet paths of tears glistened on her cheeks in the lantern light.

She gently touched the baby's forehead and whispered to her. "I'm so sorry, little Aiden. You will never know how amazing your mother was. You will never know the safety of your father." She kissed the baby's forehead. "I will make sure you are safe, and someday, we will return here. This is your birthright."

Venn mounted her horse with the infant tucked inside her jacket and the dark cloak she'd pulled on over it. She angled the horse toward the large stable door and disappeared into the night.

Aiden felt as if she couldn't breathe. She clutched at the collar of her shirt, and as she did she let go of the wolf and tumbled backward into blackness.

CHAPTER SIXTEEN

K athryn left her cabin and paused in the narrow passage, confused. It was well past daybreak; why wasn't the ship moving? She thought she'd go up on deck and ask, but first she wanted to locate Aiden and apologize, or try to apologize, for her outburst the previous night. She had no idea what she was going to say to explain herself, but she held out hope that inspiration would find her once she saw Aiden.

She knocked softly on the door to Aiden's room. After waiting for an appropriate amount of time, she knocked again. Nothing. Not to be denied an audience for her apology, she eased the door open and peeked inside. Aiden's bunk looked as if it hadn't been slept in. That seemed odd.

She hurried down the passage and up the stairs to the quarterdeck.

Raised voices greeted her as she stepped onto the deck of the ship. The sun had only just crested the horizon an hour ago, and already the air was beginning to warm.

"Why aren't we underway?" Venn and Nilah paused their intense discussion and turned to her as she walked toward them.

"We're missing a passenger." Nilah was annoyed. "Aiden is gone."

"Gone?" Kathryn swore her heart seized for a few seconds. "What do you mean she's gone?"

"She's not on the ship." Strain was evident on Venn's face.

"Someone explain to me what's going on." Kathryn wanted answers. Venn, Nilah, and two of Nilah's crew stood in a small cluster near the gangway. All of them faced her but none spoke. Finally, Venn broke the silence.

"Aiden left the ship last night for some reason." Venn gave Kathryn a purposeful glare that cut right through her. She apparently wasn't intimidated by Kathryn's status as a monarch.

"What do you mean she left the ship?" She realized she was repeating herself, but she couldn't help it. Panic filled her lungs. She focused on breathing.

"It seems last night she left the ship to take a walk and hasn't come back. There was a change in the watch. The first crewman reported Aiden's departure to the second watch." Nilah's recap was matter-of-fact. As if she were relaying the weather report for the day.

"So, the prince of nothing has left the boat." Gareth had joined the group, his arm still in a sling.

"That will be enough." Kathryn didn't appreciate his sarcasm.

"Well, we have to go look for her. She could be hurt." Kathryn began to run through scenarios in her head.

"What person in their right mind walks into the desert at night?" Gareth ignored Kathryn's glare.

"I don't like your tone." Venn faced off with Gareth.

"Deal with it. My concern is Kathryn's safety. And sitting here, stalled in the open while we wait on Aiden to return, puts her at risk. For all we know, you and Aiden planned this together. You might still turn out to be a backstabbing spy for Balak." Gareth barely finished the taunt before Venn punched him in the face. Her fist caught him in the jaw and caused him to stumble backward. He lunged at Venn with his good arm, but Nilah stepped between them.

"Enough! This isn't helping." Nilah's hand was on the handle of her dagger. "I'm in command of this vessel, and what I say goes. Stand down!"

Gareth and Venn glared at each other, but backed away.

"Can we send out a search party for Aiden?" Kathryn was annoyed at both Gareth and Venn, but her main concern was finding Aiden.

"We've checked from the eagle's nest in every direction, since sunrise. The moment I knew she was missing, I initiated a search. She's not here or within a mile of the craft in any direction." Nilah nodded at the two crewmen who'd stood at the ready in case Gareth and Venn had more blows to exchange. "Dismissed. Back to your duties."

"Well, what can we do?" Kathryn asked.

"We wait." Venn rubbed the knuckles of her hand.

"For how long?" Gareth asked.

"I leave that to Kathryn. Your Highness?" Nilah was in command of the ship, but she was obviously willing to defer to Kathryn for the moment.

"As long as it takes." Kathryn shielded her eyes with her hand and scrutinized the horizon. As she scanned the empty landscape, dizziness threatened to overwhelm her. Thoughts of Aiden lost or injured filled her head. Kathryn thought she was going to be ill. She swayed on her feet. Venn caught her before she crumpled to the deck. She scooped Kathryn up and carried her close to her chest into the shade of the main cabin wall.

Venn filled a cup with water and brought it over. "Here, drink this."

Kathryn took a few sips in between shaky breaths.

"Better?"

Kathryn nodded. But really she wasn't better. She was very afraid for Aiden's safety. The desert was no place to get lost. And worse, she worried that Aiden's late night departure was all her fault. She should have gone back and talked with Aiden. She should have tried to explain her emotional outburst. But how could she have done that? She didn't understand it herself.

Aiden coughed and squinted against the harsh light. She blinked a few times and then opened her eyes to the pulsating orange orb just above the western horizon. It was nearly sunset. She sat up and tried to swallow. Her throat was as dry as the brittle soil that surrounded her.

Where was she? Oh yeah, the salt flats.

She searched the landscape and tried to get her bearings. In the distance, she saw a shimmering shape. From this distance, it was nothing more than a lump on the shoestring that signaled the edge of the earth in front of her. That had to be the ship. She began to walk in that direction.

She'd taken a few steps when she remembered the wolf. She glanced around, but the wolf was nowhere in sight. She flexed her shoulders, which were stiff and sore. Was that real? Aiden had experienced something she wasn't sure she'd be able to describe in any sort of believable way. It had been an out of body experience where she saw her mother on her deathbed, and as far as she could surmise, felt what Venn felt in that moment twenty-one years ago. Venn had known her mother. They'd evidently been quite close. That was a revelation.

She clutched at her shirt again. She gathered a fistful of cloth in her fingers and pressed her closed fist against her chest. Her heart hurt. It ached. A knot rose in her throat, and before she could swallow it down, she felt tears on her face. They evaporated almost as soon as they materialized in the arid breeze so she let them come. She wailed into the nothingness that surrounded her. Aiden gave over to the despair she'd felt from Venn and let the tears fall.

She walked toward the boxy outline of the wind ship on the razor thin horizon. Maybe there was power in grief. If so, she would harness herself to it.

CHAPTER SEVENTEEN

The hours had dragged by, and the *not knowing* and the *what ifs* kept Kathryn from being able to settle into any sort of comfortable rest during even the hottest hours of the afternoon.

Nilah and her crew had done everything possible to make them comfortable. All the shutters had been opened to allow what little breeze there was to circulate through the lower decks. Doors on all sides stood wide open so that the interior temperature wouldn't rise any higher than the outside air. The dark stalls where the horses stood were actually the coolest part of the ship, so that eased Kathryn's mind somewhat.

But where was Aiden? As time dragged on, she feared the worst.

In the late afternoon, the breeze began to pick up. Dust devils appeared on the horizon, dancing and whirling until they depleted themselves and disappeared.

Kathryn was seated on a bench anchored to the main wall of the cabin. Long shadows fanned out across the polished plank deck of the ship. Rowan took a seat beside her.

"What happened last night?" Rowan had left her alone all day, but Kathryn had known that questions would come. Rowan could always tell when she was upset.

"I'm not sure."

"Did you two argue?"

"I wouldn't call it an argument." Kathryn closed her eyes and sighed. "We kissed. And then I got upset and left."

"Okay, I'm not really following. Explain."

"Well, after dinner I went to Aiden's room and we kissed. And I mean we really kissed and then things were progressing..."

"That sounds promising."

"Then I noticed the stitches on her arm and I asked how she got cut."

"And?"

"She got in a pub fight because she flirted with some woman." Kathryn heard herself relay the story and couldn't help thinking she sounded more like a sulky teenager than a twenty-four-year-old monarch. Now that she'd recounted the details, the whole thing sounded silly and stupid.

"And what did you do when she told you?" Rowan wasn't judging her. Kathryn was harder on herself than Rowan ever was.

"I acted like a jealous brat and stormed out."

"I'm sure it wasn't that bad."

"Yes, it was." Kathryn covered her face with her hands. "It's all my fault. I should have gone back and apologized."

Before Rowan could respond, someone shouted from high in rigging. A lookout stationed at the yardarm for the topgallant sail was waving and pointing north. Kathryn stood and strained to see into the shimmering distance. Now she saw it too. Someone was walking toward the ship. Heat waves rising from the ground made the image blurry, fuzzy, but someone was definitely walking toward the ship from the north.

Venn crossed the deck from somewhere behind Kathryn's position and trotted down the gangway. Kathryn and Rowan followed. Kathryn stood, breathless, until she could see the approaching figure more clearly. Minutes lasted an eternity until she was at last certain it was Aiden.

Tendrils of dark hair swirled around her face. Her shirt hung loosely about her, untucked and fluttering in the wind. Her face and arms were pink from the sun, but she wasn't horribly sunburned. How was that possible?

"Something has happened." Rowan had spoken softly so that only Kathryn could hear her.

All eyes were on Aiden. Nilah and the members of her crew that were above deck gathered at the railing above them and watched Aiden's approach. Venn stood apart from Kathryn and Rowan.

"What do you mean something has happened?" Kathryn asked.

"Look at her face."

Rowan was right. There was something different about Aiden's face. Her expression was serious, and her focus was locked on Venn as she approached and stopped to stand before Venn. Kathryn had done nothing but think of Aiden every minute of the day, but Aiden hadn't so much as glanced in her direction. Kathryn chided herself for even thinking such a selfish thought.

"Aiden, it's foolish to walk into the desert alone. You could have been hurt or killed." Venn's words were stern, but her expression was more hurt than angry. Venn had obviously been worried, too. That realization surprised Kathryn a little. "Where have you been?"

Aiden stood within arm's reach of Venn, her expression unreadable.

"I've been with my mother."

"That's impossible, Aiden. Your mother is dead." Venn's voice was raspy with emotion.

"It is possible. I have seen things."

"Aiden…"

"Venn, I was there, with you, with her, in the room that night."

Venn coughed. No, she hadn't coughed; she'd choked back a sob. Kathryn and Rowan stepped closer. Kathryn wanted to go to Aiden, but she was stopped by Rowan's hand on her arm.

"I'm telling you the truth. I can't explain exactly how, but I've been with my mother. I know what you did for her. I know what you did for me. I know the truth."

Venn dropped to her knees and covered her face with her hands. Her shoulders shook with silent sobs. Aiden placed her hand on Venn's head. It was a touching gesture that made Kathryn press her fingers to her own lips to hold back a sob. To witness a warrior such as Venn on her knees and in tears sliced through Kathryn's heart. Her own throat began to close with emotion.

Aiden put her hand at the back of Venn's head and drew her into an embrace. Still kneeling, Venn wrapped her arms around Aiden's waist and gave over to her tears. She buried her face in Aiden's shirt, and Aiden spoke softly to her as she stroked her hair. "Thank you. Thank you for my life."

"I didn't want to leave her." Venn's words were barely audible between sobs.

"I know."

"I loved her so much."

"I know. She loved you, too. I could feel it."

"Oh, God, it still hurts so much." Venn pressed her face against Aiden.

"Let it go. You've carried this too long. It's time to let it go."

She bent to kiss the top of Venn's head as she stroked her hair and then looked up to meet Kathryn's gaze for the first time. Her eyes glistened, and Kathryn sensed no anger from Aiden. Whatever had happened in the desert, Aiden had seen things. Rowan was right. She was strangely different, older and more mature somehow, and exuding a new sense of peace.

Relief washed through Kathryn. Aiden was back. Aiden was safe. Everything was going to be okay now.

Aiden held Venn until the sobs subsided. Finally, Venn released her. She took several deep, shuddering breaths before she got to her feet. She didn't look at Kathryn or Rowan. Aiden was sure that Venn never allowed herself to feel the things she'd just felt, and she'd done so in front of strangers.

She put her hand on Venn's back. "Just take as much time as you need."

Venn nodded and wiped at her face with her sleeve. She walked away from Aiden a few paces and faced the open landscape, still not looking at anyone.

"I'm sorry if I worried you." Kathryn was nearby, and it took every bit of self-control not to reach for her. After what had happened between them the previous night, Aiden wasn't sure Kathryn wanted to be touched. Not by Aiden anyway.

"Aiden, we were so concerned about you."

She saw nothing but worry in Kathryn's eyes. Maybe she was no longer angry.

"I think you should have some water and food," Rowan said.

"Yeah, I am very thirsty." Aiden looked down at her shirt, smeared with dust. She figured her face was too. "Maybe I should eat something and then wash up a bit."

"Yes, of course." Rowan took Aiden's arm.

She saw concern on Kathryn's face, but Kathryn made no move to reach for her. Instead, she allowed Rowan take the lead. With Rowan on one side and Kathryn on the other, they walked up the gangway back to the main deck of the ship. Venn lingered alone on the ground.

They sat in the galley at a long table in the center of the large space. The timbers began to creak as the ship started to move. Nilah had decided to set sail while they still had a few hours of daylight. A steward set food and water in front of Aiden. She downed the liquid, and Rowan reached for the pitcher to refill her glass. Kathryn sat across from her, Rowan at her side. Neither of them spoke, but Aiden could see the questions in their eyes.

After a few mouthfuls of food and a second glass of water, Aiden began to feel better. Her body felt strangely tingly. It was as if her arms were covered with goose bumps despite the fact that the air was quite warm. She looked up from the bowl of chicken and potatoes to see that Kathryn and Rowan were both watching her. She set down her spoon and smiled at them.

"Could you hear what I was saying to Venn?" Aiden wondered how much they'd overheard.

"Some of what you said, but truthfully, I'm confused by what I heard." Rowan refilled Aiden's water glass.

"I walked into the desert last night." She looked at Kathryn as she spoke. "I know I shouldn't have, but I was…upset." Kathryn broke eye contact and looked down at her hands on the table. Aiden wanted to make things right with Kathryn, but she wasn't sure how to do that. She pushed on with her story. "The white wolf found me, and when I sank my fingers into the animal's fur, I was transported to another place, another time."

"What white wolf?" Kathryn asked.

"Aiden has been seeing a white wolf since she left the monastery." Rowan relayed this detail to Kathryn as if it were the most normal thing in the world.

"A white wolf has been following you?" Kathryn sounded doubtful.

Aiden nodded. "I know it sounds strange, but when I filled my fingers with the wolf's fur, I was suddenly in my mother's bed chamber. Venn was there and I was there, only I was just an infant."

"So Venn really was in Belstaff." Rowan's voice sounded soft, contemplative.

"Yes. She and my mother…well, I don't know how, but I could feel how much they loved each other. My mother asked Venn to hide me from my uncle. I was there. I saw and heard the entire exchange between them. I feel pretty sure my mother died that same night. She seemed extremely ill and weak."

Retelling the experience felt like a weight sinking onto her shoulders. Aiden released several deep breaths and fought the urge to cry. She didn't want to break into tears in front of Kathryn. She met Kathryn's gaze, but couldn't tell from her expression what she was thinking. Probably that Aiden had gotten lost in the desert and lost her mind.

"I think I'll go lie down for a while." The wooden legs of the small bench loudly slid across the rough flooring as Aiden pushed back from the table.

"Of course," said Rowan. Rowan and Kathryn both stood up. Aiden nodded at them and left the room. She'd had the sudden strong desire to be alone. She needed to get her feelings under control. Every time she revisited the encounter with her mother she felt seized with sadness and on the verge of tears. She was unsure if the sadness was hers or Venn's. Maybe it was both.

Kathryn sank back to her seat after Aiden left the room. She and Rowan sat in silence as the steward came to claim the remnants of Aiden's unfinished meal.

"What are you thinking?" Kathryn wasn't sure what to think.

"I believe Aiden had a vision in the desert." Rowan had a far-off look in her eyes. She finally let her focus return to the room, and she turned to face Kathryn. "I believe she was somehow given a chance to see her mother, to travel back in time. Strange things can happen in barren places. In a place where every bit of life and the living has been stripped away, I believe the dead walk."

"You're scaring me a little." Chills traveled up the back of Kathryn's neck.

"The dead shouldn't frighten you. The living are the ones to fear."

Kathryn might have laughed at such an ominous statement, but she could see from the expression on Rowan's face that she was completely serious.

CHAPTER EIGHTEEN

An hour later, Kathryn found Aiden leaning against the ship's railing looking as if she were focused on something far away or lost in deep thought.

"See anything interesting?" She'd tried to think of something casual to lead with. But she was afraid that her question just sounded lame. *Excuse me while I tiptoe along the edge of the chasm that now exists between us.*

Aiden graced her bland question with a friendly smile. "Nothing but the night."

Kathryn joined her at the rail facing out on the seemingly endless dark. Thin, wispy clouds partially hid the moon and the stars. *Just say what you want to say.*

Silence stood between them like an unseen presence.

"Aiden, I owe you an apology." Kathryn didn't look at Aiden; she wasn't sure she could. When there was no response, she turned to see that Aiden was looking at her. There was a softness in her eyes that melted Kathryn's heart. Was that forgiveness?

"You don't owe me an apology." Aiden sounded dejected. Had Kathryn managed to kill the spark between them so easily?

"Yes, I do." Kathryn tucked a long strand of loose hair behind her ear and summoned the strength to be honest. "I had no right to get so upset with you. I'm…well, I was upset, and I didn't handle it very well. I should have stayed and talked with you instead of running away, but I didn't, and then when you left the ship I thought you were angry with me, and it was all my fault that you…" The words had come out in a rush, but she lost her train of thought when she felt Aiden's fingers entwine with hers.

"To be perfectly honest, I was pretty mad." Aiden turned Kathryn's hand over and traced the lines of her highly sensitive palm with her fingertip. "I didn't handle it well either. I should have followed you instead of marching off into the desert like an idiot." Aiden furrowed her brow. She released Kathryn's hand, as if she'd taken possession of it absentmindedly and regretted doing so.

Kathryn lamented the loss of contact. She pressed down the swell of need in her chest. She wanted Aiden to touch her again. She wanted Aiden to kiss her. Then she remembered what Rowan had said about who'd have to make the first move. Kathryn was used to having the world at her feet. She wasn't used to having to ask for forgiveness or make the first move.

"Will you tell me more about what happened out there?" Kathryn thought maybe getting Aiden to explain further would offer them some neutral ground. But as soon as Aiden began to recount more details about the experience, she realized the topic was anything but neutral.

"I was here and then instantly somewhere else, some time else. I don't know how to describe it really. But I saw myself as an infant, and my mother was there and Venn was there. But no one could see me. I think I was feeling everything Venn was feeling that night. The night my mother died."

"You're sure it was Venn?" This explained Venn's emotional breakdown upon Aiden's return. And she realized she hadn't seen Venn since.

"Yes, I'm sure. She was younger, closer to my age now, but it was definitely her. Something, some deep connection, obviously existed between my mother and Venn. I haven't gotten to speak with her about it yet."

"So that's why she left Belstaff's royal guard?"

"I assume so. I want to talk to her more about what happened that night, but she was so upset earlier that I thought it might be better to give her some time."

With the mention of time, Kathryn felt that time was running out. They would be back in Olmstead in another two days, and then Aiden would likely decide whether to stay or go or try to claim her throne in Belstaff. The latter could go badly, and knowing Aiden better now, she wasn't sure she'd even want Aiden to try. Maybe Gareth had been right. Maybe Aiden was no match for Balak. Even if defeating Balak would help Kathryn, she wasn't sure she was willing to possibly sacrifice Aiden to do that.

"Aiden, I…" Aiden looked at her, but she was having doubts about finishing the thought out loud.

"What is it?"

"Nothing. I think I'll turn in."

"Can I walk you to your room?"

Given her current state of mind, Kathryn reasoned she should have refused the offer, but she allowed Aiden to walk her to her chamber. Only the night watchman was on deck as they passed. Everyone else was probably either in their own rooms or in the galley drinking ale. The ship was anchored for the night, and the hour was late.

Once they reached the narrow doorway, Kathryn hesitated. When she turned around, Aiden was standing so close in the small space that her breasts brushed against Aiden's shirt. She closed her eyes and tried to quiet her libido. What was wrong with her? She'd never been so wrought up over anyone before. Why now? Why Aiden?

With her eyes still closed, Aiden brushed her lips with a soft kiss.

"For whatever I said the other night that upset you, I'm truly sorry."

Kathryn shook her head.

"Oh, okay, I understand." Aiden started to step away from her.

Kathryn caught Aiden's arm and tugged her back.

"You misunderstood. I was saying no to the part about what you said, not the kiss." She glanced up and down the passageway and then pulled Aiden into her room.

"Listen, just don't talk about other women, even if I ask. And especially if you thought they were pretty." Kathryn stroked Aiden's exposed forearm as she spoke.

"I've never met anyone as beautiful as you. Ever." Aiden sounded so serious that Kathryn had to laugh. "I mean it."

"Thank you." Kathryn titled her face up to gaze into Aiden's. "You're so handsome that I'd be a fool to think you haven't been with other women. And normally, I'd be able to handle that. I mean, I don't want you to think I'm the jealous sort, although maybe I am." Once again, the words came tumbling out. She'd hardly taken a breath.

"I haven't."

"Sorry, what?"

"I've never been with anyone before."

"What?"

"I understand if that means you don't want to—"

Kathryn covered Aiden's lips with her fingers. "You've never been with a woman before? Ever?"

Aiden shook her head. The moment the words left her mouth she'd second-guessed confiding this to Kathryn, but she'd already upset Kathryn once, and she didn't want to do it again due to lack of experience. She didn't want Kathryn to mistake inexperience or ineptitude for disinterest.

"Our kiss last night was my first real kiss." Aiden waited to see what Kathryn's response would be.

"Oh, my." Kathryn tottered back, seeming a wee bit unstable, and the wind ship wasn't even moving at the moment.

"Are you all right?" Aiden put her arm around Kathryn to steady her.

Kathryn didn't respond other than to wrap her arms around Aiden's neck and pull her into a deep kiss. She pressed the soft curves of her body firmly against Aiden.

Aiden realized that things were happening that were causing her heart rate to spike. Her face felt hot and her insides ached. She wasn't sure what to do with her hands. At first, she let them hover, afraid to touch Kathryn, but then she let them land at Kathryn's hips.

Kathryn moved against her, insinuating her thigh between Aiden's legs so that there was pressure against her crotch.

Aiden couldn't breathe. Everything that was happening between them felt amazing and utterly frightening at the same time. Having just experienced some sort of vision in the desert, reliving the night of her mother's death, all the emotion she'd experienced, Aiden's chest felt tight. And things were getting mixed up. Was she feeling something intense for Kathryn? Or was the crush of emotion the result of witnessing her mother's passing? Blood rushed in her ears like a raging storm. Panic constricted her throat. She fought to the surface of it and pulled away from Kathryn, her breathing shallow and rapid.

"What's wrong?" The look on Kathryn's face was somewhere between concern and confusion.

"I'm sorry...I can't...I'm sorry..." Aiden couldn't look at Kathryn as she stumbled out the door and down the narrow passageway fighting for air. She felt ashamed but didn't really know why. She wanted to cry or run away or hide or all three.

She ducked into her room and leaned against the door, trying to focus on slowing her rapid breathing. Aiden balled her fists and pounded against her thighs. *God!* All of it was too much: her mother, Venn, Kathryn, an uncle who wanted her dead. It was all too much and there was no way to escape any of it.

Kathryn stood staring at the empty space where Aiden had just been. Everything disintegrated so quickly that it now felt as if it had never happened. But it had happened. Something was happening between them, and she wasn't going to run away from it this time, or let it run away from her. She followed Aiden.

"Aiden?" Kathryn knocked softly. When there was no answer, she opened the door. Aiden was wiping at tears on her cheeks. Aiden shook her head.

"I'm sorry, but you should probably go. I'm—" Aiden's voice broke.

"It's okay. It's okay to feel whatever you're feeling right now." She put her hands on Aiden's arms and pushed her toward the narrow bunk so that she could sit down. "I shouldn't have kissed you." Kathryn should have sensed that Aiden was feeling overwhelmed, but she'd been selfish and she'd let her attraction direct her actions.

Aiden sniffed. "I really like kissing you."

"There's plenty of time for kissing." She brushed a clump of hair from Aiden's forehead. "For now, why don't you try to get some rest. Here, let me help you." Kathryn took the heel of Aiden's boot and tugged it free. Then she did the same with the other. Aiden shifted on the bed and Kathryn sat back down on the edge near the pillow. She pulled Aiden's head into her lap and lightly caressed her hair. "Just rest."

Aiden sighed and Kathryn reached over and dimmed the lantern near the bed. She propped her head against the wall and continued to stroke Aiden's hair. This was nice. She'd wanted nothing more than to be close to Aiden. She felt Aiden relax against her, and her breathing slowed to a more even pace. It was rare that Kathryn ever had the chance to comfort someone in such a way, and it felt good. It felt good to be the person that Aiden needed, to be the woman in whom Aiden found comfort.

Kathryn looked down at Aiden's face. Long dark lashes rested on her elegant sun-kissed cheekbones, and Kathryn thought hers was the most beautiful face she'd ever seen. She closed her eyes too and allowed herself to daydream about the future.

CHAPTER NINETEEN

Motion jarred Kathryn awake. She blinked and tried to get her bearings. The last thing she remembered was stroking Aiden's hair as she coaxed her to sleep. She must have fallen asleep too. Kathryn looked down and realized that Aiden's arm was draped around her waist. They'd obviously cuddled up to each other in their sleep. *I fell asleep. We slept together. All night.*

Kathryn wasn't sure what to do. This had never happened to her before. Well, she'd slept with a woman before, but not like this. She wasn't sure what if anything to read into this. Maybe she could slip out without waking Aiden.

She shifted, and Aiden stirred next to her. She rotated, which put her mouth dangerously close to Aiden's. She was so beautiful when she was asleep that Kathryn couldn't tear herself away. She rested on her arm and watched Aiden sleep for a few minutes until Aiden's eyes fluttered open. She appeared as surprised as Kathryn had been that they'd spent the night together.

"Good morning."

"Hi." Kathryn touched Aiden's cheek. "We must have fallen asleep."

Aiden smiled and snuggled closer to Kathryn. "I'm glad we did. Thank you for staying."

Kathryn tried not to move against Aiden. They were in a compromised position. Aiden probably wasn't even aware of the effect her proximity was having on Kathryn, and it would take very little friction to make Kathryn's libido hum.

"I should go." Kathryn said the words aloud but made no motion to leave. She felt as if her head and her body were in a tug-of-war with each other. It was early. The soft rocking of the ship indicated that they were underway. Why did she have to be in such a hurry to leave?

"Don't go."

It was such a simple request, but the implication was huge. Kathryn felt Aiden's arm around her waist. She put her arm across Aiden's hip, and as she did she realized Aiden's shirt had pulled free during the night. Her hand had a mind of its own. Like some heat-seeking creature, her hand slid under Aiden's shirt. Her palm rested against the bare skin of her back. She closed her eyes and sighed softly before she could stop herself. Aiden's skin felt so good.

She opened her eyes. She sensed Aiden had drifted back to sleep. She listened to Aiden's steady deep breathing. Meanwhile, every cell in Kathryn's body was wide-awake.

Kathryn slid gently out from under Aiden's arm, kissed her on the cheek, and slipped quietly out of the room. She let her forehead rest against the door for a moment after it clicked shut. She knew she was doing the right thing. This wasn't the way she wanted the first time with Aiden. But she was sure she'd probably regret this decision to wait. Opportunities for personal pleasure were rare these days.

"Good morning, cousin." Rowan's voice made Kathryn jump. When Kathryn looked up, Rowan quirked one side of her mouth in a knowing smile.

"It's not what you think."

"Well, that's too bad, because I was thinking some very nice things." Rowan brushed past Kathryn in the narrow hallway with a devilish grin on her face.

Rowan's grin had been infectious. Kathryn smiled all the way back to her quarters. It was still early. She'd freshen up and then go in search of coffee.

❖

When Aiden woke up, she was alone. As she struggled to clear the fog of sleep from her brain, she wondered whether cuddling with Kathryn had only been a wishful dream. She pulled the pillow to her face and inhaled. A hint of Kathryn's perfume lingered on the fabric. Aiden inhaled deeply and then rolled onto her back smiling at the ceiling.

As she pulled on a fresh shirt and splashed water on her face from the basin in the corner of the small room, she felt light as a feather. As if some emotional weight had been lifted off her chest during the night. She wondered if the feeling came from having some knowledge of her mother, having some idea of where she came from. Even though she still had no home to call her own, at least knowing she'd had a home at the beginning of her life made her feel just the least bit grounded. She couldn't quite decipher every new sensation swirling around inside, but she knew something was different.

The galley was empty when she arrived, but she managed to find an apple and some bread with butter still out in the center of the main table. She ate the apple first and then carried a slice of bread with her, taking bites as she wound her way down the narrow hallway past the sleeping quarters and up to the main deck. The boat creaked, and she heard the muffled sounds of shouted commands between the crew as she climbed out of the belly of the ship.

The craft was moving at full speed, the sails trimmed to the wind, and the boat rocking with a smooth cadence when Aiden stepped onto the deck into bright morning sun. Various shipmates were going about their duties, rolling lines, tying down supplies, climbing rope ladders high up the mast to the yardarms. This was her first passage on a ship of any kind, so she was captivated by the constant buzz of activity that it took to keep everything untangled and moving in the right direction.

She'd watched with rapt fascination the first day they'd set sail. The unfurling of the great white squares of cloth one after the other was like an orchestrated dance, a waltz of motion.

Aiden shielded her eyes with her hand as she gazed up into the broad square sails bowed out, full from the wind.

"Is this your first time on a wind ship?" Venn casually leaned against the railing nearby.

"Yes, it is." Aiden had wanted to talk with Venn since she'd had the vision, but not about ships. She sensed awkwardness between them, probably because Venn had broken down into tears in front of her. She didn't know Venn well, but she knew enough to guess that showing emotion in that way was not something Venn made a habit of doing.

Should she give Venn more space or should she push through the awkwardness and get to the questions she really wanted to ask?

"I have something for you." Venn hadn't given Aiden time to decide. She pulled her sword from the leather sheath on her belt and handed it, handle first, to Aiden.

Aiden took the sword, but she wasn't sure what she was supposed to do with it. She held it out in front of her with both hands. It was beautiful. The handle was well worn. This sword looked as if it had seen lots of action. There was also a brilliant red stone encased in silver and mounted at the end of the handle.

"I'd like for you to have it."

Aiden looked up from the sword. "Why? Isn't this your sword?" She'd noticed that today Venn was wearing a second sword in a case that hung between her shoulder blades. Leather straps crossed her chest, holding the second sword sheath in place.

"This has been my sword, but I'd like to give it to you now."

Aiden shook her head and tried to pass the weapon back to Venn. "This is too much. I can't accept."

Venn pushed the sword back. "That stone is carnelian. It imparts an acceptance of the cycle of life and removes the fear of death. It came from a pendant that belonged to your mother, so I had it crafted into the handle of the sword."

Aiden studied the ornate handle more closely. The stone was a brilliant red, not translucent, but solid in color, like a rock. There were other markings on the cross guard, a crisscross pattern, and just next to the stone, where the grooves of the handle ended, an engraving of a crescent moon and three stars. The unmistakable Roth family crest of Belstaff.

"Is that the mark that's on my shoulder?"

Venn nodded.

Aiden traced the engraved shapes with her fingertip. The red wax seals used the same emblem. And this red stone had belonged to her mother. The Roth family crest had some close kinship with red. She recalled the red uniform Venn had been wearing in her vision.

But this was too great a gift. She felt uncomfortable accepting such a gift. Once more, she tried to return the sword to Venn.

Venn wrapped her hand around Aiden's fingers on the grip of the sword. "I want you to have this sword, Aiden. Please take it." She removed the sword belt she'd been wearing and handed that to Aiden also. Aiden draped it over her shoulder because she needed two hands to put it on, but her right hand was occupied with cool steel.

She stepped away from Venn and swung the broadsword through the air to get a feel for the weight of it. This instrument was well balanced, much nicer than the heavy, clumsy sword she'd lost while held in captivity in Eveshom. After a few more strokes through the air, she put the sword in the sheath and the belt around her waist.

"Were you and my mother in love?" Aiden waited expectantly for Venn to answer. Venn was slow to respond.

"It was complicated, and our timing was off, but yes, we were in love." Venn looked sad.

"What do you mean your timing was off?"

"Isla was already married to your father when we met."

"Oh." Aiden wanted to understand. "Did she not love my father then?"

"She cared for your father very much. They had a good relationship and had been friends before marriage. She wanted to have children, and she knew they would have a good life together. He was, after all, a king. And he was a good man. So, yes, she did love him, but in a different way I suppose." Venn looked off into the distance. "If she and I had met first, who knows?"

Aiden took a seat on a wooden storage bin anchored to the railing wall. She looked up at Venn waiting for her to continue.

Hearing details about her parents was like a dream come true. A wish she'd carried since childhood that she never thought would be granted.

"Your mother discovered she was pregnant just after we met. She would never have left your father and deprived him of knowing his child. She was a very loyal person, true to her word. Maybe once you were older she'd have decided…" Venn's voice became gruff with emotion. She coughed to clear her throat.

"What happened to my father?"

"He was killed in a skirmish right after you were born. I wasn't there so I'm still not sure what happened, and I don't trust that Balak didn't have some hand in his death."

"Balak is really as bad as everyone thinks then?"

"Yes. He's motivated by self-interests and greed. And his moods are incredibly erratic and volatile. I think he's only gotten worse with age."

"And you? All these years later, do you ever regret leaving your life in Belstaff because of me?"

"With your mother gone I had no life there. Everything I cared about was gone. Everything in Belstaff would have reminded me of her."

Aiden felt sadness for Venn. She'd given up what she'd wanted for others. She'd lost the woman she loved so many years ago. Aiden was trying not to pelt her with questions, but she had many more bubbling up.

"This mark on my shoulder, how—"

"As royal born, you were marked as an infant, but only your mother's inner circle knew of your birth. For your safety she tried to keep it a secret." Venn paused. "The only person outside the castle who knew your true identity was Francis."

"Brother Francis?" He'd been her mentor and the closest thing to a father she'd had during her years at the monastery's orphanage.

"Yes, he's my uncle. He was the only person I knew I could trust completely."

"He knew? He knew the whole time and he never told me."

"I asked him not to. And he and I both agreed that you'd be safer if you didn't know your true origin."

"I didn't remember getting this tattoo on my shoulder. I just knew at some point, it was there."

"You were just two months old. Your mother considered ignoring the tradition for your safety and not performing the marking ceremony, but I convinced her to go through with it." Venn sat next to Aiden on the wooden box. "You said you remembered me from the monastery. I was there many times, but most of the time you didn't see me."

Affection swelled in Aiden's chest for this warrior who'd obviously been her guardian for years and she'd had no idea. She owed Venn a great debt.

"Thank you."

Venn looked at her, and her lashes glistened with unshed tears. "You have your mother's eyes, Aiden. There is so much of her in you. I'm glad I can finally say that to you." She sniffed and looked away, swiping at her cheek with the back of her hand.

"Were you ever going to tell me who I really was?"

"Yes." Venn hesitated. "I had planned to join you to celebrate your twenty-first birthday and then accompany you on your journey from the monastery. Regardless of where that journey led."

"I'm not sure I'd have believed you if you'd told me the truth."

"Aiden, I will help you reclaim your birthright, for you and for Isla…but only if that's truly what you want." Venn put her hand on Aiden's shoulder. "You are free to make the choice for yourself, just as your mother hoped."

Aiden nodded. She wasn't sure what else to say at the moment.

Venn playfully bumped her shoulder and smiled. "Now, let's see what you can do with that sword."

"Really? Now?" Aiden got to her feet and followed Venn toward an open spot on the deck.

"Yes, now. Defend yourself." Venn drew the sword that was strapped between her shoulder blades, and in one fluid motion, struck the blade Aiden held casually in front of her body.

She had Aiden's full attention now. Aiden volleyed three more blows from Venn, then Venn stepped back, smiling.

"Not bad, but don't use a low guard. Take a high guard, like this." Venn demonstrated by holding her sword in both hands above her head, elbows bent. She waited for Aiden to match her pose. "Defend yourself."

Venn swung downward and Aiden met the movement, blocking her strike.

"Good. Better." Venn took the high guard again. "Hold the sword straight." She motioned with her head. "Leg back, bend your knees." She gave Aiden a moment to adjust her stance and then advanced on her again.

After a few minutes, Aiden got the distinct impression that Venn was no longer holding back. Aiden deflected several advances, and then Venn got the upper hand, striking so hard that Aiden's blade hit the plank flooring. Venn stepped into her personal space and stopped short of striking her in the face with the butt of the sword handle.

"Remember, the blade isn't the only part of the sword that can be used as a weapon."

Aiden nodded and took a step back. They continued to volley, and after each advance Venn talked to Aiden about mental discipline.

"Never give in to rage." Venn circled Aiden's position. "Anger and fear are the real threats in any conflict."

"How can you make yourself not be afraid?" Aiden believed she'd have an easier time controlling anger than fear, but she knew she'd never been truly tested.

"You control your mind; you stand in front of it."

Aiden wasn't sure she understood, but she nodded anyway.

"Always keep your head clear of everything except your objective." Venn circled and then unexpectedly lunged. Aiden was ready and blocked her thrust.

They were both breathing hard; their skin glistened with sweat. Aiden was pleased to see that she wasn't too easy an opponent for Venn.

CHAPTER TWENTY

Sails!" someone shouted from high in the rigging. Aiden looked up until she spotted the crewman and he shouted again. "Sails, port!"

Aiden moved to where Nilah stood near the rudder wheel with a spyglass. Venn joined Aiden at the railing.

"We've got company." Nilah handed the telescope to a crewman nearby. "Bring us about, southwest thirty degrees. Let's see if they follow us." The man at the rudder wheel adjusted course.

Aiden watched the craft in the distance. It was still fairly far away but clear that it was a wind ship smaller than the craft they were on. The sails of the smaller ship flashed bright white in the sunlight as it altered course to follow them.

"They've changed course." Aiden couldn't help making the observation aloud even though her input was unnecessary.

Nilah already had begun to shout orders to go back to their original course and put more sails into the wind.

"What does this mean?" Aiden asked.

"If they'd stayed on their southward heading I'd have thought they were just a traveling transport like we are. But they came out of nowhere, and now they've altered course to match ours. That causes me to have serious doubts about their intentions."

The ship rocked on its spinning axles as it picked up speed, but even with the extra wind power from the numerous sails, the smaller craft was gaining on them.

"Man your stations. All hands at arms!" Nilah shouted more orders, and two cannons were rolled into position on the port side of the deck. Hatchways were thrown open, and the cannons were pushed through. They were primed and then chained to the deck to stave off recoil.

Aiden's pulse quickened. This was serious and she wasn't sure she was prepared for what was coming, but at least now she had a weapon should she need it.

❖

Kathryn was in the galley when the boat lurched without warning. She stumbled sideways when the floor tipped sharply toward the port side.

Something is wrong. Kathryn steadied herself and listened. Muffled shouts sounded overhead.

She headed down the narrow passage toward the steps up to the main deck. Twice, she had to brace herself on the wall to keep from falling as the ship jerked and bumped. Fearing the worst, she stopped by her cabin to retrieve her crossbow and quiver of arrows. When Kathryn breached the doorway, she was greeted with a frenzy of shouts and movement. She saw Gareth first.

"What's going on?" Kathryn asked.

"Sails. We spotted them a few moments ago and they're getting close." An arrow struck the railing, sinking into the wood, between where they stood. "And they're gaining on us."

"All hands to arms!" Nilah barked orders from the helm.

Kathryn loaded the crossbow. She took cover behind some wooden crates aft of the helm and peeked around to try to get a better look at what or who was chasing them.

Gareth crouched beside her. She looked around for Aiden but couldn't find her in the mayhem on deck.

"Where's Rowan?"

"I sent her below." Gareth pulled his sword free. His left arm was still in a sling, but luckily, he was right-handed.

"Who do you think they are?"

"I'm assuming more of Aiden's pals."

"How could they possibly know that Aiden is on this ship?"

"You tell me. You two seem pretty thick lately."

"If they are after Aiden, then I assure you she's as surprised as we are."

"Whatever you say."

"Gareth—" Kathryn was getting pissed, and she was about to launch into him when a grappling hook flew past them and then slid back along the decking, lodging itself against the railing.

Gareth swung his sword and cut the line.

Kathryn popped her head up for a better look. The ship was coming alongside them. It was a much smaller craft, which might have explained its speed. Kathryn heard shouts and turned to see Aiden and Venn engaged with raiders who'd swung across from lines attached to the masts of the attacking ship. Another man swung across the expanse between the ships and dropped onto the deck.

Venn dispatched one of the men swiftly and then dumped his body over the side, but Aiden was having a tougher go of it. She was wielding a broadsword and was fully engaged with one of the men who'd swung over from the other ship.

Kathryn tried to get a clear shot with her crossbow, but Aiden kept shifting in front of her attacker, blocking the shot. Kathryn tried for another shot, but a shadow passed over her as another raider dropped down a few feet from her position. She pivoted and fired. The arrow hit the main square in the chest. She knelt to reload.

"Come up on the wind! Get us broadside!" Nilah shouted at her crew. The ship leaned and began to turn on the smaller craft. "Ready cannons port!"

There was a deafening boom, and splinters exploded from the other ship. A second cannon fired and struck the runners under the smaller boat, pitching it to the ground. It came to a sliding stop, the friction of its grounded hull pulled against Nilah's ship where it was still tethered by several remaining grappling lines. Members of the crew scrambled to sever the lines with axes.

A skirmish was still underway on the main deck. The high pitch of clanking steel echoed in the crisp air as Aiden volleyed with one of the raiders who obviously was unaware he was outnumbered and now separated from his ship. Kathryn held her breath as Aiden dodged and then lunged, knocking the man's sword from his hand. He backed away from her. She backed him against the thick timber of the main mast and held him pinned there, her sword point pressing against his chest. Aiden turned her head and Kathryn captured her gaze. They held each other for a moment with their eyes. Aiden was glistening with sweat and breathing hard, but she appeared otherwise unharmed. Kathryn let out the breath she'd been holding and stepped over a fallen raider while Gareth and Venn heaved another dead one over the railing.

"I want him alive." Nilah moved past Kathryn to where Aiden held her raider captive. "Put him below deck in irons and get this ship moving. Bend every sail. I want distance between us and anyone else who might be following!"

A couple of Nilah's men roughly grabbed the man Aiden had captured and dragged him below deck.

Rowan rushed to Kathryn. "Are you hurt? Is anyone hurt?"

"I think we're all okay." But there were three more bodies lying motionless on the deck in the debris of smashed crates and broken vats.

Gareth walked among the fallen. He stepped over the first two and then stopped at the third. He searched the man and found nothing. But in the next jacket he pilfered, he found something. He stood up with the folded parchment in his hand. Kathryn's gut clenched when she saw the flash of red where the Roth wax seal had been broken.

Gareth opened the document. He studied it for a moment and then handed it to Kathryn. "I hope she's worth it." He stepped over the prone body, leaving Kathryn and Rowan to read the note.

"Don't listen to him." Rowan touched Kathryn's arm.

Kathryn nodded to Rowan and then read the message. *Suspected heir traveling east. Wind ship, central region. Mark on shoulder. Reward, dead or living.*

Kathryn handed the paper to Rowan and then waited for her to read it.

"How could they know we're on this route?" Kathryn was beginning to feel as if she'd been set up. This was the third attack if she counted the initial skirmish at the jail, but she'd chalked that up to random bad luck. Maybe there was no such thing on this journey.

The ship tilted as their speed picked up. She reached for the railing to steady herself. Rowan held the paper out to Kathryn.

"What does it say?" Aiden walked up just as Kathryn was reaching for the parchment. The look on her face told Kathryn that she already had a pretty good idea what the note said.

"Somehow, someone knew you were on this ship." Kathryn felt tired. She wanted to get all of them back to Olmstead and under the safe care of her imperial guard. Maybe she'd been wrong not to accept Frost's directive to bring guards along with them. Maybe she'd been naïve.

Aiden took the paper and studied it for a moment, then handed it to Kathryn. "I'm sorry. All of this is my fault."

"No, it's Balak's fault." Venn wiped her blade and slid it into the sheath strapped between her shoulders. "And don't forget that, Aiden. This is all Balak. You couldn't have stopped this. He'd have found you one way or the other, sooner or later."

Aiden seemed a bit crestfallen. Strands of hair clung to her sweaty forehead. Her shirt wafted in the wind, still untucked and rumpled from sleep. Aiden nodded in agreement, but she sheathed her sword with a heavy, discouraged sigh.

Kathryn wanted to reach for Aiden and pull her into a hug, but not in front of everyone who'd gathered. For some reason, she wanted to give the appearance of distance between them in front of Nilah's crew and in front of Venn, and especially in front of Gareth, although he'd gone below deck and hadn't resurfaced.

"Venn is right, Aiden. This isn't your fault." She waited for Aiden to meet her gaze. "I chose this. I chose to be here."

Aiden smiled weakly at Kathryn. She probably owed Kathryn her life. First Venn and now Kathryn. If Kathryn hadn't come for her, she suspected she'd have died in that cell. Or been killed the moment she was released. And if it hadn't been for Kathryn she'd have never even known why.

"Throw these bodies overboard." Nilah was still shouting orders to her crew. "Get this mess cleaned up." She stopped when she reached the spot where Kathryn was standing. "I'm going to question the prisoner. Do you want to join me?"

"Yes." Venn answered even though Nilah had been speaking to Kathryn.

"Only if the queen agrees." Nilah was clearly still taking her lead from Kathryn.

"It's fine for Venn to join us. Thank you, Nilah." Kathryn followed Nilah below deck with Venn close behind them.

Aiden watched as the limp bodies were hoisted over the railing. They thumped to the hard earth with a cloud of dust as the ship left them, speeding onward.

Life and death so close to each other. One person alive, another dead. Was death what they'd expected? If they'd known the risk, would they still have come? To challenge an heir they'd never even met. Balak must be a powerful man to hold such sway over others. How could she possibly defeat such a man as this? She felt a strong desire to understand more fully what was really going on behind his greed so that she could reclaim her throne in order to protect Kathryn from this destructive tyrant.

Aiden had been lost in thought and hadn't realized Rowan was still standing nearby.

"Kathryn needs you as much as you need her." Rowan spoke as if she had just read Aiden's thoughts.

"I doubt that."

"Maybe not in the same way, but she needs you." Rowan put her hand on Aiden's arm. "You've given her hope. You've fueled her dreams. Trust me. I see it, even if you don't."

Aiden stood speechless as she watched Rowan walk away.

CHAPTER TWENTY-ONE

Kathryn listened as Nilah questioned the prisoner. He was seated in a chair with his hands bound behind his back and his shoes were missing. He didn't seem particularly tight-lipped. Gareth had punched him twice with his good arm and threatened to set him on foot in the desert without water, and that was all the motivation he needed to spill details of the raid on the ship.

"When did Balak give you this message?" Nilah held the folded parchment inches in front of his bleeding nose.

"Who's Balak?" He spit blood on the floor and then flinched when Gareth made a move as if he were going to punch him again. "I never talked to Balak!"

Nilah looked in Kathryn's direction. Kathryn stepped forward. "Who gave you this message?"

"I don't know a name. Only that they came from Olmstead and said there would be a reward."

Kathryn's insides knotted into a fist. "Olmstead? You're sure?" The man nodded. "How were you to receive this reward if you succeeded?"

His eyes darted from side to side. When Gareth moved toward him, he blurted out his answer. "We was to meet at a spot on the map. That's all I know, I swear."

"What map?" asked Venn. She'd been standing in the shadows, but now stepped to Kathryn's side.

"The cap'n has it on the other ship. I swear I never got a good look at it."

Kathryn walked away from the group. She rubbed her fingers against her temples and squeezed her eyes shut. If this man was telling the truth then this message didn't come from Balak but from someone in Olmstead, someone from her own kingdom. What about the other messages they'd found? Had those come from Balak? Someone had to be working closely with Balak because the wax seal bore the Roth crest. Only Balak himself or someone in his cabinet would have access to that seal. Was it possible that someone in her own court would betray her, one of the nobles perhaps? She racked her brain in an attempt to identify a likely candidate. No one rose to the surface.

"I don't think he knows anything else of value." Venn interrupted her thoughts. She nodded. "You're thinking what I'm thinking?"

"I'm thinking that someone in my own cabinet may be working with Balak."

"I had the same thought, but I don't want to jump to conclusions. This is just one questionable witness telling us this. It could be that Balak simply wants us to think the message came from Olmstead. It would serve his purposes to undermine your trust in your inner circle." Venn put a hand on her shoulder. "Don't let him get to you."

She nodded but didn't have a chance to say more because Nilah joined them.

"I'm going to keep him in the hold until after you disembark. Then I'll hand him over to the authorities in Fainsland, near Eveshom." Nilah's decision left no room for discussion. Kathryn considered telling Nilah that she feared the magistrate in Eveshom was also in league with Balak in some way. But she had no proof of that either, only a feeling. She decided she'd rather have this man in a cell in Eveshom than anywhere within the territory of Olmstead anyway, so she let it go.

After a few moments, she returned topside. The crew had done a quick job of clean up. Had she not witnessed it herself, she'd have hardly believed they'd been under attack. Except for some splintered crates piled nearby, everything seemed in order and the ship was moving at a good clip heading due east. She squinted to shield her eyes from the sun. She was just barely able to see the dark line of wooded foothills on the horizon.

"Thank you for last night." Aiden stood beside her looking in the same direction. She hadn't even seen Aiden walk up. And she'd been so distracted with everything that she hadn't had a moment to let her thoughts dwell on the previous night.

"You're welcome, but you don't need to thank me." Kathryn turned to face Aiden. Sleeping in the comfort of Aiden's arms was as much a gift to her as Aiden. She'd slept better than she had in weeks. The sunlight bounced off the polished steel as Aiden shifted her stance, and Kathryn noticed the sword at Aiden's belt. "The handle of that sword is beautiful."

Aiden followed Kathryn's gaze to the ornate carving that encased the brilliant red stone. "Venn gave this to me." She pulled the sword free so that Kathryn could see it more closely. She held it in front of her, balanced on her outstretched hands.

"It suits you." Kathryn looked from the sword to Aiden's face and back again.

"I've never owned anything so beautiful." Aiden focused on the details of the gleaming weapon as if she were seeing it again for the first time.

Kathryn was struck by the irony of that statement. Here was a woman who by birth should have inherited a kingdom but who instead knew nothing of the trappings of wealth. By chance, Aiden had lived the life of a common monk. Maybe she would be the better for it, but Kathryn worried that Aiden might not be prepared for the fight ahead should she decide to lay claim to her throne.

CHAPTER TWENTY-TWO

Kathryn shifted in the saddle atop Blaez. The day was upon her with a vengeance, voraciously stealing minutes and hours, chasing the sun across the sky. They'd left Nilah's wind ship in the mid afternoon, disembarking at the edge of the Great Salt Desert into lowland scrub brush. As they began to climb, juniper scented the air. And as the forest around them thickened with each change in elevation, Kathryn's unease began to ebb.

They'd have to spend one more night on the trail, but by late afternoon the next day they'd be within the walls of Starford Keep in Olmstead. She'd be home and they'd be safe. The prisoner's words nagged at her thoughts, but she pushed them back.

"I see smoke." Gareth pulled up next to her. A thin tendril of black rose above the treetops just ahead of them.

"Probably the York homestead. We should be close by now." They'd stopped at the Yorks' farm as they traveled to Eveshom in search of Aiden. The Yorks had been generous with both water and food for their horses. It was late enough in the day that they might even be able to camp on the farm for the night.

As they rounded the bend along the rutted road, the thickly wooded forest gave way to an open pasture, and Kathryn immediately had an uneasy feeling. There were no animals about and the place was quiet. Too quiet. Gareth rode ahead and swiveled to look back at her. The look on his face said he, too, felt something was wrong. He signaled for everyone to stop. They dismounted and tied the horses to the fence. If there was trouble ahead, then sitting atop the horses made them easy targets.

"Something doesn't feel right." Kathryn untethered her crossbow from her saddle. The others armed themselves and they split up. Kathryn and Gareth followed the fence line toward the dwelling, while Aiden and Venn began winding their way along the edge of the small animal enclosure and around the far side of the barn. Rowan stayed with the horses. The grass was almost waist high in the pasture, and there was ample brush to provide cover as they approached the log house.

The door of the cabin stood ajar, a black rectangle cut through the rough logs of the exterior. Even though dusk was upon them, no lamps were lit. Kathryn raised the crossbow in front of her. Gareth was to her left, a few steps ahead of her.

She almost tripped over the body of a sheep. Kathryn was watching the open door so intently that she hit the animal's body with her foot. She knelt down and sunk her fingers into its shaggy coat. The sheep's body had no heat. Two arrows protruded from its side.

Gareth was watching her from just outside the cabin door. Then he slowly eased the door open and peered inside. After hesitating for only a moment, he stepped inside. Kathryn waited, crouched near the body on the ground.

Aiden and Venn eased around the side of the barn. Kathryn stood up as they approached, at the same time Gareth exited the cabin. "No one is home. Everything inside has been ransacked. Furniture smashed. Food gone. I think they ate before they left because the embers in the hearth are still smoking and hot. I think that's the smoke we saw."

"It looks as if whoever was here butchered a calf and carried most of it with them. There are no other animals on the place." Venn knelt and began to examine the staff of the arrow protruding from the sheep. "This is from Belstaff."

"How can you be so sure?" Kathryn asked.

"These markings here, this arrow definitely came from the armory at Windsheer Castle." Venn pointed to a pattern just below the fletching, a crescent moon bounded top and bottom by three lines.

"How long do you think it's been dead?" Kathryn wondered how much they'd missed the attack by. If they'd have gotten here sooner maybe they could have done something.

"Several hours. Maybe since this morning," said Venn.

"Damn him." Kathryn ran her fingers through her hair. "Do you think they harmed the Yorks?"

"Either the Yorks left or they were taken, but there's no sight of them inside." Gareth put away his sword. "Maybe they had some warning and escaped on foot before the raiders sacked the place."

The Yorks weren't in their youth. They were probably past fifty, so the thought of them being routed from their home or worse, taken captive, made Kathryn's blood boil.

"I don't understand. Why would someone do this?" Aiden stood next to Venn looking down at the dead animal. "They butchered one animal and left part of the meat. Then they killed this animal for no reason and then ransacked the house. I don't understand why."

"Fear is a means of control. He gets his thugs to burn a few farms, and it's like Balak lights a fire that spreads across Olmstead." Gareth kicked the dirt with his foot. He sounded angry. "Fear gives him a foothold here before his army even puts boots on the ground."

"What does he want?" asked Aiden.

"You mean besides your head on a stick?" Gareth stopped pacing and faced Aiden.

"Gareth, enough." Kathryn was in no mood for his sarcasm.

"No, she should hear this. Balak wants Kathryn's throne. He wants Olmstead for himself. That's what this is about. If he claims Olmstead then he'll control the North River and all commerce between Belstaff and the mines in the Arranth Mountains. He's been chipping away at the border lands for months, and he's not going to stop until he gets what he wants." Gareth was definitely angry. It was as if Aiden's question had tipped a pot that had already been set to boil. He pointed his index finger at Aiden but stopped short of making contact.

"Gareth, enough!" Kathryn squared off in front of him.

He exhaled loudly and took a few steps back. "What do you want to do, Your Highness?" He sounded annoyed and impatient. Aiden looked as if she wanted to say something, but she kept quiet. It was just as well. Gareth would turn whatever Aiden said into an argument. He needed some time to cool off.

"I want to get to the castle as soon as possible."

Gareth nodded but didn't speak.

Kathryn wanted to keep moving. The sooner they could get to Olmstead the better. Balak clearly saw her as no threat if he was boldly attacking more farms along the boundaries of her kingdom. If the mineral rich mines in the mountains were his goal, then he needed her off the throne and out of the way.

Kathryn walked through the cabin before they left. There were no messages or signs left behind, other than the markings on the arrow. It looked to be a simple act of thievery and violence. What a tragedy. Whether Aiden could reclaim her throne or not, it was becoming apparent that doing nothing in the face of Balak's aggressions was no longer an option.

She exited the dark interior and stepped outside. Rowan was nearby with the horses. Kathryn leaned her forehead against Blaez's neck for a moment before she climbed into the saddle.

The mood of the group was somber as they continued east along the roadway. They rode for another half hour before deciding to camp. Kathryn had needed to put some distance between them and the York homestead, although the smoke was still visible even from this distance, rising above the treetops. In another half hour they'd no longer be able to discern the black smoke against the night sky. Nightfall was upon them. They'd pushed as far as they could toward the keep before setting up camp.

Aiden pulled the saddle from Sunset and placed it on the ground next to her bedroll. Sunset was tied near some saplings and other greens that she was enjoying. Aiden watched Kathryn toss her bedroll on the ground a few feet away. Kathryn had hardly uttered a word since they'd left the raided farm.

Gareth was building a fire while Rowan dug through one of her side bags for food rations. Everyone seemed lost in their own thoughts.

"Hey, are you all right?" Aiden knelt to help Kathryn spread out the corners of her blanket.

"I'm fine."

But she didn't seem fine. "Did you know the people that owned that farm?"

"Not well, but they offered us shelter when we passed by here a few days ago." Kathryn sat on the blanket and rested her arms on her knees. "We just saw them, and now they're...gone."

"What can I do to make you feel better?" Aiden wanted to soothe Kathryn like she'd done the previous night for her. She supposed it wasn't ideal to ask a person how to help, it should be the sort of thing you just intuitively knew, but she didn't know what to do. She had a strong urge to put her arm around Kathryn, but she was feeling a bit shy to do that in front of Venn, Gareth, and Rowan.

Gareth glared at her across the fire pit. He definitely didn't like her. He took every opportunity to let the group know that. Aiden should've known better than to ask stupid questions out loud. She'd set herself up for his ridicule. Aiden was nobody; Gareth could say whatever he liked to her. But why did Kathryn allow him to be so argumentative with her? She was the queen, his monarch. Aiden wanted to punch him for lashing out at Kathryn, but she'd held back. She didn't fully understand the relationship Gareth and Kathryn had, and she didn't want to do anything that would cause Kathryn to be more upset. Now, watching his smug expression from across the fire, she once again had the urge to punch him.

"I think I just need to rest." Kathryn gave her a weak smile.

She rocked back on her heels and watched as Rowan handed Kathryn a strip of dried venison and some water. Then Rowan handed the same rations to her. Aiden moved a few feet away to her own blanket and settled against her saddle. She chewed the dried meat slowly, savoring the salt and smoked flavor.

Kathryn didn't need or want anything from her. She was obviously troubled by the events of the day, but she didn't seek any comfort from Aiden. That hurt.

Darkness fully enveloped them, except for the flickering flame of their small campfire. Rowan boiled water for tea and handed a cup to Aiden. Kathryn was either asleep or pretending to be. Gareth rolled over with his back to the dying fire. Venn was lying on her side, propped on her elbow. She nodded to Aiden as if to silently bid her good night and then rolled onto her back and closed her eyes.

Rowan moved over to sit next to Aiden with her own cup of tea.

"We'll be in the heart of Olmstead tomorrow. We should make it to Starford Keep by early afternoon. Maybe even midday if we make good time." Rowan watched the flickering embers and sipped her tea. She'd spoken as if she were talking to no one in particular, but Aiden appreciated the details of their journey. She had no idea where they were in relation to Kathryn's home.

"I'm glad. I'm sorry you've been away for so long because of me."

"Kathryn wanted to make this journey herself. The head of her imperial guard wanted to make the trip instead, but Kathryn insisted. So don't take this on. This was her choice. Even though today was hard, I think it was important. Now it's real."

Aiden sipped her tea and watched the red coals spark and flicker. She wasn't sure why Rowan was talking to her in this way, and she wondered if what Rowan said was also for Kathryn's benefit. She didn't expect that Kathryn was soundly asleep so she could very well be listening.

"What was it before?" asked Aiden.

"What?"

"You said that now it's real. What was it before?"

"Supposition and speculation."

They sat quietly for a few minutes. Aiden mulled over what Rowan was saying.

"I think I complicate things." Aiden finished her tea and set the cup near the fire ring.

"I don't think that's true."

"You can't really mean that." Aiden rested her forearms on her knees and turned to look at Rowan. The remnants of the fire reflected in her dark eyes.

"I do." Rowan put her hand on Aiden's arm, and the most soothing sensation traveled up her forearm to her shoulder. As if Rowan had some healing touch. "Life is complicated, whether you participate in it or not."

"To be honest, I thought I wanted complications. I mean, I didn't really use that word, but I wanted to experience something beyond the simplistic way of life at the monastery. Now I see how much I was shielded during my youth there."

"You should prepare yourself for tomorrow because once we arrive at the court, things will likely seem even more layered with complexity."

"Great. I can't wait."

"Get some rest and don't take anything Gareth says to heart." Rowan patted Aiden's arm and then moved to her blanket to settle in for the night.

Aiden lay on her back watching the stars overhead. After a time, she sensed the others were asleep. They were very still, and their breathing was deep and even. The embers only held the faintest glow and not enough to cast even the smallest light against the darkness. A slight glow began to materialize in her peripheral vision, and she slowly rotated her head in that direction.

She flinched but quickly realized it was the white wolf. Her guardian. The white wolf had returned and was lying several feet away watching her. It was the strangest sensation to have this large animal lying so close. She wondered if this was simply another vision. If the others woke, would the wolf disappear like fog in the heat of the day?

Aiden didn't move and neither did the wolf. She wasn't sure why the wolf had come, but the animal appeared content to simply lounge nearby. After a little while, exhaustion claimed Aiden, and she drifted into a deep, dreamless sleep.

CHAPTER TWENTY-THREE

R elief rippled through Kathryn's body when the towers of
  Starford Keep came into view. Covering the final distance
seemed to happen quickly. Maybe it was the unspoken urgency that
hastened time. The unmistakable stone towers of the keep were
visible as they left the thick woods for the open grassy field that
surrounded the walls of Kathryn's domain. Her stomach seemed to
settle a bit just at the sight of the stone gateway into the village's
interior.

Kathryn turned to look for Aiden. She should say something.
They'd made a plan not to reveal Aiden's true identity to anyone
except Frost. Just until they were sure what course of action they
should take, if any. Aiden would simply be a guest of the house,
along with her woman-at-arms, Venn. Even still, Kathryn thought
she should say something more to Aiden. The next few days were
inevitably going to be difficult for Aiden, or at the very least
confusing, and Kathryn would be tied up with other matters. She
didn't want Aiden to misunderstand her distraction with the political
affairs of Olmstead as disinterest.

Aiden was at the rear of the small company of riders, with Venn
trailing her. Kathryn peeled off and circled back. As she got closer,
Aiden's brilliant smile stirred things in Kathryn's chest—a sense of
longing and desire for her that had yet to be fulfilled. She'd had such
plans for their transit aboard the wind ship, but things had conspired
against her libido at every turn.

"How are you feeling?" Kathryn pulled Blaez alongside Sunset, matching her pace.

"I feel good. And you? You must be relieved to be so near your home." Aiden sounded calm, relaxed, a sharp contrast to the intensity of her gaze.

"I am happy to be home. Listen, Aiden, I know we talked briefly about what things will be like when we arrive."

"Yes, was there something else?"

"No, I just… Well, I will have many demands on my time when we first arrive. I don't want you to think it's my choice to not spend time with you."

"I think I understand."

"Good, well, if there's anything you need once we arrive, the servants in my house are at your disposal. Just ask them."

Aiden nodded and Kathryn offered her a weak smile as she rode away to resume the lead as they neared the large stone gate. Venn materialized at her side as she watched Kathryn's back, her hair blowing in the wind as they approached the looming gray walls of Starford.

"What do you suppose that was about?" asked Aiden.

"That sounded like a woman who wants you to know she's interested."

"You think so?" Aiden looked at Venn, who was amused by Aiden's doubt.

"Absolutely. Trust me on that." Venn slapped Aiden's back and laughed.

They rode single file past the gatehouse with its complex of towers, bridges, and barriers whose only purpose was to keep those unwanted from gaining entrance to the inner sanctum of the keep and the small clustered dwellings of the village that surrounded it. The scene within the walls reminded Aiden of the street market in the small town near the monastery. Vendors sold meat, vegetables, and other goods from carts and makeshift shelters. Chickens squawked and pranced about as they scurried to be away from the horses' path.

Kathryn still rode at the front, and as she passed through the central aisle of the stalls, some of the merchants recognized her. One portly woman wearing a long apron handed Kathryn flowers as she passed. A few others called out and waved to her. Clearly, she had a friendly rapport with those who lived nearest the castle.

Small stone dwellings crowded the roadway as they ambled toward the towers that Aiden could see just ahead. When they arrived at the stables, Gareth and Kathryn dismounted, and two grooms took their horses. Rowan, Aiden, and Venn followed. Gareth took the reins of their horses and tugged them lightly toward stalls and fresh hay. Aiden remembered now that Gareth ran the castle stables. He seemed comfortable and at ease, back in his realm.

As Aiden shouldered her bag and her bedroll, she realized how fatigued she was. This wasn't her home turf, but for some reason she felt more relaxed here than she had in days. Maybe Kathryn's calm was spreading to her.

Venn and Aiden followed Kathryn and Rowan into the entry hall of the castle. Torches mounted in iron cages on the rock walls on either side of them cast a warm light into the small, high-ceilinged dark room. The moment Kathryn crossed the threshold, servants began to scurry about her. They accepted her cloak and took the satchel she carried and her crossbow along with the quiver. Then other servants did the same for Rowan.

Aiden stood uncomfortably apart from the brief frenzy of activity, taking it all in. She wondered for the first time where she and Venn would stay. The stable building was solid and dry, a bed of fresh hay piled high sounded appealing at the moment. She was just about to turn and leave when Kathryn pulled a maid in her direction. The girl was young with blond hair and bright blue eyes. She was shorter than Aiden, and the dress she wore swirled around her slim figure as she moved.

"Aiden, this is Juliet. She will see to your needs and get you settled into our guest quarters." Kathryn pulled Juliet closer. She was a bit shy.

"You mean I'm to stay here? In the castle?"

"Yes, of course. You and your woman-at-arms are my guests." Kathryn tipped her head in Venn's direction.

Kathryn was following their planned disguise by announcing Venn's role. If Aiden were going to play the part of a royal-born, she would have to try to be a bit less self-conscious about her surroundings. That was a tall order considering this was the first time she'd ever set foot inside a castle. She had no idea what to expect or how to behave. She looked in Venn's direction.

Another chambermaid was relieving Venn of her gear and indicating that she should follow up the stairs to the second level.

Kathryn touched Aiden's arm. "Aiden, rest and bathe, and I will see both of you for dinner later."

Aiden nodded mutely and followed Juliet up the stairs on Venn's heels.

Kathryn watched Aiden climb the stairs. She wanted nothing more than to follow her, but she needed to find Frost and check the status of things before she'd have the luxury of relaxation. Rowan excused herself as Kathryn headed toward the throne room. Frost would likely be in the map room, which joined the throne room and the library. Before she reached the map room, she saw the outline of Frost's tall frame approaching in the dimly lit corridor.

"It's so good to see you, Your Highness. The steward told me you'd arrived and that you brought two guests with you."

"Yes. Can we speak privately in the throne room?" Kathryn knew they would be undisturbed. She didn't want anyone to overhear the details of her excursion to Eveshom, even innocently. Frost was the only person she trusted with her discovery of the missing heir to Belstaff.

"So you were successful then?" Frost asked.

"Yes, but I'd prefer to keep Aiden's identity private until we've had a chance to deliberate about what, if any, path of action we should take."

"His name is Aiden?"

"Her name is Aiden," Kathryn corrected Frost, who was obviously still operating under the same original false assumption that the heir was male.

"My apologies. When the steward informed me of your arrival, he mistakenly identified her as a young man."

"She's not." Kathryn feared that if she weren't cautious she'd reveal more of her feelings for Aiden than she intended to.

"It shouldn't be difficult to explain having noble born visitors at the moment. Since the solstice celebration is tomorrow night." Frost had thankfully not acknowledged Kathryn's obvious personal interest in Aiden.

"Oh, no, with everything that's happened, I completely forgot about the solstice feast." Kathryn ran her fingers through her hair. The tangles she encountered reminded her of how much she wanted to bathe and wash her travel-dusted hair.

"Everything is arranged. The chancellor stepped in during your absence with preparations. No one will even suspect that you've been away."

"Thank you. And I'll be sure and offer my gratitude to the chancellor as well. The celebration is important and anticipated by everyone in the village. I wouldn't want to disappoint them." The solstice feast was one of Olmstead's largest events in celebration of the harvest. People came for miles to feast, drink wine, and dance. Kathryn couldn't believe she'd let the date slip her mind. She must be more fatigued than she realized.

"You should get some rest. We can speak further later." Kathryn nodded. "Thank you."

She left Frost and climbed the tower steps to the solar chamber, her small fortress of solitude. Well, not complete solitude at the moment. Her maids-in-waiting had laid out a dress for her, and one of the women, Lillian, was adding steaming water to a large tub as she entered the room. She was grateful that they'd anticipated her desires and prepared a bath for her. She eagerly discarded her soiled, dusty blouse and trousers. Lillian offered Kathryn her hand as she stepped onto a small stool and then over the high-sided tub into the deep water. Kathryn moaned in response to the luxurious warmth that enveloped her weary muscles as she sank chin deep into the hot water scented with rose petals.

Kathryn relished the occasional adventure, but at the moment, a hot bath was all the adventure she craved.

CHAPTER TWENTY-FOUR

Aiden sloshed water around as she scrubbed at her feet and legs. Then she sank completely under the surface, holding her breath in the noiseless depth of the bath for a few minutes as she washed soap out of her hair. When she resurfaced, Juliet was leaving with all of her discarded clothing under her arm.

"Um, excuse me, but if you take those what am I to wear?" Aiden was concerned she'd be left stranded in strange quarters with nothing more than a towel.

"Not to worry. I'll return straightaway with some clean clothes. I just needed these for sizing, and then we'll put them out for the steward. He'll see that they get washed." Juliet smiled and closed the door.

Aiden sank back into the sudsy water. She'd never experienced such a place of luxury as this room. In contrast, she now realized how stark the monastery had been. She catalogued the elements of the room from her watery perch. The bed had a high frame built around it with a heavy post at each corner. Fabric was draped around the crosspieces and had been allowed to drape down the side of each column. The bed was well outfitted with pillows and coverings. At the bedside was a small table with a lantern. The sun had not set for the day so the candle under the lantern's glass had not been lit yet. There was a desk and a cushioned chair with ornate carvings all along its wooden arms. And a small hearth set with a fire that had also not been lit.

She'd never had this much space to herself. The rooms within the orphanage weren't much larger than the cabins aboard Nilah's ship and nearly as sparse. Things were a distraction. Things weighed humanity down. In too many instances, the thing man thought he owned actually owned him. At least that was the perspective of the monks, and by association, the children raised under the monastery's roof.

The stone walls of the monastery were surrounded by lands tended by peasants who had no hope of owning land of their own. So it was easy to see how the perspective on ownership had developed. It seemed to Aiden that there should be enough to grant each household ownership of a small plot for farming. That was only fair, but she was beginning to see that fairness played by its own rules in the world that existed outside the community of faith she'd been raised in.

Aiden lounged in the bath until the heated water began to cool. She was just about to climb out and reach for a towel when Juliet returned.

"The tailor says these things should fit you. He'll sort out something more formal for the celebration tomorrow night." Juliet laid several items on the bed and brought a towel over for Aiden.

"What celebration?"

"The feast of the summer solstice." Juliet gave Aiden a questioning look, as if she was surprised that she didn't already know about the event. That probably did seem odd. Why else would Aiden be visiting the castle? Right?

"Oh, yes, I didn't realize that was tomorrow." She tried to pretend she'd just gotten confused about the day, but Aiden suspected that Juliet saw right through her. She was a terrible liar.

Juliet held the towel out as if she expected Aiden to climb out of the tub in front of her. Aiden was far too shy for that. She gave Juliet a confused look.

"Go ahead, miss. I won't bite."

"Um, thank you, but I can manage myself. I won't be needing any assistance to get dressed." Aiden sank down to her chin, hoping the suds on the surface offered her some covering.

"As you wish." Juliet smiled, and if Aiden wasn't mistaken, there was a playful glint in her eyes. She tossed the towel over a wooden bench near the tub and left the room.

The bath water was lukewarm at best now so Aiden wasted no time climbing out after Juliet's exit. She wrapped the towel around her shoulders and used one end of it to dry her hair. She looked at the clothing on the bed. She fingered the material of the white shirt, which was a similar style to the one she'd been wearing, although this shirt had no tears or obvious distress from too many washings. The trousers were a blue-gray. She liked the fit when she pulled them on. They were slim through the hips and legs and hung low, just below her waist. She tucked in the long shirttail and reached for her belt. The well worn leather of the belt and her dusty boots were in stark contrast to the clean, pressed clothing. Maybe she would have a chance to polish her boots tomorrow. But for tonight, she was hoping for some food.

She finger combed her hair and walked toward the door. She stopped as she passed one of the narrow windows that overlooked the interior green space of the keep. It looked like a courtyard of some kind. There were rose bushes and other flowering plants, and a labyrinth of pathways wound through the greenery in every direction. It looked as if several of the pathways ended in front of a small stone chapel. She made a mental note to investigate the garden when she got the chance.

The sun was going down, and just as she reached for the door, she heard a knock. She opened it to find Juliet carrying a candle.

"I was coming to light the lantern for you."

"Thank you, but I won't need it right away. Maybe you could direct me to the kitchen." Now that she was clean and dressed, Aiden realized she was starving. Dry venison for two days wasn't much.

"Oh, dinner is being served in the great hall shortly. I'll show you the way." She stepped aside for Aiden to pass through the doorway. "You look very nice, if you don't mind me saying so."

Aiden felt heat in her cheeks. The compliment had been unexpected. "Thank you." She knew she was blushing. At least the light in the hallway was fairly dim so perhaps Juliet hadn't noticed.

They walked down the lengthy hallway outside her chamber toward the grand staircase. Paintings she assumed were Kathryn's ancestors lined the walls on both sides. She sensed their disapproval but did not look up to meet their gazes. Juliet directed Aiden to the main dining hall, and when she arrived she saw that Venn was already there. She'd bathed and dressed for dinner also. She wore tailored pants similar to Aiden's. They fit her muscled thighs snuggly. She wore a dark gray shirt, in contrast to Aiden's stark white. Venn had also added a leather vest. This vest looked nicely broken in, soft, with scuffs from wear. There were two ornate buttons pulled through leather loops that pulled the soft leather of the vest snug against Venn's torso. Venn struck quite an imposing figure, and she was at ease in these environs that were so incredibly foreign to Aiden.

Rowan joined them. She was wearing a lovely mahogany colored dress that brushed the floor as she crossed the room. She smiled warmly as she approached, and for a split second Aiden could have sworn Venn fidgeted as Rowan approached. But whatever nervousness Aiden had witnessed she quickly covered.

The extravagantly long heavy table had place settings for four. Aiden was just about to ask Rowan a question when Kathryn entered the room, and any thought Aiden had evaporated. She was so struck by Kathryn's beauty that she had to remind herself to close her mouth.

Kathryn had exchanged travel clothes for an emerald dress. Like Rowan's, the hem reached to the floor, and the layers of her slip under the skirt made soft swishing noises as she walked toward them. The bodice of the dress fit snug to her slim waist and pushed up her breasts in a tasteful display of cleavage. Her hair had been swept back and up and was gathered in place by an ornate comb.

Venn cleared her throat and lightly bumped Aiden's arm. Aiden had been in a trance. She realized she'd been unabashedly staring at Kathryn as she moved fluidly around the table and motioned for them to sit.

Aiden managed to pull her chair out and take a seat, but she could hardly pull her eyes from Kathryn. She'd been transformed, and Aiden wasn't even sure she was the same woman that she'd kissed in the small cabin aboard Nilah's ship. If she were just meeting her now Aiden would have been far too intimidated to even speak to her. Her palms were damp. She rubbed them against her thighs under the table and tried to read cues from Venn. She was completely out of her element, and so lightheaded she feared she was moments from passing out.

She ran an unsteady hand through her still damp hair.

"Aiden, are you feeling all right?" asked Rowan.

"Yes, thank you. I think I'm just a little hungry." *And I'm so taken with Kathryn that I'm forgetting to breathe.* Aiden lectured herself to calm down.

Servers began to bring dishes around to the four of them; each one contained something different, and it wasn't long before Aiden's plate was piled high. As she looked at her heaping plate, contrasted against the others' more reasonable servings, she had to admit that maybe she'd gotten a little carried away. She'd never seen so much food or such a diversity of food at a single meal. Meals at the monastery had consisted of potatoes and one other vegetable; twice a week there'd be beef, lamb, or venison.

Kathryn had to cover a laugh as she watched Aiden respond with unrestrained joy on her face to each entrée presented by the serving staff. She was trying to imagine how all of this felt to Aiden, but having grown up without ever wanting for anything, it was hard to imagine.

Rowan had been insightful when she'd said that Aiden was incredibly open. Whatever she was feeling was written all over her face. That wouldn't always be a bad thing. Like just now, when Kathryn had entered the room, she could tell that Aiden was attracted to her. As she drew closer, the glistening in her eyes signaled a deep and simmering desire. And as Kathryn now knew, that desire had yet to be tapped. She wanted to be the first to test those waters.

Only now she found that she was as nervous as a schoolgirl with no experience at all. As soon as everyone began to eat, she worried that things weren't perfect. And she wanted them to be. She'd hosted guests before, but not really since her father's funeral, and most of that had been taken care of by the chancellor and his wife, thank goodness. Kathryn had been so laden with grief that she'd been unable to think of the simple daily needs for those visiting the keep for the funeral.

This was an entirely different occasion. She liked Aiden. She wanted to please Aiden. But at the same time, she didn't want to overwhelm her. In a matter of days, everything in Aiden's world had shifted. Kathryn hoped Aiden would allow her to assist her with that adjustment.

Thank goodness that Venn was with them, because Aiden would need a strong ally. Ever since Aiden had returned from her vision in the desert, the energy between Aiden and Venn had noticeably shifted. There was respect between them, and admiration, and maybe even love. You could see it clearly in the way they spoke to one another and in the way that Venn tutored Aiden. Once Kathryn had realized that, she could allow herself to relax a little, knowing that Venn was there for Aiden, and she would keep her safe.

Rowan reached across the space between them and touched her arm. When Kathryn turned to face her, Rowan mouthed the word *relax*.

Kathryn smiled and felt the tension in her shoulders ease just from Rowan's gentle suggestion.

"I might have neglected to tell you both that there's a summer solstice celebration here tomorrow evening. The entire kingdom is invited, and most of them will likely attend." Kathryn took a sip of her wine. Aiden and Venn listened intently from across the table as they ate. "We'll have a feast for the noblemen and their families in the great hall. Both of you are invited as my guests."

"Thank you," Venn responded. Aiden's mouth was full of food.

"It's really quite fun, one of my favorite events of the year." Rowan's eyes sparkled with mischief as she regarded Venn. "Long tables are set up in the courtyard in front of the main hall with all manner of food, desserts, wine, and ale. Everyone is invited to participate. There'll be music and dancing."

"Dancing?" Aiden sounded uncertain.

"Do you dance?" Rowan asked the question instead of Kathryn, but she was anxious to hear the response.

"Um, no, I've never danced."

"I'll have to give you a lesson then." Venn gave Aiden a friendly slap on the back.

Aiden gave Venn a horrified stare as if a dancing lesson was the thing she feared most in life.

"Is this a…what I mean is, I'm not sure I have the right clothes for something like this." Aiden took a sip of wine and leaned back in her chair. She'd done an amazing job polishing off the healthy servings of food she'd taken.

"I've spoken with the tailor, and he will visit you in the morning to fit you for a jacket." Kathryn paused. She realized in that instant that she'd arranged this without speaking with Aiden first. "I hope that isn't a problem. I should have asked you first, but I realized while I was arranging other details for tomorrow with the chancellor that you might need a fitting." Kathryn was accustomed to making decisions for others. She realized now that maybe she shouldn't do that where Aiden was concerned.

"That's not a problem. Thank you for thinking of me."

I've hardly been able to think of anything else, is what Kathryn wanted to say, but she stopped herself. "I think he'll be able to fit you with something you'll like."

Coffee and dessert was served as they continued to talk. Every time a servant reached around Aiden's shoulder, she jumped a little, as if caught by surprise. Kathryn found her curiosity about everything that was happening in the room endearing, her hopeful innocence like a child in a toymaker's shop.

"Do I need to seek out the tailor tomorrow, or will he find me?" asked Aiden.

"He'll announce himself tomorrow morning, and one of the stewards will show him to your quarters. That's assuming you don't plan to be out too early." Kathryn's tone was playful. She had to remind herself that Aiden was completely out of her element. She wouldn't know even the smallest thing about life in the royal enclave.

Venn had hardly said a word during dinner, obviously content to listen and enjoy her meal. Rowan had her work cut out for her if she was going to break through the stoic woman's defenses.

"There is a courtyard I could see from my window. It looks almost like someone's flower garden." Aiden finished the last bite of a slim slice of finely layered cake.

"That was my mother's garden. Would you like to see it?"

"Yes, very much."

"You two should go for a walk while Venn and I finish our coffee." Rowan clearly wanted Venn to herself for a moment, and Kathryn was grateful for the excuse to escape the formal room and the curious eyes of the castle staff.

"Only if Aiden is finished. Are you?" asked Kathryn.

"Yes, I'd love to see the garden." Aiden stood and spoke to the servants standing nearby. "Thank you for a fine meal." They nodded, acknowledging her thanks, and then Kathryn stood to lead them out of the dining hall.

"I'll find you tomorrow for that dance lesson." Venn called to Aiden as she left.

"I'd say I can't wait, but I'm not so sure." Aiden grinned.

CHAPTER TWENTY-FIVE

Aiden got the chance once again to admire Kathryn's elegant emerald dress unnoticed as she followed Kathryn from the dining hall. Their footsteps echoed on the stone floors as they passed through the mezzanine and then two smaller sitting rooms before finally stepping into the courtyard. Kathryn mentioned a few details about each room as they passed through them, but Aiden could only focus on the delicate line of her shoulders and the small area of pale skin showing from the scooped neckline at the back of her dress as she followed a few feet behind.

Kathryn's demeanor had definitely shifted since her return to the castle. She'd been distant, serious, and politely aloof. Aiden missed the moments of casual contact they'd shared while traveling. Kissing Kathryn, holding her while they slept in the tiny cabin aboard the wind ship, now felt like nothing more than a dream. Maybe this distance between them was just a symptom of adjustment to the more formal environment here. She hoped they could get past it. Kathryn turned to face her.

Aiden's heart beat painfully, as if it were pounding against the walls of her chest to escape. The moonlight softly lit Kathryn's blond hair and her delicate features; her sheer beauty was making it hard for Aiden to breathe. Kathryn was like the uncharted depths of the great Taiga Forest—mysterious, mythical, unknowable—and Aiden longed for the chance to know her.

Kathryn seemed to be lost in the moment as well. She'd turned to face Aiden, but she hadn't spoken. Her breathing quickened, and there was a hunger in her eyes that matched what Aiden was feeling, although she couldn't yet give it a name.

They were alone in the moonlit courtyard, surrounded by the perfume of roses. Aiden was drawn to Kathryn as if a tether had been strung between them, pulling her in. She tenderly traced Kathryn's cheek with her fingers, and when Kathryn closed her eyes, Aiden kissed her.

It was a tentative kiss at first. Aiden brushed her lips lightly across Kathryn's, then she pressed her lips more firmly to Kathryn's mouth. Kathryn's lips parted, and their tongues danced and teased. Desire flamed hot inside Aiden's chest, and before she could stop herself, she wrapped her arms around Kathryn and drew her close.

Through the fog of want, she felt Kathryn's hands pushing against her arms to separate them. Kathryn broke the kiss and whispered urgently against her cheek. "Not here, not in the open."

Aiden took a step back, releasing her. Her lips felt hot and swollen, and she ached for more. Kathryn grasped her hand and tugged her into the small, darkened stone chapel at the edge of the garden. Within seconds, they were in each other's arms again, feverishly kissing. Aiden felt as if she couldn't get close enough. Kathryn's dress was beautiful, but it was also cumbersome, and the layered skirt filled the space between them, creating a barrier that Aiden couldn't breach.

She, on the other hand, was much more accessible to Kathryn.

Kathryn kissed her neck through the open collar of her shirt. Kathryn's hands were on her ass. Then Kathryn put her hand at the back of Aiden's head and pulled her mouth down to her soft, rounded breasts, exposed above the bodice of her dress. Kathryn moaned quietly as Aiden delicately feathered kisses across her skin.

Kathryn placed her hands on Aiden's cheeks and tilted her head up so that she could see her eyes. Kathryn searched her face.

"Aiden, I want you."

Aiden wasn't sure what she meant; she just responded with a questioning look.

"I want to make love to you. But only if you want that, too."
Kathryn still held her face in her hands.

Aiden nodded and then answered softly. "Yes."

"We shouldn't be seen going upstairs together."

Aiden nodded again. She wasn't sure why, but she figured
Kathryn had her reasons.

"You go to your room and I will come to you. Okay?" Kathryn
kissed Aiden softly on the lips.

Aiden forced herself to leave Kathryn in the shadows of the
chapel. She ran her fingers through her hair and smoothed the front
of her shirt. She adjusted the crotch of her trousers. She worried
that anyone she passed on the way back to her quarters would know
what she'd been up to. Her cheeks felt hot, and she was sure they
were blazing red. She took a deep breath and stepped back into the
cool interior of Starford Keep.

CHAPTER TWENTY-SIX

Aiden had taken off her boots and her belt, but left her trousers and her shirt. She'd pulled the shirttail free. It draped around her, falling to mid-thigh. She'd paced barefoot back and forth across the room at least fifty times. Maybe Kathryn wasn't coming. She felt lost and adrift with the waiting, and the notion that she had such a strong longing for Kathryn annoyed her. She willed herself to rise above her own base needs.

She stopped pacing and stood in the center of the room. A fire had been lit by Juliet to chase away the cool evening air. There was water in a pitcher on the bedside table, and the lantern had also been lit. Shadows from the candle's flame danced up the stone walls on either side of the high four-poster bed.

Should she just get undressed and go to bed? That seemed as if it would be awkward if Kathryn did finally appear. What if *making love* to Kathryn meant something else? What if Aiden really had no idea what making love meant? Uncertainty threatened to relieve her of the fine evening meal she'd eaten. She poured herself a glass of water and tried to calm down. As she drank she heard a soft knock at the door.

She rushed to open it for fear that in the twenty seconds it took her to cross the room, Kathryn would change her mind.

Kathryn quickly slipped inside. The elegant emerald dress was gone. Kathryn was wearing a simple white linen nightgown beneath a velvet robe. Her hair was down and loosely hung past her shoulders. Aiden's first thought was that it hadn't been the green dress after all that was so lovely but Kathryn herself. She was just as gorgeous in a common nightgown as she'd been in the emerald dress.

"I was afraid you weren't coming," Aiden blurted out and then regretted it. She didn't want to seem like some nervous beginner, even though that was exactly what she was.

"I'm sorry. It took me longer than I expected." Kathryn smiled sweetly, as if she hadn't noticed how anxious Aiden was. "I hope it wasn't too presumptuous of me that I dressed for bed."

Aiden looked down and was reminded that she was still in the clothes she'd worn to dinner. "No, that's fine. I...I wasn't sure if I should get undressed or..." Her voice trailed off when she felt the warmth of Kathryn's hand on the center of her chest.

"I can help you get undressed."

Aiden's pulse rate increased exponentially as she watched Kathryn drop her velvet robe over a nearby chair and then return to face her. She could see that Kathryn was nude beneath the sheer fabric of the loose fitting nightgown. The fabric clung to the sensuous curve of her hips and then draped loosely from the swell of her breasts. Aiden swallowed and tried to focus on Kathryn's face.

"Let's get in bed." Aiden felt Kathryn's fingers moving next to her skin as she unfastened the buttons of her trousers and pushed them down until they pooled at her feet. She stepped out of them, and then Kathryn assisted her in pulling her shirt off over her head. She was now only wearing boxy undershorts that were tied at the waist.

Kathryn realized that Aiden was allowing her to take the lead. She had to fight the urge to throw Aiden back onto the bed and ravish her. Hopefully, there would be time for that later. This time, Aiden's first time, she needed to focus on going slow. This would certainly test her self-control since she'd done little else but imagine making love to Aiden since the second time she'd seen her with her shirt off bathing beside that stream.

She put her hand in the center of Aiden's chest and gently pushed her back onto the bed. As Aiden sat watching, she pulled the drawstring at the neck of her nightgown untied and let the sheer fabric slowly glide off her shoulders onto the floor. Aiden stared, wide-eyed, at her teasing display.

They pulled the covering back and slid into the cool sheets. Kathryn wondered if Aiden had ever slept on a feather mattress before. The wonder on her face indicated that she hadn't. Or maybe that expression had to do with other things.

Kathryn wanted to rid Aiden of her last bit of clothing, but she also wanted to give Aiden a little time to adjust. She snuggled next to Aiden and let her fingertips trace the contour of Aiden's broad shoulder, across her ribs, and then down to her pronounced hipbone. Then she followed the waistline of her undershorts; she felt Aiden's stomach muscles shudder as her fingertips touched skin.

"Don't be afraid. We won't do anything you don't want to." Kathryn spoke softly as she slowly tugged the knot of drawstring at the front of her undergarment.

"I'm not afraid."

"But you're trembling."

"That's not fear. That's…something else."

Kathryn smiled. She left the drawstring to hang untied and let the shorts stay for the moment. Right now, she needed to focus on Aiden's mouth. She moved partially on top of Aiden and kissed her, as she continued to explore the landscape of Aiden's chest and torso. Her small breasts came to sharp points as Kathryn pressed her palm on top of them, massaged them tenderly, and then let her hand drift down across Aiden's clenched stomach muscles. She sensed underneath the taut muscle a building fire. Aiden's skin was warm to the touch.

Kathryn wanted to become intimately acquainted with the topography of Aiden's body and intended to study its secret spaces in depth. Kathryn was emboldened by the knowledge that she was the first to explore this sensual terrain. Her desire was to tread gently for now and focus on reading the signals Aiden's body was sending her.

Aiden felt Kathryn's fingers at the waistband of her shorts. She teased them across her hyper-sensitive stomach just before she slipped her fingers inside Aiden's shorts and teased at the stiff patch of curls at the apex of her thighs. Aiden made no move to stop her, so she traveled farther south to explore the place between Aiden's legs.

Aiden felt unmasked, as if her chest was a dark cavern of need; the need to be touched, the need to be held, the need to be seen. Aiden felt the muscles in her thighs stiffen as Kathryn continued to caress her.

She'd touched herself before, but to be touched by Kathryn was something else entirely. She had no control over her body's response to Kathryn. She wondered if Kathryn sensed the power she wielded over Aiden in this moment. The instant Kathryn's skin had pressed against hers she'd burst into flame.

Kathryn kissed her deeply, and with the fingers of her other hand, fisted Aiden's hair. She filled Aiden's mouth with her tongue, and Aiden imagined Kathryn's tongue in other places. Aiden moaned against Kathryn's mouth. A tremendous, magnificent rush began to build and pulse through her body emanating from Kathryn's touch between her legs. The tension in her body was excruciating. Every nerve and every fiber of every muscle was strained, pulled painfully taut. Release would be her only salvation, and only Kathryn could release her. She stood at the edge of infinity prepared to be splintered into fragments and cast into infinite nothingness should Kathryn pull away.

Kathryn sensed Aiden's rising climax. Aiden's hands tightened on her ass, pulling their bodies firmly together. Aiden's hips matched the insistent caress of her fingers between Aiden's legs as they moved in a sensual dance, grinding their bodies into a singular exploration for release.

"Oh, Kathryn." Aiden broke the kiss and buried her face in Kathryn's neck. She wrapped her arms around Kathryn and held tightly.

"That's it, let me take you there." Kathryn increased the rhythm of her caress. She felt Aiden tighten around her fingers and the strength of her body as she shuddered beneath her.

Aiden muffled a cry against Kathryn's neck, and as the orgasm rippled through her body, she trembled in Kathryn's arms. For Kathryn, this was just a taste. She wanted more. She wanted to be inside Aiden, and even beyond that, she wanted Aiden inside her. She desired possession and to be possessed. She pressed her lips to Aiden's forehead.

Kathryn focused on her face as Aiden released a shaking breath and let her head drop back onto the pillow. Her eyes glistened beneath heavy lids. Kathryn stroked her face and then trailed her fingers down the center of Aiden's chest, lingering momentarily in the hollow space above her pounding heart.

"Can we take these off?" She tugged at Aiden's undershorts.

Aiden simply nodded. Aiden pushed the shorts over her hips and then kicked them free somewhere under the covers. Warmth and desire coursed through her body when she draped her thigh over Aiden's. The sensation of skin on skin sent shivers up Kathryn's arm and along the fine hairs at the back of her neck. Aiden's body was exquisite.

Intellectually, Kathryn knew that they were apart from one another, distinct, separated by their own experiences, but she felt sure this sensual communion brought them nearer. The connection she felt for Aiden was untested, but strong. Kathryn smiled down at Aiden, braced as she was on her elbows.

"How are you feeling about all of this? Is this okay?" Kathryn punctuated the question with a light kiss.

Aiden guessed that Kathryn was trying to be solicitous knowing it was her first time with a woman, but she couldn't imagine anything that Kathryn might do that she wouldn't enjoy. Even if that meant doing nothing except holding each other, even if that meant doing everything, whatever *everything* entailed. She was smitten with Kathryn. Her heart felt huge and aching. She felt consumed, exposed, but for some reason unafraid.

Lost in the soft perfection of Kathryn's skin, Aiden realized she'd forgotten to answer Kathryn's question. "I want to do whatever you'd like to do, as much as you'd like and as often as you'd like." Aiden hoped that covered *everything*. Even though she still didn't quite know what that word, in this context, meant.

Kathryn laughed softly. "I like the sound of that." She brushed hair away from Aiden's forehead and searched her face.

"Kathryn, you are so beautiful." Aiden had thought this many times; she wanted to make sure she'd remembered to say it out loud.

"So are you. I don't think you have any idea how attractive you are."

Aiden felt heat rise to her cheeks.

"You're blushing. So cute." Kathryn kissed the tip of her nose. "I'm serious. Once my tailor gets through with you there won't be a single maiden in my kingdom that won't have the inclination to drag you into bed."

Aiden laughed at the obvious absurdity of that. "Not likely."

"I'll have to place armed guards around you. Mark my words, Aiden Roth."

Aiden felt a shiver run through her body, and she was filled with a sudden realization that she was more than some nameless orphan.

"What's wrong?" Kathryn shifted her weight to one side.

Aiden shook her head, and despite her best effort to hold it back, a tear trailed down her cheek.

"Oh, Aiden, what happened? What did I say?"

"It's nothing, really. It's just…that's the first time anyone has ever used my full name." And she was marked with a birthright. She didn't know what all that meant yet, but she would think about it later. All she could think about now was Kathryn.

Kathryn pressed her lips to Aiden's. Then she kissed the wet path of the tear on her cheek. She held Aiden's face in her hands. "Aiden Roth, you are stunning, beautiful, sexy, and I'm begging you to make love to me."

Aiden couldn't help but smile. "Show me."

Kathryn returned the smile and shifted their positions, pulling Aiden on top of her. She spread her legs so that Aiden's could slide her thigh between them. Kathryn began to grind slowly against Aiden's leg. She could feel wetness against her thigh. She knew she didn't really have any idea of the proper technique, but she had an insatiable urge to touch Kathryn, so she did.

She covered Kathryn's body with hers and traced the soft rounded contour of Kathryn's stomach until she found the place between her legs. Tentatively, she began to explore. Kathryn directed her fingers showing Aiden where she wanted them.

Aiden watched Kathryn's face. Her eyes were closed and she bit her lower lip as she moved against Aiden's hand. Then she opened her eyes, darkened with desire, and smiled up at Aiden. She pulled Aiden's ear close to her mouth.

"I want to feel you inside." She guided Aiden's fingers, and Aiden slowly pushed inside. Kathryn moaned softly and spread her legs farther, moving against Aiden's hand. "Deeper...more."

Aiden adjusted her position, braced on one arm, and began to thrust deeper. Kathryn's breasts heaved as she rose to meet each thrust. Aiden bent down and took Kathryn's breast into her mouth.

"Yes." She felt Kathryn's fingers at the back of her head, pulling her more firmly against her breast.

As their movements became more fevered, Aiden relinquished Kathryn's breast and focused on what she was doing with her fingers. She felt herself getting close to climaxing again with just the friction between their bodies. She tried to push back her own desire so that she could focus on pleasing Kathryn.

Kathryn arched up and kissed her deeply. And as she did, she moved her hand between them and slid her fingers inside. Aiden inhaled sharply and then allowed herself to adjust to the sensation of Kathryn's fingers inside. She slowed her movements as she wrapped her head around the fact that she was making love to Kathryn.

"That's it, Aiden. Slow and deep."

Kathryn's voice snapped her back to the moment. She moved on top of Kathryn, against her hand, while she continued to thrust inside Kathryn. Aiden felt every muscle in her body hum as she drew close to the edge. Beneath her, Kathryn's body tensed and thrust with force against her once, twice, a third time, and then Aiden felt her own orgasm push her over the threshold. Her entire body tensed as she climaxed. Kathryn pressed against her, holding her in place until Kathryn cried out. Kathryn's eyes were closed, her body convulsed. She pressed her open mouth against Aiden's shoulder, and then drew her close, not moving her hand. Kathryn shuddered beneath her.

Aiden started to withdraw her fingers, but Kathryn stopped her.

"Don't. Not yet." She kissed Aiden's neck and held her tightly.

They were both breathing hard and covered with a light sheen of sweat. Aiden couldn't brace herself any longer on one arm and allowed her full weight to sink onto Kathryn. She felt weak and sated and content. She had the unfamiliar sense of belonging, for maybe the first time ever. Emotion threatened to overwhelm her. She focused instead on tactile things—the warmth of Kathryn's skin against hers, the candlelight flickering beneath the glass of the lantern, the scent of Kathryn's hair.

Kathryn pressed her lips to Aiden's.

Aiden could have lain there all night, never moving, just to soak in Kathryn's essence. But after a little while, they separated. Aiden rolled onto her back, and Kathryn snuggled into the hollow space in her shoulder. Kathryn's leg was draped over Aiden so that she could still feel how wet Kathryn was. She fought the urge to touch her there again.

They lay luxuriously in each other's arms. The fire had died to glowing embers, and the bedside candle had burned to a nub. Moonlight danced through the room. Aiden caressed Kathryn's back with her fingertips, tracing small circles on her velvety skin.

The reality of what had just happened began to slowly sink into Aiden's brain as she lay looking up at the heavy timbers cutting across the ceiling above them. She wondered if Kathryn thought this was a big deal or if Kathryn had other women she slept with. Surely as a queen she could have whatever or whomever she wanted. Aiden began to doubt their connection. Could she really hope that the first woman she slept with would fall madly in love with her? That seemed unrealistic, regardless of how Aiden felt about her.

Kathryn held herself apart. She was with Aiden but somehow still slightly distant. Aiden could see it in her eyes despite their physical closeness. She had the insatiable desire to reach Kathryn and win her heart; she just had to figure out how. Aiden drifted off, to thoughts of possibility.

CHAPTER TWENTY-SEVEN

The creaking of the door woke Aiden the next morning. She blinked and then panicked, thinking that Kathryn was still in her bed. It was probably best if the entire royal household didn't find out through gossip that she'd slept with their queen.

A second later, her sleepy brain caught up with the present, and she was reminded that Kathryn had left her side in the wee hours of the morning. Well before the sun was up.

Aiden leaned up on one elbow and rubbed sleep from her eyes. Juliet carried a tray to the bedside table. The smell of food made Aiden's stomach growl. And then she realized she wasn't wearing any clothing. Quickly, she sank back under the covers, pulling the blanket up to her chin.

Juliet smiled and pretended not to have noticed.

"Good morning, miss. I've brought you some breakfast."

"Thank you." Aiden's voice cracked and she cleared her throat. "Do you know the time?"

"Oh, it's almost eight. The queen told me I should bring your breakfast because she said you might be tired." Juliet stood over her with her hands on her hips. "Well, are you?"

"What?"

"Tired."

"Um, no, but obviously I overslept. Please thank the queen for me."

Juliet smiled slyly as if she had a pretty good idea of what had happened the previous night. Aiden felt heat rise to her cheeks. She was sure she was blushing.

"Thank you for the food." Aiden thanked Juliet again in hopes that would be the cue she was waiting for to leave. She wasn't about to sit up and eat with Juliet still lingering.

"All right then. I'll be by later to retrieve the tray. Oh, and the tailor is due to arrive at nine." She pulled the heavy door closed behind her.

As soon as she'd gone, Aiden reached for the plate of eggs. She couldn't believe she'd slept so late. She'd still be asleep if Juliet hadn't woken her. As she chewed her food she wondered where Kathryn was and what she was doing.

She put a generous slathering of butter on one of the slices of bread and sank back into the pillow reminiscing about the previous night with Kathryn. She'd been a bundle of nerves, and she hoped it hadn't showed too much. Kathryn was a remarkable woman. As she evoked Kathryn's touch, she shivered. Chewing contemplatively, she sank further into the feather mattress. So far, her time at Starford Keep had been nothing but an indulgence for the senses.

Aiden polished off breakfast and then pulled on the clothes she'd been wearing when Kathryn arrived. They were strewn about on the floor and a bit wrinkled. She shook them out as best she could and then used water from the basin to wash her face. She felt almost awake and presentable when she heard another knock at the door.

A portly man, probably in his fifties and a few inches shorter than Aiden, stood on the threshold. He had an intricately patterned, deep red jacket draped over his arm and a basket of sewing tools. A lanky teenaged boy hovered at his elbow. He was holding a small stepstool and a wooden case with latches and hinges at the sides.

Aiden invited them in. She had never been to a tailor. She prepared herself for yet another unfamiliar experience.

❖

Kathryn looked up from the stack of papers on her desk as one of her servants set a cup of hot tea beside her. She sighed and again attempted to make sense of the dispatch she'd been trying to read repeatedly despite her distraction. Lack of sleep wasn't what was hindering her ability to focus this morning. Her thoughts kept drifting to Aiden. And when she allowed them to go there, she completely lost the thread of what she was reading.

This was ridiculous. She'd never been this unbalanced by sex. She knew that she deserved the comfort of companionship, but the simple act of ruling the small kingdom she'd inherited carried great responsibility. She couldn't afford to allow herself to be this distracted, especially now, with Balak's constant subtle threat to her reign. Every waking moment since she'd returned held strain and tension.

After returning to her room, Kathryn had slept for a couple of hours, then woken at dawn and stood quietly while servants dressed her. The attention in any other similar scenario might have felt intimate, but the distance of birth separated Kathryn from the women who attended her daily needs. She was physically close to them, but separate from them. Apart.

But this was somehow not the case with Aiden, despite her provincial upbringing.

She recalled the brush of Aiden's fingers across her skin. Chills ran up her spine to the back of her neck, and she squeezed her eyes shut.

Kathryn had started to read dispatches that she hadn't finished the previous day. And she had a few more to wade through. She hoped the tea would give her a boost. She thanked the server for delivering it and then he backed respectfully out of the room.

Luckily, Kathryn was skilled at thinking on her feet, giving the appearance of outward calm even if uncertainty hovered in her chest.

As she signed each document, she handed it to the chancellor who stood patiently in front of her desk. She wondered if he'd noticed her distraction, and if so, what he attributed it to. Chancellor Rhodes was a kind man. She didn't know his exact age, but she guessed he was close to sixty. He and his wife had raised two sons who'd taken wives and moved north to claim the land granted to them by her father. The Rhodes boys had grown into fine swordsmen, and Kathryn knew if the crown called they would return to defend the keep.

"I think this is all for now." Kathryn handed the documents to the chancellor.

He nodded. "Very good, Your Highness." He started to leave and then turned back. "Would you like for me to return to discuss details for tonight's festivities?"

"Oh, yes, that would be good, thank you."

He nodded and left.

Kathryn finally had a moment to sip her tea and enjoy the silence. She allowed her mind to drift to thoughts of Aiden, then frowned when she heard the unmistakable sound of boots on the stone hallway leading to her study that adjoined the throne room.

Frost stepped into the room.

She seemed tense. Frost was always tense. Kathryn supposed that came with the uniform, but still, it wasn't as if they were under attack at this very minute. Regardless, she was grateful for Frost's diligence. Frost Sylven was a serious soldier and a steady, confident leader. What more could she ask from the person who lead the imperial guard?

"Your Highness, I'm sorry to disturb you."

"Not at all. Please enter."

"I wondered if I might speak with the heir."

"Aiden."

"Yes, my apologies, Aiden." Frost stood with her arms at her sides and her feet shoulder's width apart. Anyone else might have assumed Frost was standing at attention, but Kathryn knew that for Frost, this was at ease.

"Is there something specific you wanted to speak with her about?" For some reason, Kathryn had the desire to shelter Aiden as long as possible from outside pressures. Those pressures would be upon her soon enough. Kathryn had hoped to give Aiden a bit more time to adjust before she had to make any serious decisions about next steps.

"I would simply like to have a better sense of who she is." Frost cleared her throat. "In the event that I'm asked to advise her in any capacity regarding the current situation in Belstaff."

"I'd prefer we give Aiden a few days to acclimate to Olmstead." Kathryn leaned forward, resting her arms on the edge of the desk. "At the moment, you and the rescue party are the only individuals who know her true identity. I believe this grants us a bit of time."

Frost nodded. "As you wish." There was a moment when Frost looked as if she might say more, but instead she adjusted her sword belt and shifted her shoulders back. "I will see to the security details for this evening's celebration. Please let me know if you have any specific requests."

"Thank you, Commander. I will."

Frost pivoted and left. Kathryn had gotten an odd feeling from Frost that she couldn't quite decipher. Not for the first time, she wished Frost were easier to read and a bit more transparent.

CHAPTER TWENTY-EIGHT

Aiden had been roaming around the castle grounds when Venn found her. Aiden had returned to the small courtyard that she could see from her window, the place where she and Kathryn had kissed the night before.

"There you are. If I didn't know better I'd think you were trying to avoid your dance lesson."

Aiden had buried her nose in one of the blooming roses. The heavenly scent reminded her of Kathryn's hair. She laughed. "On the contrary, I've been anxiously awaiting your instruction."

"Right. Then, get over here." Venn motioned for Aiden to follow her to the open central area of the small courtyard. The ground where Venn stood was covered with flagstone, and while it wasn't completely smooth, it would be adequate for a limited amount of footwork, provided the steps weren't too intricate.

"Okay, face me. And put your arms out like this." Venn waited for Aiden to get in position. She held her hand up and put her other hand at Aiden's waist. "You'll likely lead, so let me see if I can think in reverse."

"Am I supposed to hold your hand?"

"Yes, wait, if you're leading then my hand is on your shoulder and your hand is at my waist. I had that the other way around." Venn switched positions with her hands.

"This feels strange." Aiden had always envisioned that her first dance would be with someone a bit more—feminine.

"The steps aren't difficult. I'll show you." Venn looked down at her feet to position them properly.

"No, I mean, *this* feels weird. Holding your hand, leading you around in a dance."

Soft laughter caught her attention.

"I have to agree with Aiden about this." Rowan grinned at them.

Aiden wasn't sure how long Rowan had been watching from the doorway, but she now joined them in the center of the courtyard. Aiden and Venn each took an awkward step back. Aiden nervously rubbed her palms on her trousers.

"Why not let me teach you?" Rowan stepped between them. She turned and gave Venn a playful smile as she took Aiden's hand.

Aiden tried to focus on where she was supposed to hold Rowan.

"Elbow up, cradle my hand in yours, you don't have to hold so tightly." Rowan moved Aiden's other hand to her hip. "And this hand here." Rowan was wearing riding trousers that hugged every curve of her shapely legs, and tall boots, so it was easy for Aiden to see her feet. Venn stepped to the side and watched with an amused expression on her face.

Aiden was a bundle of awkward nerves. There was no music, so Rowan began to hum in between coaching Aiden's steps.

"The basic step for a waltz is a box step. It's called a box step because that's the shape we will create on the floor with our feet." Rowan took one step back, but Aiden didn't immediately follow her. "I'm teaching you the lead part, so you step forward when I step back, okay?"

Aiden nodded and tried to shadow Rowan's footwork and movements.

"A box step can be divided into two parts, a forward half box and a backward half box. Each half box has three steps." Rowan began to count as she moved her feet. "One, two, three, one, two, three... Good. Take a step forward or backward, a step to the side, and a step to bring your feet together."

Aiden tried a few times to get the rhythm right, but she felt inept. She even stepped on Rowan's toes once.

"The leader starts with the left foot and executes a forward half box, followed by a backward half box." Rowan exuded patience, but still, Aiden was frustrated with her own clumsiness. "See, I start with the right foot and execute a backward half box, followed by a forward half box." Rowan watched Aiden's feet as they moved together and began to count again. "That's it. One, two, three, one, two, three, good."

Aiden was still looking down and trying to imagine the box shape she was outlining across the flagstones.

"Relax, Aiden. And you should look at your partner, not at the ground."

As soon as Aiden looked up, she lost track of where her feet were and went forward when she should have gone sideways and bumped into Rowan.

"That's it. I'm cutting in." Venn had obviously stood by as long as she could. "Aiden, stand aside and watch."

Venn took Aiden's position. She held her hand out for Rowan, and when Rowan stepped into her arms the energy between them shifted. Aiden watched as Rowan and Venn relaxed into each other's embrace as if they'd been dancing together for years. Venn was poised, her stance erect but not stiff, and her movements were smooth yet firm as she led Rowan through the steps of the dance. Aiden was momentarily jealous of Venn's confidence.

Rowan's cheeks gained color as they continued to move together, and their stance became more intimate as the space between their bodies lessened. It was if they'd become lost in their own world and had forgotten that Aiden was watching.

After a few more elegant turns, Venn snapped out of whatever trance she'd been in. She abruptly stopped, released Rowan, and stepped away from her. She cleared her throat, gave Aiden a sheepish look, and motioned for Aiden to take her position.

"Aiden, now you try it again."

She nodded and stepped up to accept Rowan's outstretched hand, but she knew she'd never be able to dance as well as Venn with only one afternoon of lessons.

"Just relax, Aiden. Dancing should be fun." It was as if Rowan had read her thoughts, and the simple statement calmed her down. She smiled and nodded.

CHAPTER TWENTY-NINE

By late afternoon, the bustling activity leading up to the festival was at a fever pitch. Aiden left the castle to stroll around the village. Mostly to have some time to herself, but also to stay out of the way. She'd offered to help, but it looked as if every servant had a task already and there was nothing that she could do except be a hindrance.

She'd grabbed an apple off a tray near the kitchen as she scuttled down the broad rock steps from the main entrance of the great hall to the commotion of the main square in front of the castle. Tables and stalls were being set up for the night's event. Wooden casks of ale were being hoisted onto large racks, and benches were brought round to accessorize each of the long tables.

The common area outside the castle was as frenetic as the inside had been, so Aiden decided to venture farther into the web of winding dirt lanes that comprised the village surrounding the keep. Everyone she passed seemed occupied with some task—wresting chickens from their coops, carrying baskets of vegetables toward the castle, making candles, washing clothing. Laughing children ran past her trailing ribbons of gold and green. No one paid her any attention, which was nice. Before she realized it, she'd wandered in a circle and had ended up near the castle stables.

She saw Gareth and changed direction, but it was too late. He'd seen her before she could slip back into the flurry of activity in the nearby street. The barn turned out to be a small area of calm at the center of the storm.

"Aiden." He nodded a greeting to her as he walked a horse into one of the stalls and shut the gate. She noticed that his left arm was still in a sling.

"Gareth." Maybe she'd be lucky and just say hello and leave. She still had the distinct feeling that Gareth didn't like her, so what could they possibly have to say to each other beyond the most insincere greeting?

"I'm surprised to see you." He leaned against the railing near the gate he'd just closed.

"I was trying to stay out of the way, so I took a walk. I didn't mean to disturb you."

"Oh, you disturbed me before I even saw you. You've been disturbing me since we fought our way out of that dingy dungeon in Eveshom." Her hunch had been correct. Gareth didn't like her. He wasn't even subtle about it. And that was starting to make her angry.

"Look, Gareth. I don't know what I've done to annoy you—"

"Breathing, talking, existing."

"I guess we're finished here then." Aiden turned to leave, but Gareth stopped her by stepping in front of her to block her path.

"No, we're not done. I have a question for you."

Aiden glared at him. "Well, what is it?"

"Are you going to try to take back the Belstaff throne?"

Aiden didn't respond.

"Well, are you?"

The truth was, Aiden didn't know the answer to that question. Was she willing to risk her life to claim a throne she had no attachment to or memory of? She hadn't had time to sort any of that out. She'd been too busy taking dance lessons and losing her virginity. The last thing she felt like doing was getting into a fight over a birthright that she still wasn't completely convinced was really hers to claim. So Aiden just stared at Gareth and said nothing.

"That's what I thought. You put Kathryn at risk. For nothing."

There was that same accusation again. She hadn't asked Kathryn to come for her. It wasn't her fault that Kathryn had taken the risk to do so. But in truth, wasn't she grateful that Kathryn had?

Aiden was about to argue the point with Gareth but then decided against it. *Walk away. This has nowhere to go but badly. Just walk away.* Gareth obviously wanted a fight, but she wasn't in the mood to give him what he wanted.

She strode away from the stables and tried her best to trace her steps back to the castle. Once she'd returned, Aiden sought shelter in the one place where she thought she might find refuge from the noise and the crush of people, too many people.

The interior of the small chapel in the courtyard was cool and dark. Light filtered through a broad-leafed maple tree just outside the door and cast a shifting pattern of shadows onto the stone floor. There were two high, narrow windows near the front of the chapel, but they shed very little light on the interior. The air was still. Aiden became mesmerized by the shifting patterns on the floor.

She assumed this chapel's purpose was meditation because there was no altar and no iconography of any kind. Just an array of simple wooden benches organized in the center of the small space. And stone outcroppings low along the walls that could also be used for seats.

Aiden moved farther into the dark space and ran her palm across the rough cool stone that insulated the interior from the heat of late afternoon. Touching the rock felt soothing. She sank to one of the stone outcroppings, let her head settle against the wall, and closed her eyes. The silence of this place was a gift. She realized how unaccustomed she was to so much stimulation in her life. At the monastery there'd been long hours of quiet and solitude that now she missed.

She sensed some presence in the room and opened her eyes. The white wolf sat on its haunches in front of her, watching. The animal cocked its head and then moved to sit next to her. The wolf leaned against her leg and looked up as if it wanted to be petted. The wolf was much larger than a dog, its head almost at her level even while seated. Aiden reasoned that she should be afraid, but for some reason she wasn't. She now realized that every time the wolf came to her she had felt safe. She felt comforted. Aiden couldn't explain why, but genuine affection pulsed from the animal to her.

She ran her hand over the short fur at the top of the animal's head and then sank her fingers into the thick mane at the Wolf's shoulders. As soon as she closed her fingers around a handful of fur, she knew why the wolf had come. The wolf had come to show her something. She tightened her grip and closed her eyes. A sense of being in motion caused her to open them again.

Aiden stood on a high cliff, overlooking the sea. Dry golden grass almost to her knees rustled in the salt-scented breeze. She didn't recognize this place. To her right was a walled village with dark stone towers visible at its center. A well-trod path followed the undulating contour of the black rock cliff in the direction of the village. She looked toward the towers and wondered if she should venture in that direction, but then she heard something from the opposite way.

"I am the wind that blows across the sea. I am the wave of the ocean." The stanza was familiar from the same poem she'd repeated to herself that night in the Eveshom jail.

She turned and felt her heart rate spike when she realized who'd spoken. Her mother, Isla, stood a few feet away looking out toward the churning water. Isla looked to be the same age as when Aiden had seen her before, only this must have been what Isla looked like prior to her illness. Her black hair fell well past her shoulders. It swirled around her in the light wind, as did the fabric of the dress she wore. The skirt of dark crimson draped to her ankles. Isla was beautiful and young.

Aiden tightened her grip on the wolf, which sat calmly at her side.

"The sea is immense from this elevation isn't it?"

"Yes." Aiden wondered if her mother could see her, or if this was only a one-way vision like the last had been. At the sound of her voice, her mother turned to her and smiled.

"Aiden, I wanted you to see this. I wanted you to feel what I feel when I stand here on the black cliffs and look at our land, our view of the southern Abbasson Sea, our home."

This must be Belstaff. Her mother smiled and nodded as if she'd heard her silent thought aloud. "You can see me." It was a statement, not a question.

"Yes, I see you." Isla stepped closer and placed her hand on Aiden's cheek. "You've grown into a handsome, strong person. It's time for you to come home."

Warmth spread through Aiden's body from her mother's touch. She wanted to close her eyes and relish the moment, but she was afraid if she closed her eyes her mother would somehow evaporate.

"How can I come home? Balak doesn't want me here."

"Balak is a truly unhappy man."

"Why does he hate me so much?"

"He was second born to your father, Edward. The only way he would ever sit on the throne was if his brother died. Unfortunately, Edward lived long enough to father an heir, so the only thing that stood between Balak and the throne was you."

So it was as simple as greed and ambition. Aiden could be anyone, but by birthright, the throne was hers so Balak wanted her dead. If she didn't return and face him, would she have to live in fear for the rest of her life? Could she even hide from him if she tried? And what about Kathryn and his threats to invade Olmstead?

"I know what you're thinking, sweet Aiden. But this is a thing you cannot escape."

"I want to do the right thing." Aiden's voice cracked with emotion. She longed to embrace her mother. She wanted to fall at her feet and weep. "I just don't know what the right thing is, and I'm not sure I'm as strong as you think I am." Aiden wiped at tears with the back of her hand, careful not to release the wolf with the other.

"When the time comes, you will know." Isla brushed a tear away. Her blue eyes pierced Aiden's soul. "And the strength of your ancestors will be with you when you need them most."

Aiden wanted to ask more, but something caught Isla's attention. She looked over her shoulder and then back at Aiden. "Someone is looking for you. You should go." Isla stepped away from her, and the scene began to falter and fade to darkness.

Someone touched her shoulder and Aiden flinched.

"I'm sorry. I didn't mean to startle you." Venn was leaning over her in the chapel. Aiden looked for the wolf, but she already knew the animal was gone. It had retreated as fast as the vision of her mother.

"I must have dozed off." Aiden didn't want to explain to Venn that she'd seen her mother again. Venn looked at her as if she doubted what she was saying, but she let it go.

"The dinner celebration will start soon. When you weren't in your room getting ready, I thought I might find you here."

Aiden nodded and got to her feet. "Thank you for finding me."

"We can get changed and then go down to the great hall together. It might be better if you aren't alone since you've probably never attended an event like this before."

Aiden was grateful to Venn for looking out for her. Not just in the bigger way of saving her life so many years ago, but in the little ways too. And with any luck, she wouldn't be required to dance. Despite her afternoon lessons, she wasn't sure she could pull it off. As they climbed the staircase to the second level and then parted for their separate quarters, Aiden was lost in thought. She puzzled over the things her mother had said. But at least now she understood why she'd had such a strong desire to travel to the sea when she left the monastery. She now knew that her people lived on the shore of the southern sea.

It was an odd sensation to have new details of her origin revealed to her and at the same time have some sense that she'd known those things all along.

Chapter Thirty

Kathryn admired herself in the long mirror propped against the wall of her chamber. She'd chosen a gown with a deep golden color. The fabric had a slight sheen so that when she moved, the long full skirt caught the light. One of her personal maids knelt on the floor making final adjustments to the hem.

Someone knocked.

"Enter."

Rowan closed the door behind her and crossed the room. "Kathryn, that dress!"

"Yes?"

"Stunning. Truly."

"Thank you." She pulled at the sides of the skirt to check the length. "That will be all." She dismissed the maid, who curtsied as she retreated with her sewing basket.

"I came to claim you. The head cook is impatient to put the feast on the table before it cools. Besides, all your guests are eagerly awaiting your arrival."

Kathryn nodded. She'd taken longer than she'd intended to get ready, but she'd had a hard time deciding how to style her hair. In the end, she pulled it up to highlight the elegant neckline of the gown she'd chosen. She could tell by the look of approval on Rowan's face that she'd made the right decision.

"Is Gareth coming tonight?" Rowan fingered the cloth of a dress that had been considered for the night but then tossed over a chair.

"He's invited to sit in the great hall, at one of the lower tables, but I haven't seen him since we returned." Kathryn dabbed a bit of powder on her nose and cheeks. "If he's going to be in such a horrible mood I'd just as soon he not come."

"He's not at his best when forced to deal with reality."

"What do you mean?" Kathryn put the small container of powder on the vanity and smoothed the front of her dress.

"For Gareth, you falling in love was only ever in the abstract until now."

Kathryn's heart skipped a beat at Rowan's suggestion. "I'm right aren't I? You are falling for Aiden."

Kathryn felt herself blushing, and there was no way to stop it. She hadn't had the chance to tell Rowan that she and Aiden had spent the night together, but she could see that her perceptive cousin already suspected.

"We spent the night together last night. But I haven't seen her today."

"I have. And she was glowing." Rowan tucked an errant strand of Kathryn's hair back into place. "And so are you."

Kathryn smiled. "I do care for her. And last night was…well, I don't quite have the word for it."

"Sexy, amazing, electrifying, earth shattering, romantic—"

"Yes, yes, yes. All of those things and more." Kathryn laughed and tugged her cousin toward the door. "Now let's make an entrance and get this evening started."

Rowan and Kathryn descended the grand staircase with arms linked. The crowd of nobles at the bottom of the stairs, dressing in finery, looked up with smiling faces to greet them. Kathryn searched the crowd for Aiden but didn't find her.

She welcomed her esteemed guests, announced that dinner was being served in the great hall, and asked that everyone join her in taking their seats. As she turned, a flash of deep red caught her eye. She spotted Aiden at the far side of the room. She was wearing a fitted jacket with a rich crimson pattern. The collar was stiff and stood up at each side just touching her jawline, but the jacket was open to reveal a hint of flesh and the brilliant white open-collared shirt underneath. The dark gray pants she wore were fitted also and tucked into almost knee-high black polished boots. Her tailor had done well. Aiden was stunning, and as she'd predicted, it likely wouldn't be long before every eligible woman in the room noticed.

Maybe calling for her tailor had been a bad idea. Deep down, her ego desired for Aiden to reach her full potential, and then Kathryn wanted that full potential on her arm. Was that so wrong?

Kathryn felt the intense heat of Aiden's penetrating gaze as if her skin were too close to a flame. She looked away, as one of the guests spoke to her, but feared she was already blushing.

Aiden followed everyone through the large arched doorway of the great hall, but never took her eyes off Kathryn. She'd thought Kathryn looked lovely in the emerald dress she'd worn the previous evening, but the gown she wore tonight was truly spectacular. How could she hope to be with a woman such as Kathryn? Forget that Kathryn was royal born; even if she weren't, her sheer beauty and grace made Aiden doubt her worthiness. Yet last night Kathryn had chosen her. That had to mean something.

She'd wanted to speak with Kathryn all day, but every time Aiden caught a glimpse of her she'd been busy with some business affair or at least tasks that appeared official in some way. Aiden could now see how demanding Kathryn's daily schedule must be. Some of the comments Kathryn had made to her about things being more layered and complex once they returned to Olmstead were beginning to make sense. She'd had no real context for them before now.

Venn was walking at Aiden's elbow as they found their seats at one of the lower long, elegantly appointed tables. Venn had explained to Aiden that the seating for the feast would be based on status. The most important guests would be at the table on the raised dais at the front of the Hall. Everyone else would be seated at the lower tables. Since no one knew Aiden's true identity, that included her. The central area of the hall had been left vacant for dancing following dinner.

As she settled into her chair, Aiden saw that Gareth was seated almost directly across from her. Perfect. And next to him was some formidable woman in a military looking blue dress uniform.

"That's probably the commander of the imperial guard." Venn must have followed her gaze.

Aiden nodded to Venn and took a sip of wine to settle her nerves as soon as it was poured. Then the food began to arrive in waves, and Aiden tried to focus on her plate rather than on the people she didn't know seated around her. She had an unhindered view of Kathryn from her seat, and that only served to upend her already nervous stomach further. Every time they caught each other looking, they held each other with their eyes. And every time, Aiden felt the tug of Kathryn's gaze as if it were a physical force.

She wanted to hold Kathryn. She wanted to take Kathryn away from all of this noisy gleeful mayhem and take her to bed. Aiden wondered if Kathryn could read her thoughts. If she could, would she like what she saw there?

CHAPTER THIRTY-ONE

Aiden watched those seated around her to glean social cues—when to ask for more food, or not, which silverware was for which purpose, when to sit and when to stand. Toasts had been offered to the queen and to other honored guests in attendance. None of whom Aiden knew. She was trying to sip the wine slowly. She felt she'd more than learned her lesson at the pub in Eveshom, and she wasn't going to make the mistake of over indulgence again, especially in a situation where she needed her wits intact.

She and Venn had moved away from the table and were watching couples begin to dance in the center of the great room. The large hall had extremely high ceilings constructed of successive archways supported by marble columns. The acoustics in the room were very good. The orchestra didn't have to play very loud for the music to reach every corner and reverberate off the arched stone ceiling.

Aiden was studying that ceiling, probably a dead giveaway that she was from somewhere else, when she heard someone speak to her.

"Aiden, I'd like to introduce myself. I'm Frost Sylven, commander of the imperial guard." Frost extended her hand to Aiden.

She'd been right in her assumption that the blue uniform had military roots. She figured Gareth had told Frost who she was since he'd been sitting next to Frost during the meal. She looked for him now, but he was nowhere in sight.

"It's a pleasure to meet you, Frost." Aiden shook Frost's hand. Beside her, she sensed Venn stiffen. "This is my commander at arms, Venn."

Venn and Frost gave each other a terse nod. According to Kathryn, Frost was the only other person in the castle who knew Aiden's true identity. Aiden wasn't sure how she felt about Frost, her first impression gave her little information about the stiff soldier.

"I trust your journey here was pleasant."

That seemed like an odd thing to say. Surely Kathryn, or at the very least Gareth, had told Frost about the attacks they'd suffered en route. Maybe she was waiting to see what Aiden would reveal. "I enjoyed traveling by wind ship. I'd heard about them but had never been aboard one of them before." A neutral, yet friendly response.

"If possible, at your earliest convenience, I'd like to brief you and Venn about the current status of Belstaff."

"Thank you for the offer." Aiden wasn't sure what the proper response should be. She also wasn't sure what sort of information Frost could relay that would be helpful or that she didn't already know. After all, she already knew her uncle wanted her dead. He'd made that painfully clear. And she'd been to Belstaff earlier today, with her mother, but she wasn't about to bring that up. She didn't know Frost, but she exuded the sort of strict disapproval likely to scoff at visions brought on by enchanted white wolves.

Frost looked as if she were about to say something else, but she was interrupted by a very attractive redhead in a flowing dress. The bodice of the dress fit snugly, pushing up her breasts until the fullness of them spilled out the top of the gown. A garnet necklace hung just low enough to dip into the top of her deep cleavage. Aiden tried not to notice, but that was impossible.

"Captain Frost, you always look so serious." The woman flirtatiously brushed her hand across Frost's arm. "And at such a gala event as this too." She looked in Aiden's direction with sparkling green eyes. "Aren't you going to introduce us?" She held her hand out toward Aiden.

"Yes, of course. Miss Lauren Jeffers, this is Aiden—"

"Lyons. Aiden Lyons." Aiden cut Frost off. She wasn't sure what Frost was going to say, but she and Venn had decided earlier that if necessary she would use Venn's last name. Aiden held on to Lauren's hand for a moment. Then Lauren's grip tightened.

"So charming. Let's dance, shall we?" Lauren tugged Aiden onto the dance floor.

Well, at least this had given her a chance to get away from Frost. There was something about Frost that Aiden found a bit unnerving. She glanced back to see Frost say something to Venn and then walk away. Venn looked at Aiden, but it was impossible to read her expression.

"Your jacket is quite handsome." Aiden sensed Lauren's hand on her shoulder. Lauren let it slide down Aiden's chest and then back to her shoulder.

"Thank you." As they moved to the center of the dance floor, Aiden thought maybe she should compliment Lauren's dress, but she was too busy struggling to remember the dance lesson Rowan had given her earlier. Make a box with your feet, that's what she'd said. One, two, three. One, two, three. Aiden felt as if everyone was watching her, but she quickly realized that in reality all the couples around her were in their own world.

Lauren seemed like a nice enough woman. Aiden surely didn't want to injure her toes as a result of inept footwork, so she tried to focus.

Kathryn kept her seat as the small orchestra began to play and couples moved to the floor to dance. The raised platform gave her a good view of the entire room. But she spent most of her evening watching Aiden. She wanted to ask Aiden to dance, but she didn't want to seem too eager.

Then she saw Frost cut across the room in Aiden's direction. Kathryn was just about to attempt to intervene when the chancellor who'd been seated beside her pulled her attention away to make an introduction. When she looked back a few minutes later, Aiden was gone. Kathryn slowly scanned the crowded hall until she caught a flash of crimson and black hair. Aiden was on the dance floor with

Lauren Jeffers. Kathryn felt her pulse quicken at the sight of another woman in Aiden's arms, especially that woman. Lauren was noble born, well-endowed, and sexually aggressive.

Kathryn left the raised dais and cut across the floor toward Aiden. Someone stopped her as she passed through the revelers. She was polite but brief so that she could keep moving before Lauren pulled Aiden into some dark corner of the castle. Not that she didn't trust Aiden, but she suspected Aiden had no experience with women like Lauren. It was her job to protect Aiden. However, even as she lifted her skirt to hasten her steps, she knew in her heart that she had motives other than protecting Aiden's honor in mind.

"May I cut in?" Kathryn could tell Lauren was about to protest when she realized who'd asked the question.

"Of course, my queen." She curtsied with respect and stepped aside. "Another time, Aiden." She winked at Aiden as she turned to exit the dance floor.

Kathryn placed her hand in Aiden's. And Aiden lightly settled her other hand on Kathryn's hip.

"I'm so happy to see you."

Kathryn could barely hear her over the string orchestra. And she wasn't sure she'd heard what she'd said. "What did you say?"

Aiden leaned in, and when she spoke, her breath caressed Kathryn's cheek. "I'm happy to see you and you look beautiful."

Kathryn smiled. "Thank you. This jacket suits you. I'll have to offer my tailor a bonus for his fine work."

They circled the room slowly, as if they were dancing to some music of their own.

"What are you thinking about?" Kathryn couldn't read Aiden's expression, but she seemed far away.

"I was just thinking about how stupid I am."

"That's what you were thinking? At this very moment? I'm not sure what that says about me."

"Oh, no, I'm not stupid about this. Not about dancing with you. I just meant I'm dumb, in the classic sense of the word. In the larger scheme of things."

Kathryn smiled as Aiden tried to retract her words.

"I'm glad to hear I'm not included in your assessment of intelligence."

"Absolutely not." Aiden's fair complexion reddened. "I was thinking about the day I left the monastery and how I thought I knew everything, when in fact, I knew barely anything."

"I think you're being a little hard on yourself." Kathryn squeezed Aiden's hand.

"Maybe. At least I was smart enough to follow you when you asked me to."

"Yes, at least there's that." Kathryn smiled. "And now I'm following you."

"Rowan deserves the credit, or I daresay your toes would be in mortal danger."

Kathryn laughed and moved closer, lessening the open space in their embrace. Aiden was gorgeous, and the air between them pulsed with desire. Kathryn wondered if she was the only one who felt it. She wanted to steal Aiden away from the crowded room. She looked around the hall for a moment, mentally calculating how soon she'd be able to sneak away.

"Thank you, Kathryn."

"For what?" Kathryn looked up to meet Aiden's glistening eyes.

"For everything."

CHAPTER THIRTY-TWO

Aiden watched from several feet away as Kathryn prepared to toss the bouquet into the small crowd gathered at the base of the broad stone steps at the front of the castle. As it was explained to Aiden by Rowan, this was Kathryn's final task for the evening. To toss several bunches of fresh cut flowers into the crowd as a ritual of good will and abundance to her subjects. The crown had provided a feast with plenty of ale, and everyone was in top spirits. As the last bouquet was tossed, cheers went up. It was obvious that the residents of Olmstead loved their queen. And she appeared to care for them with equal fervor.

Before Kathryn could retreat to the castle's interior, several young families brought their infant children to the steps so that Kathryn could offer them a blessing. The more Aiden knew of Kathryn the more she felt drawn to her. The more she wanted to be the sort of person that Kathryn would admire and care for.

Aiden watched as the chancellor and other members of the royal cabinet encircled Kathryn and ushered her back inside. Cheering erupted again from the lantern and moonlit courtyard as the revelers went back to tables for more ale. Once back inside the mezzanine, Kathryn surprised Aiden by walking over and taking her arm. She hadn't expected Kathryn to be so open, but then she remembered how many turns they'd shared as the orchestra played. By the end of their display on the dance floor, all eyes had been on the queen and her mystery dance partner in the crimson jacket.

"Would you mind escorting me upstairs?"

"Of course." Aiden couldn't think of anything she wanted more than a chance to be alone with Kathryn again. The thought of it made her stomach begin to somersault as they climbed the grand staircase.

"I suppose now I've really given everyone something to talk about." Kathryn smiled.

"Well, maybe they've had enough wine that no one will notice." But as Aiden looked back down into the crowd, she spotted Frost's humorless expression. She figured there wasn't enough wine in the entire kingdom to get her to smile.

They walked down the long corridor, past all the portraits, toward the stairs that lead to Kathryn's private chamber in the tower. From the second floor landing, Aiden heard the orchestra begin to play again.

"The party will go on for a while, but I needed a break. Thank you for leaving with me." Kathryn leaned into her shoulder a little as they climbed the narrow, spiral staircase.

"It's my pleasure. I missed you today." She felt Kathryn squeeze her arm.

"I missed you too."

Aiden was a knot of nerves. As Kathryn lead her into her private quarters, Aiden wondered if she'd ever get to the point where Kathryn didn't make her nervous. On the one hand, the butterflies in her stomach were nice, mostly because no one had ever made her feel them before. But on the other hand, she wanted to be able to relax. She wanted to be on even footing with Kathryn so that Kathryn would take her seriously as an equal, rather than a novice at practically everything.

Kathryn poured a small glass of some cordial from a jeweled crystal decanter and handed it to Aiden. It had the faintest taste of blackberries as she sipped it.

A fire had been lit in anticipation of Kathryn's return to her chamber, and the flames danced shadows around the spacious room. The tower windows were tall but narrow and reached almost to the floor. Aiden leaned through one of the openings, braced against the wide stone windowsill, and looked out over the nighttime landscape. She could see the tile and thatch roofs of the village dwellings below and beyond that the open, grassy field that surrounded the exterior wall of Starford Keep. Beyond that lay thick forest and darkness. She felt Kathryn's hand on her shoulder, pulling her attention back to the softly lit room. Kathryn began to open the buttons of Aiden's jacket, and she let her. Kathryn's pale delicate fingers mesmerized Aiden as they slowly worked each of the ornate metal fasteners free. Aiden felt herself shiver as she imagined Kathryn's fingertips against her skin.

"Will you stay with me tonight?"

Aiden nodded. She traced the outline of Kathryn's face tenderly with her fingers. "I'm not sure I deserve you."

"Oh, Aiden, I was just thinking the same thing."

Kathryn slid her hands inside Aiden's jacket and slipped it from her shoulders. Her heart thumped so loudly in her chest that she was sure Aiden must have been able to hear it. She didn't want to think about who deserved what or whom. Or who was worthy or unworthy. She didn't want to be the queen of Olmstead. She wanted the freedom to simply be a girl falling in love.

"Let's don't think those things." Kathryn fingered the front of Aiden's shirt. "Let's just be you and me. Let's be together in this moment, just as us, two people who care for each other."

"Okay."

Somehow saying what she'd said tilted the axis of power between them. Maybe Aiden needed to hear her say those things so that she could feel as if she were on more equal footing. The entire situation had to be intimidating for Aiden, or at least that's what Kathryn assumed. She wanted Aiden to feel empowered to act on her impulses. Kathryn craved the intimacy she'd felt with Aiden when they'd made love. She wanted to feel that again. She wanted to linger in that rare space between night and day, between desire and possibility, between the unknown and the known.

More than anything, Kathryn desired to be known by Aiden. This was something she was usually afraid to allow, because given her position she could never truly trust someone's motives in getting close to her, but she felt safe with Aiden. What she felt for Aiden and with Aiden was so different from anything she'd felt with anyone before that it scared her a little, but not enough to withdraw. She relaxed against Aiden's chest and willed herself to let her guard down. It felt good.

Aiden bent down and kissed her. Aiden's hands were warm as she cradled Kathryn's face. She deepened the kiss and teased Kathryn with her tongue. Despite her inexperience, Aiden was a very good kisser. She knew how to allow a kiss to slowly build from the softest brush of her lips to possession: deep, searching, craving possession. Kathryn felt this kiss in the hard points of her breasts and the throbbing between her legs. She pressed her body against Aiden's and decided that there were way too many layers of clothing separating them.

"You'll have to help me with this dress." The dress had buttons at the back of the bodice so she needed Aiden's assistance to take it off. She presented her back to Aiden. She could feel Aiden tugging each button free so that the shoulders of the gown began to droop. She pushed the gown down over her hips and stepped out of the garment and laid it across a small sofa nearby. A slip and corset remained.

Once again, she turned her back to Aiden who dutifully loosened the laces, and Kathryn tossed the stiff corset on top of the dress. The thin cotton slip hung loosely about her body. Her breasts, now free of the corset, swayed as she turned into Aiden's arms. Aiden's hands settled on her hips as she reached back and pulled the clasp from her hair, releasing it to cascade about her shoulders.

Aiden's hands were strong as they explored the curve of her shoulder and then her neck. Aiden tilted Kathryn's head up and kissed her again passionately. So passionately that Kathryn's knees threatened to give way. She wanted to be taken. This was exactly what she'd hoped for. Aiden cupped her breast through her slip, and she moaned softly against Aiden's mouth.

Aiden pulled away from Kathryn. Raw desire filled her eyes. Aiden pulled her boots off and knelt in front of Kathryn. She never took her eyes from Kathryn's as she slowly slid the hem of her slip up. Aiden eased her undergarments down and off. She shuddered when she felt Aiden's warm mouth trail kisses up each thigh and then along the low curve of her stomach. She filled her fingers with Aiden's hair and held on for fear she'd topple from the excruciating ecstasy of Aiden's lips on her responsive skin.

Aiden teased the place between Kathryn's legs with her tongue, and Kathryn knew her arousal was no longer a secret. Aiden cupped her ass with her hands and pressed further with her tongue.

"Aiden." Kathryn's voice was low and a little hoarse. "Please take me to bed."

Aiden stood, and as she did, she pulled the hem of the slip along with her until it was over Kathryn's head and gone. The stiff fabric of Aiden's trousers brushed against her sensitive flesh before Aiden lifted her, cradled in her arms, and carried her to the bed. Kathryn watched with rapt attention as Aiden disrobed at the side of the bed and then she slid next to Kathryn. But Kathryn wanted Aiden to finish what she'd started. She wanted Aiden between her legs.

"Do you want me to touch you there?" Aiden must have sensed her longing. She touched Kathryn's sex lightly as she asked the question.

"Yes." Kathryn opened her legs for Aiden, and she felt Aiden's thigh against hers as Aiden moved partially on top of her.

"I want to be here every night. Not in this room, not in this bed, but here." Kathryn inhaled sharply as she felt Aiden's fingers slide teasingly inside her.

Something had shifted in Aiden. The shy, uncertain woman that Kathryn had taken to bed only the previous night had been replaced by someone else. Somehow she was more confident, more sure of herself. Kathryn liked this change. She moved against Aiden's hand, raising her hips to meet each thrust. Aiden's possessiveness didn't frighten her; it only made Kathryn's desire crest.

"I want you so badly, Aiden. I've been able to think of little else today but having you in my bed. Feeling you inside." Aiden was thrusting deeply while slowly increasing the pace and using her thumb to take Kathryn higher. "Oh, God, yes. I'm yours, Aiden. Yes."

Kathryn allowed herself to be swept into the vortex of swirling desire that Aiden's exploration was creating. She tossed her secrets aside and let Aiden in.

She felt Aiden moving against her thigh, wet and in need of release. She pulled Aiden firmly against her leg urging her to climax with her.

"Kathryn, I'm going to—" Aiden stiffened and then shuddered on top of Kathryn as the orgasm ripped through her body. Somehow she managed to continue to thrust in and out until a moment later, Kathryn joined her, slipping over the edge into the bright light of liquid brilliance.

She cried out and gripped Aiden's arm with one hand while clinging to her neck with the other. A second orgasm raged through her body an instant later, while Aiden was still inside her. She closed her legs around Aiden and held on tightly as wave after wave of ecstasy coursed through her body.

Slowly, they untangled and Aiden sank to the soft mattress beside her. Tendrils of sweat-dampened hair clung to Aiden's forehead, and Kathryn brushed them aside. Kathryn felt cherished and content. She pressed her lips to Aiden's forehead and pulled her close. She wanted to stay in bed forever. She wanted to keep Aiden safe.

Kathryn lightly trailed her fingertips down Aiden's arm.

"What are you thinking? You seem far away." Aiden draped her arm over Kathryn's stomach, caressing her skin with the palm of her hand as she moved.

Kathryn smiled weakly. "Nothing."

"It must have been something."

Kathryn didn't want to allow the reality of their situation to intrude. She shook her head. "Really, it was nothing."

"Talk to me, Kathryn." Aiden pushed for more; she obviously didn't believe her.

A tear gathered at the edge of Kathryn's lashes and slid down her cheek.

"Hey, don't cry. Please tell me what's wrong." Aiden moved on top of her, bracing herself above Kathryn on her elbows.

"I'm afraid for you." She tried to speak around the knot rising in her throat. There, she'd said it. She'd given her fears a voice and allowed them into the sacred space between them.

"I'm right here. Everything is going to be okay." Aiden gently stroked her hair and kissed her tenderly. "Nothing is going to happen to me."

"Stay here with me." She didn't want Aiden to think she was weak or afraid, but it felt good to share her fears.

"I'm here." Aiden pulled Kathryn close. Kathryn snuggled into the curve of Aiden's neck and willed herself to relax. The firelight flickered and ebbed to nearly nothing, and after a little while, as she lay nestled in Aiden's arms, sleep claimed her.

Aiden opened her eyes, and for a brief moment couldn't get her bearings. Then she sensed the press of Kathryn's warm body against her and a sense memory of their coupling came rushing back. She had the strongest urge to kiss Kathryn, but she seemed to be sleeping so soundly. Aiden rolled onto her side and watched Kathryn. The moonlight filtered into the room. It softly lit the contour of her pale shoulder and the curve of her hip beneath the light blanket.

As gently as she could, Aiden slid from the bed and poured herself a glass of water from the pitcher on the table in the center of the room. She stood at the open window. As she took long gulps, she looked up at the moon's etched surface. There were no clouds to block her view.

One clear thought came to Aiden as she stood staring up at the night sky. She needed to travel to Belstaff. She'd clearly seen the fear in Kathryn's face. She didn't want to be the cause of it. And she was the only person who could do something about that.

If she'd left Kathryn right after her escape from the cell at Eveshom, then she'd never have had to see that look of fear. But something was happening between them. Something she could deny or look away from or possibly live without, but she didn't want to. After tonight, she only wanted more of Kathryn, not less. If she and

Kathryn had any hope of being together, free from fear, then she needed to deal with Balak.

The thought amused her.

She'd planned to avoid any trap of responsibility the day she'd left the monastery and here she stood, naked, unarmed, seriously considering the capture of the Belstaff throne. Sex had obviously affected her ability to make wise decisions. Or maybe it enhanced it. Maybe she was thinking clearer right now than she ever had.

Aiden smiled when she felt Kathryn kiss her shoulder. Kathryn wrapped her arms around Aiden's waist and leaned her cheek against Aiden's back.

"Are you coming back to bed?" Kathryn kissed her shoulder again.

"Yes, I'm coming back. I didn't mean to wake you. I was thirsty."

Kathryn stole the glass from her hand and took a drink. Aiden rotated in Kathryn's embrace and kissed her. Kathryn's lips were cool from the water. Kathryn entwined her fingers with Aiden's and tugged her back to bed.

CHAPTER THIRTY-THREE

"Venn." Aiden shook her shoulder. "Venn, wake up."
Venn blinked and glared at Aiden. "What time is it?"
"Time to get up."

"That's not an answer." Venn rubbed her eyes and squinted toward the window. Just the faintest hint of pink was visible.

"It's early."

"I can see that. What's going on?"

"You ask a lot of questions for someone who's barely awake. Get dressed. I want you to ride to Belstaff with me."

"What?" Venn sat up and regarded Aiden with a wide-eyed expression.

"I've had an epiphany and it involves you and me riding to Belstaff. My hope is that if we leave now we'll almost make it there by nightfall." Aiden stood up to leave the room so Venn could dress. "I just need to do something quickly and then I'll be back to fetch you."

"When you return we'll discuss whether this is a wise choice of action or not. That's what we'll do." Venn sounded grumpy. Obviously, she wasn't a morning person.

Aiden walked to her room, just down the hall from Venn's. With great effort, she'd left Kathryn sleeping soundly in bed. She was afraid if Kathryn knew of her plan she'd try to talk her out of it, but she didn't want to travel to Belstaff without leaving a note for Kathryn.

She pulled out a slip of paper from the desk drawer in her room and dipped the quill into the ink. She tapped the side of the small glass jar so that she didn't have too much ink on the nib. Aiden hesitated, her hand hovering just above the paper as she struggled for words. What did she want to say to Kathryn? Ink dripped on the paper. She wadded up the sheet and took another.

Dearest Kathryn,

It was very difficult to leave you this morning. More than anything, I wanted to snuggle against you and breathe you in. But there is something I must do. Not just for myself but for you also. Don't worry. Venn is with me, and we will return in three days' time. Think of me fondly while I am away, for I am yours.—Aiden

On her way to deliver the envelope to Kathryn's chamber, she passed Frost in the long hallway where all the portraits resided. She spoke a brief greeting and thought she'd get past Frost without incident, but Frost had other ideas.

"Those are the stairs to the queen's private quarters." Frost stepped in front of her, blocking her path.

"Uh, yes, I wanted to leave this letter for Kathryn." Aiden held the envelope up in hopes that Frost would let her pass. She didn't want to reveal to Frost that she'd just spent the night in the queen's bed so she knew full well what lay at the top of those stairs. What she didn't know was why Frost was lurking about at the base of the tower steps at such an unreasonably early hour.

"I'll be sure that she gets it." Frost held out her hand.

Aiden felt some reluctance to turn the letter over to Frost, but she didn't see any other option. She wanted to retrieve Venn and be underway as soon as possible. She simply nodded and handed over the envelope.

"Thank you. Please see that she gets the letter."

"May I escort you back to your quarters?" Frost clearly didn't like the idea of Aiden roaming the castle without supervision.

"I know the way." Aiden headed back the way she'd come. She looked back to see Frost still watching her. The woman had an unnerving way about her.

By the time she returned to Venn's chamber, Venn was dressed, and within another half hour the two of them were saddling horses in the stable. The sun had yet to fully crest the horizon, but it was light enough not to need a lantern. Aiden was happy to see that Gareth was nowhere in sight. A very bleary squire who'd been sleeping in the barn helped them with their gear, but he was so groggy from too much ale during the celebration that Venn sent him back to his bed in the hay.

"Aiden, are you sure you want to do this?" Venn leaned against her saddle.

"I need to see Belstaff for myself. Don't you think it will be easier if just the two of us go? I don't want to announce myself. I simply want to look around." Aiden still hadn't told Venn about her most recent vision.

Venn nodded, but the expression on her face told Aiden that she wasn't convinced.

"Venn, I want to know things. Things I can't know without seeing them for myself." Aiden climbed into the saddle and patted Sunset's neck. "I'm going to Belstaff. Are you coming with me?"

Venn mounted her horse. "Yes, I'm with you, Aiden."

They had enough supplies for four or five days, bedrolls, and weapons. Aiden hoped they'd be back in three days, but she was prepared to take as much time as she needed to get the answers she was looking for. They rode side by side past the gatehouse and out across the open field. Ribbons of pink stretched across the sky as the sun rose to claim the day.

Chapter Thirty-four

K athryn's day started as usual with maids helping her dress, breakfast, then papers and requests from the previous day. Through all of these tasks, she thought of Aiden. She was surprised to find that Aiden had risen before her and gone, but she appreciated the gesture. No doubt Aiden didn't want to be there when the maid arrived in order to protect Kathryn's privacy.

There was no need to be concerned, in Kathryn's opinion, as everyone had seen them dance at the celebration. She was certain that especially those who worked in the keep had already figured out some relationship was developing between the two of them. If anyone knew Aiden's true identity, they would heartily approve the match.

Still, by mid-morning Kathryn was surprised that she hadn't seen Aiden.

By the time she joined Rowan in the dining room she was starting to become worried that something was wrong. Was Aiden avoiding her? She wracked her brain in an attempt to remember something that might have happened to upset Aiden, but she could think of nothing.

"Have you seen Venn today?" Rowan's question caught Kathryn by surprise.

"No. And I haven't seen Aiden either." Kathryn took a seat across from Rowan as the server placed a bowl of steaming soup in front of her. "I was actually going to ask you if you'd seen them." Kathryn didn't want to worry, but this seemed odd.

"I'm sure they're just out for a ride or something." Rowan took a few sips from her spoon. Kathryn could tell that Rowan was trying to make her feel better, but the look on Rowan's face didn't instill confidence.

"By the way, thank you for Aiden's dance lessons." Kathryn hoped to distract herself with a subject change.

"I saw you two dance. I think she's a natural."

"Did you manage to get Venn on the dance floor?" Kathryn felt bad that she hadn't noticed, but she'd been completely absorbed with Aiden. For all she'd cared the rest of the room could have dropped away into oblivion.

Frost walked by the open door as they chatted, and Kathryn called her over.

"Frost, I wonder if you've seen Aiden or Venn recently?" Kathryn leaned back in her chair as the server delivered the main course of their meal.

"No, I haven't seen them, Your Highness." Frost dipped her head in greeting to Rowan.

"If you see either of them will you tell them I need to speak with them?"

"Certainly. Will that be all?"

"Yes, thank you, Frost."

After lunch, Kathryn had to meet with the chancellor and other members of her cabinet to discuss a land dispute between two barons. She asked Rowan to go to the stables. It was late in the afternoon before she found herself alone in her study.

"Kathryn, Gareth hasn't seen Venn or Aiden either, but one of the squires helped them find tack for their horses this morning. He said they left very early. The squire was quite hung over and didn't remember hearing them say anything about where they were going."

"This just doesn't seem like Aiden." Kathryn began to pace. "I can't believe she would leave without saying something. Not after last night."

"What happened last night?"

Kathryn stopped pacing and looked at Rowan.

"Oh."

Maybe what happened between them had meant more to her, but she didn't think so. She brushed her fingers through her hair and began pacing again. She'd let her guard down with Aiden. She'd let her in, she'd trusted her, wanted to protect her, and now Aiden was gone. Then she remembered something.

"I told Aiden last night that I was afraid for her."

"So?"

"Do you think I frightened her away by saying that?"

"I think we're going to find out in a few hours that we were worried for no reason. We're making it sound as if she's not coming back. She and Venn probably just went for a long ride."

"Is that what you really think?"

"No."

Kathryn was grateful for Rowan's honesty. "I don't either. I can't explain why, but I feel as if something has happened." Kathryn extended her route into the library that adjoined her study and resumed her pacing. Moving sometimes helped her think.

Rowan followed her and stood looking into the small fire in the grate. Even though the first day of summer had arrived, the thick stone walls kept the castle's interior cool enough to require a small fire for warmth most days.

"What's this?" Kathryn turned to see Rowan fish something from the coals. It looked like a partially burned letter. "This is addressed to you. Did you mean to burn this?"

Kathryn stepped closer and examined the partly burned envelope in Rowan's hand. "I haven't seen this. I didn't burn it."

They moved to the small desk on the other side of the library, and Rowan gently separated what was left of the envelope from what remained of the letter inside. The parchment had been folded in half so that only the first line and the last line were unsinged and legible.

"*Dearest Kathryn, It was very difficult to leave you this morning. More than anything...*" Kathryn read the words aloud but the words evaporated at the edge of the burned paper. Then she read the only other line that was still visible, although some of the words were blackened and unreadable. *"Think of me…I am away… yours.—Aiden"*

"Who burned this letter?" Rowan asked the question that was on Kathryn's lips.

"I don't know." And what had the missing words said? The not knowing burned inside her head like a fever. At least now she knew that Aiden had left word for her. But where had she gone?

❖

Kathryn found Frost at the stables talking with Gareth.

"Frost, may I speak with you?" Kathryn lifted her skirt as she stepped through the dirt surrounding the stalls. There'd been a light rain in the early afternoon, just enough rain to make the streets muddy.

"There's no need for you to come here, Your Highness." Frost held out her hand to assist Kathryn as she navigated the uneven ground. The soft earth had been chewed up by the passing of hooves. Kathryn wondered why so many horses had obviously been traveling through the area in front of the barn. This sort of traffic only happened if troops were being mobilized.

"It's urgent that I speak with you, and I wasn't sure when you'd be back to castle."

Kathryn hadn't spoken to Gareth in days. She'd seen him at the celebration dinner, but he'd left before she got a chance to talk with him. She suspected that Rowan was right and that he was jealous of Aiden. If he saw them dance then he'd have to know that Kathryn had feelings for her. At the moment, he was watching her intently, but she couldn't quite read his expression.

"Frost, I'd like to request that you send a patrol out to look for Aiden and Venn."

"I'm afraid that isn't possible at the moment." Frost rarely declined a direct request, so this was unexpected.

"Will you explain why?"

"The last battalion of troops just left to offer reinforcements to the north. We received word yesterday that raiders had crossed the border into Olmstead. I didn't want to worry you or ruin the celebration, so I dispatched two regiments of cavalry yesterday before the celebration began."

"The chancellor didn't inform me of this."

"The chancellor didn't know."

"What?" Dispatching troops without cabinet approval was highly unusual. This was an alarming breach of protocol, especially when enacted by someone as by the book as Frost.

"I felt it was in the best interest of our citizens to the north to act quickly and decisively. I believed that had I presented you and the cabinet with the details I'd received, that you would have endorsed this course of action." Frost cleared her throat. Her tone had not been condescending but there was something in her voice that sounded foreign to Kathryn. "Given that everyone was busy with preparations for the celebration, I made the decision myself."

Kathryn was stunned. She was usually good at thinking on her feet, but she had no idea how to respond to this brazen breach in procedure. She trusted Frost, but that didn't mean she approved of Frost making unilateral decisions without consulting the cabinet.

"If you'll excuse me, Your Highness, I'll go now to discuss these matters with the chancellor."

After Frost left, Kathryn turned to Gareth.

"You knew about this deployment also?"

"I just saddle and care for the horses, right? That's all you need from me." Clearly, Gareth was upset about other things.

"Didn't you think this was something you should have told me? You see battalions mounting horses and leaving the keep and you don't even tell me?" Kathryn was ignoring his passive aggressive comments about what she needed him for. What she needed from him at the moment were answers.

"Look, I assumed you knew. Why would I think otherwise? Unless you were so distracted by someone that you don't even know what's going on in your own cabinet?"

He was right. She should have known. Frost should have told her. Or she should have somehow figured it out. She should have taken her head out of the fog and paid attention. But it was too late now to call them back. Frost had dispatched three battalions of troops leaving Starford Keep woefully undefended. And she'd done it right under Kathryn's nose. But also under the chancellor's nose. Frost was right; they'd all been so distracted with details of the solstice celebration that none of them had noticed what was happening at the stables less than a quarter mile away from the castle.

"You're in love with her aren't you?"

The question had come out of nowhere. Kathryn looked up at Gareth. She was confused. "What? What are you talking about?"

"Aiden. I saw you with her last night. I saw you dancing. You're in love with her aren't you?" Rather than combative, Gareth sounded genuinely crestfallen.

"I don't know." Kathryn searched her feelings. She owed Gareth an honest answer. "Yes, I think I am."

"She doesn't deserve you."

"Gareth, I—" But he didn't wait to hear what she had to say. He'd already disappeared into the dark interior of the barn.

Kathryn thought about going after him, but she had other more distressing matters to sort out. She lifted her skirt out of the mud and trudged back to the castle.

CHAPTER THIRTY-FIVE

Aiden leaned back on her bedroll, propped on her elbow, watching the fire. They'd ridden all day and were well inside the boundary of Belstaff, but darkness had caught up to them so they made camp. Ever since they'd crossed into Balak's territory, Aiden's senses had been highly aware of everything. Every tree, every stream, every sound, every detail of the terrain and the air itself called to her. Like something remembered from a dream. She'd never experienced anything like it before. She felt sure she'd never be able to settle down enough to sleep.

"We should be near Windsheer Castle by late morning." Venn stoked the fire.

"Is that what it's called?" Aiden never knew the name of the place she'd seen in her vision, the place with the dark towers near the sea.

"Yes, Windsheer Castle. A place I've not seen in twenty-one years." Venn's smile was a tight thin line.

"How do you feel about coming back?"

Venn released a long sigh. She seemed to be considering her words before she spoke. "I think I always dreamed of coming back, with you. But as the years passed and I heard of Balak's violent exploits, I was beginning to let go of that dream." Venn regarded her thoughtfully. "Frankly, I was beginning to think this day might not come."

Aiden pulled off a piece of dried beef and chewed slowly, allowing her vision to lose its focus as she stared at the dancing flames.

"I was under the impression you had no interest in Belstaff. What has changed?" Venn asked.

Aiden didn't respond. She just looked at Venn across the fire.

"Does Kathryn know about this little scouting mission?"

Aiden shook her head. "I did leave her a letter, so she may suspect we were planning to travel to Belstaff, but I didn't really spell it out."

"I don't necessarily think this is a bad idea, but we must be very careful. You cannot reveal yourself to anyone."

Aiden nodded.

"I'm serious, Aiden. We investigate and we leave. Two swords are not enough to defeat Balak on his own turf."

"I hear you. Don't worry. I have every intention of returning to Olmstead in one piece." She was curious about Belstaff, but equally anxious to be back with Kathryn.

She hoped she'd said enough in the letter to let Kathryn know how she felt, but not so much that she overstepped where they were at the moment. They'd only spent two nights together, but Aiden knew her feelings for Kathryn went way beyond their short time together. If she closed her eyes she could feel Kathryn beneath her, smell her fragrant hair, the taste of her mouth. She already knew that to consider life without Kathryn would be to feel sickeningly cast out. Did that mean she was in love with Kathryn already? She suspected she was.

Venn stirred the fire and sparks rose with the smoke, disappearing into the darkness.

A chill ran up Aiden's spine. And she puzzled over the cause of it. The night was warm and they had the fire. Venn lay across from her looking up at the stars. She was lost in her own thoughts. Aiden willed herself to relax. As she lay back and closed her eyes, she regretted the letter. She should have talked to Kathryn. She should have kissed her good-bye and told her how she truly felt.

❖

Kathryn tossed back and forth in her bed. She'd skipped dinner, and now sleep was eluding her. She couldn't relax. Ever since her discussion with Frost, a feeling of unease had settled over her. Was it just that by acting on her own, Frost had openly challenged Kathryn's authority? No, that wasn't it. She'd spoken with the chancellor, and given the evidence Frost purportedly received from the scout, he concurred with her decision to send troops. However, she couldn't help feeling that sometimes the chancellor and the rest of the cabinet relied too heavily on Frost for decisions about defense and strategy. At any rate, the chancellor had assured Kathryn that Frost's decision had been sound. So that wasn't the source of her worry. Something else was causing her to fret, and she couldn't figure it out.

The obvious answer was that she was concerned for Aiden's safety, which she was. But Venn was with her, so hopefully, they would return soon. Her letter, what was left of it, gave no indication of a timeline. The letter only said that she'd gone, but it didn't say where or how long she'd be away or even if she was coming back. And who burned a letter that was addressed to her? That unanswered question was almost as alarming as her worry over Aiden. Had Aiden decided not to leave the letter for Kathryn and burned it herself? A sick queasiness rose from Kathryn's empty stomach.

She had to believe that Aiden would come back. They had made love twice, and while the first night had been little more than an exploration, the second night had transcended anything Kathryn had ever experienced. Surely Aiden felt that too.

Kathryn was surprised when she heard a soft knock at her door. The glow of the candle that Rowan carried preceded her into the room as she gently closed the door behind her.

"Kathryn, are you awake?" Rowan whispered the question from across the room.

"Yes, come to the bed." Kathryn sat up and made room for Rowan to join her under the covers. She was grateful for the company.

"I couldn't sleep. I thought you might be having the same problem." Rowan set the candle on the bedside table and climbed up onto the high, four-post bed. Kathryn put her arm around Rowan and drew her close.

"I can't sleep either. I can't stop thinking about everything and worrying…"

"Venn didn't say anything to me before she left either. Not that she would. We haven't gotten to the same place as you and Aiden, despite my best efforts." Rowan's words caught Kathryn by surprise. *The same place as you and Aiden.* Where was that exactly? What place?

"How could she possibly resist you?"

"I know, right? I'm wondering the same thing."

They both laughed.

"Maybe she's not interested."

"Impossible." Kathryn squeezed Rowan's shoulder. "She's dealing with a lot of emotions at the moment, I think."

"Yes, you're right. I'm just being selfish."

"Hey, being selfish is okay every now and then." Kathryn was so happy to be talking about Rowan's frustrations rather than her own. She welcomed the distraction.

"Maybe when Venn returns I'll try a new tactic."

"That sounds promising and fun."

They both giggled like schoolgirls. It felt good to laugh.

They snuggled down under the covers, sharing the same pillow, just as they'd done many nights when they were younger and the world was much less complicated.

Chapter Thirty-six

A iden looked up. The black towers of Windsheer Castle loomed in front of them. They'd decided to leave the horses well away from the walls of the village surrounding Windsheer. Venn felt the saddles looked too valuable and would surely give them away as something more than weary travelers. They'd donned drab brown hooded cloaks and covered the last two miles to the main entrance on foot.

Aiden noticed the downtrodden tenor of the place almost immediately. No one looked up at them as they passed. Villagers were coming and going along the wide dirt road through the main gate at a slow pace. Some pulled handcarts, others carried baskets, some had small dirt-smeared children in tow, but with this many people about, Aiden would have expected more noise. The cheerful chatter between the residents of Starford Keep was noticeably absent here. And everyone's clothing looked as if it were three winters past wearable. Everything looked gray-brown and ragged. Even the solitary mule they passed looked as if it had not had a good meal in months.

The sword beneath her cloak offered Aiden some small amount of comfort. She'd wrapped the ornate handle with straps of thin leather so that if anyone caught sight of it they wouldn't think it was anything special. She gripped the handle as they walked past a sad looking open market. There appeared to be very little to barter, and patrons milled about in their tattered clothing looking hungry and tired.

They had passed within visual distance of a few farms as they traveled through the northern region of Belstaff. The farms were run down and generally in disrepair, but Aiden had assumed that these were isolated poor tenant farmers. Now she could see that the whole place suffered.

The minute they'd drawn close to the main gate, Aiden had sensed a shift in Venn. Her body pulsed with tense caution. She stayed close, and anytime anyone drew near she stepped in front of Aiden protectively. As they'd broken camp she tried one more time to talk Aiden out of this reconnaissance mission, but Aiden would not be dissuaded.

They hadn't spoken as they wandered through the small narrow alleyways. Stone and brick dwellings crowded close to the dirt alleys, and occasionally Aiden was able to glimpse the interior through an open door. Every place looked sad and forlorn. No wonder Balak sought to capture Olmstead. He'd ground Belstaff into the dirt.

Aiden tried to scope things out from the shielded view of the cloak. The day was overcast and cool, especially with the breeze coming in from the sea, so the warmth of the cloak was welcomed.

Raised voices caused Venn to pull to a stop in front of her. She tried to look past Venn's shoulder.

"Get back." Venn motioned for Aiden to move away from the street.

"What's going on?" Aiden strained to see.

They stilled at the corner of a small stone market building. A scuffle of some kind was happening just ahead near a seller's cart. She heard a man talking but couldn't make out his words, only his tone, which was definitely angry. She leaned around Venn for a better look. There was a man shouting at some poor merchant. The merchant cowered and kept nodding his head as the older man berated him about something. No, wait—the merchant's daughter had thrown something at the well-dressed man. The child had thrown an apple. The shouting man was holding it as he yelled.

The shouting man stood out from the rest because his clothing was richly colored and clean. There were two men with him in uniform. How had Aiden not noticed? She'd been drawn to his erratic angry movements and hadn't seen them.

Wait. The fine clothing, the polished boots, the men-at-arms, the enraged sense of entitlement.

"That's Balak," Venn hissed.

Aiden took a half step closer, but she felt Venn's arm reach across her chest to stop her.

Balak was still angrily berating the poor merchant but had also started taking swings at him with a club. The merchant's daughter was crying and trying to reach her father, but onlookers held the girl back as they edged away from the scene. Some were crying, some looked away, others had angry, dark expressions on their faces but made no move to help the man.

The man crumpled to the ground and raised his arm in an attempt to shield his head from the club. Balak was on him with ferocity, as if he were in some crazed fit of vengeance. *He's going to kill him!* Rage surged through her body. She could watch this display of violence against an unarmed man no longer. Aiden stepped from the shadows.

She put her hand to her sword and took another step forward. Venn roughly grabbed her, pulled her back into the shadows, and pressed her back against the wall with her forearm across her chest. Aiden fought against her, but Venn was too strong.

"Let me go!"

"No. Aiden, stop it, stop! This is not the time." Venn began to drag her away from the scene as more onlookers gathered, keeping themselves at a safe distance.

Aiden had never witnessed such callous violence. Her hands shook with fury. The distraught look on the girl's face was etched in her mind. She tried to break free again, but Venn held her fast and struggled to pull her into a narrow side alley out of view.

"Stop, Aiden. There's nothing you can do." Aiden felt Venn's arms tighten around hers. "Don't fight me. We're here to do something larger than defend one man. Aiden, listen to me."

The blood rushing in Aiden's ears began to subside. Her heart still pounded in her chest. She squeezed her eyes shut against the man's cries. And then there was silence. She relaxed in Venn's arms, defeated. She felt Venn stroke her hair as she held her against her chest.

"There was nothing we could do."

"We could have stopped him."

"And revealed yourself to a crowd, in front of how many of Balak's armed men."

Aiden wrapped her arms around Venn.

"Aiden, this is Belstaff now. You wanted to see it for yourself."

"I know." Aiden's voice was muffled by Venn's cloak.

"We can't win an open fight without help. We need the support of Kathryn and her troops." Venn still held Aiden with a hand on each arm. "Do you understand? I'm not saying we won't fight. And I'm not saying I won't fight by your side. But when we do fight, I intend for you to win."

Aiden nodded and brushed a tear away with the back of her hand.

"Now, let's wait for the crowd to clear and then do what we came here to do. We need to get close enough to the castle to see what sort of security he has. It's been twenty years since I set foot there. I want to know what's changed before we charge in there."

Aiden leaned against the wall and let out a long sigh. It started to rain. She leaned out past the eaves and let the raindrops cool her heated face.

CHAPTER THIRTY-SEVEN

Kathryn looked at herself in the mirror as she pulled her hair back into a clasp. Rowan had stayed in her room all night and then returned with coffee and some toast before Kathryn had even dressed. They'd stayed up most of the night talking, in an attempt to distract themselves from their worries. Rowan was seated on a nearby sofa. She sipped coffee with her feet tucked under her.

Loud footsteps echoed on the stone stairway outside her chamber. Rowan must have heard them too. She jumped off the sofa and came to stand near Kathryn. The door opened and Frost burst into the room. She had four rough looking people with her that Kathryn didn't recognize, three men and one woman. All of them carried weapons and small arms. They looked like a small force of invaders.

The first thought that came to Kathryn was that Frost was under some threat, but then she realized that Frost knew them. They seemed to be following her command. Kathryn's brain struggled to make sense of what she was seeing.

"Frost, what's the meaning of this?" Rowan stood at her side. They both faced the intruders, but they were both also unarmed. Kathryn never kept weapons in her chamber. Her crossbow was in the arms room downstairs.

"Take her. Leave the other." Frost pointed first at Kathryn then at Rowan.

One of the intruders strode across the room and grabbed Kathryn's arm. She slapped him, and he slapped her back.

"Enough!" Frost caught the man's arm before he could hit Kathryn again. "She is not to be harmed. Not in any way. Do you understand me?"

The man responded with something that sounded more like a grunt than an actual response.

"Frost, what are you doing?" Rowan tried to put herself between Kathryn and Frost.

"Step aside, Rowan." Frost's tone was icy. It was as if Frost had become someone else. Someone she didn't recognize. And for the first time, Kathryn was afraid.

The woman who'd come with Frost pulled Rowan aside and shoved her to the floor. "Stay down," she barked.

"Kathryn is coming with us. I'd advise you to stay clear. I don't want to have to hurt you, but I will if you try to intervene."

Rowan looked as if she was going to try to get up, but Kathryn gave her a look that she hoped said, *No, don't.* The man who'd slapped her pulled her toward the door of her chamber. A second man joined him by taking her other arm, and they half dragged her, half carried her down the tower stairs and along the long corridor to the grand staircase.

They passed the body of one of the maids on the floor, unconscious. As they neared the throne room, Kathryn strained to see through the open door. The chancellor's body lay face down. Panic surged in her chest. This had all been a setup. Her solders had been deployed without her consent, Aiden was away, and now the chancellor had been killed. There was no one to save her.

As they crossed the entryway, one of the burly men that ran the kitchen rushed from the doorway with a large carving knife in his hand; two other young men followed him. All were dispatched within minutes by the broadswords of the thugs Frost had brought into the castle.

Kathryn fought against the two men who dragged her to horses tied at the base of the wide front steps of the castle. They were trying to force Kathryn to get on a horse when Rowan rushed down the steps and tried to pull one of the men off Kathryn. Rowan had a small dagger in her hand and managed to slice the man's arm.

He turned on her in a fury. He punched her so hard she fell to the ground, dropping the knife. He drew his sword and raised it.

"No!" Kathryn broke free and covered Rowan's body with her own.

"Enough. Stand down." Frost commanded that the man put his sword away. "Kathryn, get on that horse or more people will be hurt. I have my orders."

"On whose orders?" Kathryn had a bad feeling that she already knew.

"Balak is expecting you in Belstaff. I'm to bring you, conscious or unconscious. I'd prefer the former, but I'll turn you over to these men if you don't cooperate."

"If I go with you no one else will suffer?"

"No. You have my word."

Kathryn almost burst into laughter. Frost's word was worth less than nothing at this point, but she'd do anything to keep Rowan safe.

"Don't come after me. Please, Rowan, I couldn't survive if something happened to you," Kathryn urgently whispered as she was jerked up from the ground. Rowan watched, her eyes filling with tears.

Other household staff had gathered at the head of the stairs above them, but they were unarmed, held back by one of Frost's men.

Frost took something from her jacket and tossed it on the ground near Rowan. "When Aiden returns, make sure she gets this." Balak's red wax seal on the envelope was unmistakable.

Kathryn's hands had been tied in front of her. She held on to the horn of the saddle, as her horse was lead by one of the other riders. They obviously didn't trust her with the reins of her own horse. They moved at a fairly quick pace through the narrow dirt streets of the village, headed toward the main gate.

Her heart seized as they galloped by the castle stables. She saw Gareth lying motionless in the churned earth. He didn't stir or acknowledge their passing in any way. Frost must have known Gareth would try to stop this. Frost had neutralized anyone who would interfere. Damn her. Smartly, she'd struck very early before any other nobles arrived at the court. Kathryn had been essentially alone and vulnerable, with only the servants of the house on the grounds. Most of the villagers must have already been out tending their crops or inside doing the baking for the day. The scent of fresh bread was in the air. Hardly anyone was about as they rode through the huge gate. And why would anyone interfere if they'd been noticed? Everyone trusted Frost, including Kathryn, until now.

As Starford Keep receded behind them, Kathryn searched her memory for some clue, some reason that Frost would have to betray her in this way. She couldn't think of anything. The thought that Frost had been given access to every part of the castle, including the arms room and the map room, gave her great concern. The deployment of troops now made complete sense. For surely at least some of them would not have followed Frost down this path. She'd had to import mercenaries from Belstaff.

These people riding with Frost were rough, hardened, and barely in control of their tempers. One of them was a woman, but not like any woman Kathryn had ever seen. Her face was scarred and her hair shorn. She wore wide metal cuffs at each wrist and had tattoos on her forearms. But none of those things made her seem less female to Kathryn. It was her manner. The hungry look in her eyes when she regarded Kathryn, as if she'd just as soon cut her heart out as take her to bed.

Kathryn drew herself in, trying to seem small. She made every attempt not to make eye contact with any of them. Frost had sold her to the devil, but at what price and for what purpose?

CHAPTER THIRTY-EIGHT

A iden was so happy to see Starford Keep come into view
across the grassy field as they broke through the trees.
They'd ridden through miserable rain off and on during their return
from Windsheer Castle. Aiden had witnessed all she could tolerate
during one morning in the village. She'd finally seen Balak for the
first time, and the image of watching him beat a defenseless man to
death was probably forever burned into her brain. She saw it every
time she closed her eyes. But Venn had been right to stop her from
trying to intervene. She needed to return with more troops and put
an end to his reign, forever.

They'd seen how his subjects suffered, hovering near the edge
of poverty in a land where they should have plenty.

Aiden had waited impatiently in the shadows while Venn had
ventured close to the main entrance of the castle. She'd returned
with a head count of sentries, and she'd been able to study people
coming and going through the main door enough to hopefully be
able to formulate a plan of attack. The element of surprise would
be their best offense. But the more they knew going in, the more
effective their assault would be.

They'd ridden hard to get back to the keep in Olmstead, only
stopping to sleep and let the horses rest for a few hours before riding
again.

The stable was quiet when they dismounted. Almost too quiet.
Gareth was nowhere in sight. One of his stable hands took their
horses from them as they unfastened their bedrolls and gear.

Aiden's back was stiff from riding and from very little sleep. She'd been too wound up on the ride to Belstaff and too upset during the ride back. Her legs felt sluggish as she climbed the steps to enter the castle. As they entered, servants gave them furtive glances and ducked out of sight. Aiden looked to Venn, confused by the manner of the servants.

"Something isn't right." Venn dropped her gear in the entryway and pulled her sword free.

Aiden didn't want to jump to conclusions, but something did seem off. She followed Venn's lead and freed her sword as well. They walked through the great hall, past the throne room, past Kathryn's study, and each room was empty. The entire place was eerily quiet. They climbed the grand staircase to the second level. Just as they crested the top step, Rowan ran toward them. She fell into Venn's arms.

"Rowan, what's wrong?" Venn held her sword in one hand and held Rowan against her chest with the other.

"I saw you ride in from the tower window. Thank the goddess you've returned." It was hard to hear what Rowan was saying clearly, her voice was muffled against Venn's shirt.

"Rowan, where's Kathryn?" Aiden felt afraid.

"Oh, Aiden, they took her." She could see now that Rowan had been crying. Her eyes were red-rimmed, and there was a nasty bruise on her cheek.

"Who took her? Took her where?" Aiden put her sword back in its sheath at her belt and touched Rowan's arm.

"Frost and mercenaries from Belstaff. This morning—" Rowan looked back and forth between Aiden and Venn. "This morning they came very early. No one was here. The soldiers are all gone—"

"What do you mean the soldiers are gone? Rowan, you're not making sense." Venn held her at arm's length so she could look at her face. "Who hit you?"

"They—"

"Did they hurt you?" Venn cut Rowan off. She was getting angry. Aiden had never witnessed Venn angry. Not even when they'd seen Balak beat a man to death. Venn had kept a cool head when Aiden had not.

A creeping sense of panic settled in the short hairs at the back of Aiden's neck. She ran her fingers through her hair.

"I'm not hurt, but Gareth is. Badly. And the chancellor and some of the staff are dead."

"What did you mean when you said the soldiers are gone?" It was hard to piece the details together with Rowan so upset, but Venn was trying.

"Kathryn told me that Frost sent them to the north to offer reinforcements for some skirmish."

"Frost is smart. She knew there was no way all of the soldiers would follow her. Kathryn is well liked. Frost had to do this when the castle was undefended."

"So you think the threat to the north was fabricated?" Rowan asked.

"That's my guess." Venn seemed to be putting some puzzle together in her mind.

Rowan covered her face with her hands. "I didn't sense this. I didn't suspect Frost. I didn't see this, because I wasn't looking." She was berating herself.

"There was no way you could have known." Venn pulled Rowan back into her arms. "None of us could have known."

But Aiden wasn't sure Venn was right. She'd had a weird feeling about Frost and she'd dismissed it. And the morning she'd been taking the letter to Kathryn, she should have questioned Frost lurking in the hallway. She should have delivered the letter herself. She should never have left Kathryn alone. Her stomach soured and turned on itself. She was forced to sit down and put her head between her knees.

When she looked up, Venn was watching her intently as she cradled Rowan in her arms.

"Venn." Aiden stood up.

"Yes?"

"I'm going after them." She wasn't asking permission.

"I know. I'm going with you."

"No." Rowan pulled away from Venn. "I sent two squires north yesterday immediately after Frost left. They're to bring the soldiers back. Wait for them. You can't do this alone."

"We'll eat, get fresh horses, and then we leave for Belstaff. If the soldiers are back by then they can ride with us. If not, we go and you send them after us when they arrive." This wasn't open for discussion. Aiden would not wait one minute longer than she had to. As it was, Frost was a full day's ride ahead of them. Damn, they'd probably have passed them en route, except that Frost likely hadn't followed the main roads.

It would take them another day and a half to get back to Windsheer Castle. The thought of Kathryn alone, in Balak's custody, made Aiden's insides clench with rage. If he hurt her in any way— no. Aiden couldn't let her mind go there.

It was early still. They could leave within the hour and still have plenty of daylight left. They could be back in Belstaff by tomorrow.

"Frost left a message for Aiden." It was as if Rowan had just remembered.

"What?" Aiden had been plotting their departure in her head and wasn't paying attention to what Rowan was saying.

"Frost left you a message. I had it with me, but I left it in Gareth's room. This way." Rowan headed back in the direction of the guest rooms, the part of the castle where Venn's and Aiden's rooms had been. They followed her. "We moved Gareth to one of these rooms so the castle doctor could tend to him more easily." Before she opened the door, she looked back at them. "I should warn you that he looks pretty bad. I don't think the men who did this meant for him to survive."

When Aiden saw Gareth, she had to cover her mouth to keep from gasping. His eyes were swollen shut, and one side of his face was dark purple with bruises. His lip was spit and bulbous, and it looked as if there was blood seeping from a bandage around his head. One arm was bound and splinted. He'd obviously put up a fight and had been beaten badly for it.

Rowan handed Aiden the envelope with Balak's red wax seal. The seal was unbroken. The room was dim so Aiden stepped close to the window so that she could see the letter more clearly.

Aiden,

I'm anxious to meet you in person. Come to Windsheer Castle. I have something you want. In truth, I want her also. But I'm willing to trade her for you. I anxiously await your arrival.—Your loving uncle, Balak Roth

She handed the disturbingly brief note to Venn. Aiden braced her hands on each side of the narrow window and focused on breathing. This was all her fault. If Kathryn hadn't come for her, then she'd have never been put in harm's way. Or if Aiden had left sooner, maybe, just maybe, this wouldn't have happened. But Frost must have told Balak that Aiden was in Olmstead. Frost must have told Balak that if he took Kathryn then Aiden would come for her. It was all so perfectly awful. So much for a strategic invasion with troops. Venn's original plan would never work now. But then Aiden had a thought. She turned to Venn.

"Balak still doesn't know what I look like."

"No, he doesn't." Venn crumpled the note. "But why does that matter?"

"It means we still have the element of surprise." Aiden was formulating a plan, but before she could say more, Gareth moaned from the bed.

Rowan had been cooling his forehead with a damp cloth. Aiden moved closer. Gareth's lips were moving; he was trying to say something. Rowan offered him a spoonful of water. He coughed, which seemed to be painful. No doubt he had a few broken ribs to go with his broken arm.

He barely opened his eyes and turned his head in Aiden's direction.

He whispered something.

Aiden couldn't hear him so she leaned down. With bloodied knuckles, he reached for the front of her shirt. He pulled her close so that her ear was next to his swollen lips.

In a raspy whisper, Aiden heard his plea. "Save her."

CHAPTER THIRTY-NINE

Aiden and Venn raided the arms room taking as many weapons as they thought they could carry: daggers, knives, axes, ropes, and one grappling hook. They loaded their arsenal onto a third horse along with other gear they might need, like torches and blankets and food. Aiden didn't know how to prepare fully, but she and Venn were trying to consider every possible scenario. Including one in which Kathryn might be injured and require a stretcher for transport. Rowan wanted badly to go with them, but Venn refused her.

"It's too dangerous." Venn had been adjusting one of the supply straps. She turned away from the horse and faced Rowan.

"I might be able to help if Kathryn is hurt."

"Rowan, I can't focus on what needs to happen if I'm worrying about keeping you safe." Venn stepped closer to Rowan and stroked her cheek tenderly. "We will come back, and we will bring Kathryn with us."

Rowan nodded and then hugged Venn. Then she turned to Aiden. She kissed Aiden on each cheek and then wrapped her into a tight embrace.

Venn was just about to put her foot in the stirrup when Rowan stopped her. She turned Venn toward her, pressed her back against the horse's side, and kissed her on the mouth. Venn looked completely surprised, and it took her a moment before she relaxed into the kiss and encircled Rowan with her arms, drawing her close.

Aiden watched the entire display with interest and amusement.

"I didn't want to regret not doing that." Rowan smiled, despite the tears that were now on her cheeks.

"Rowan, I…" Venn seemed at a loss.

"You don't have to say anything, just come back to me."

Venn nodded and climbed into the saddle.

They rode out of the village at a fast clip. It had taken them two hours to prepare, and now Aiden was anxious to cover as much ground as possible before it was fully dark. Venn had drawn a diagram of the castle from memory. Assuming not much about the interior structure had changed in twenty years, the map would come in handy as they planned their assault.

Kathryn wasn't sure how close they were to Windsheer Castle. They'd stayed mostly on rough trails, away from the main road that ran north to south. It wasn't as if she'd have known where she was anyway. She'd never traveled this far south before. They had to be well inside the boundary of Belstaff.

Frost signaled that they were stopping for the night. Since Kathryn's hands were tied, she had to be helped from her mount. The fierce looking woman tied a rope through the binding at her wrists and led her away from the horses.

"Sit."

Kathryn hesitated. She considered what the penalty might be for not agreeing to follow directives. A slap across the face was her answer. Her cheek stung from the blow.

"I said sit. Don't make me tie you to a tree." Kathryn sank to the ground, and the woman towered over her. Frost had intervened when the man had hit Kathryn earlier, but she didn't seem to care if a woman struck her because Frost said nothing.

She considered making a run for it, but she was surrounded as the group made camp in a circle around where she sat on the ground with her skirt gathered into a heap about her legs. After a little while, the woman came for her, jerking her to her feet.

"Let's go."

It was as if her world had collapsed into vast disorder. Frost was here, but Frost obviously no longer cared, or had never cared for her. She'd been forcibly taken from her home, Gareth and the chancellor had both likely been killed, and Aiden and Venn were missing. At least Rowan was safe, she hoped.

"Where are you taking me?" Kathryn made no move to follow the woman.

"This is your chance to relieve yourself. I suggest you take it." Then the side of her mouth tweaked up. "Unless you'd prefer a gentleman escort."

There were no gentlemen present, only thugs. Kathryn shook her head and willed herself not to cry. There was no way she would allow herself to cry.

"What is your name?" Kathryn thought maybe knowing who her captors were would be of some use.

The woman looked back over her shoulder as if she were considering whether to answer or not. Finally, she responded. "Miro." She turned abruptly and pulled Kathryn against her. "Why, you wanna know me better? In a personal way?" Miro gave her a calculating up and down glance.

Kathryn tried to remain calm while every cell in her body wanted to scratch Miro's eyes out for having the audacity to look at her in such a way, as if she were undressing Kathryn with her gaze. Kathryn calculated an answer and decided instead to say nothing.

Miro turned and pulled Kathryn farther into the trees. As she relieved herself, she regarded Miro, who'd taken a seat on a nearby fallen tree. She wondered what might motivate Miro to join with men such as these. Forgetting Frost, the others were a truly rough and scary lot. As she smoothed her skirt back down, she conspired to figure things out.

They walked back to camp and Frost handed Kathryn a serving of beans and bread. Kathryn touched Frost's fingers as she accepted the plate. She was trying to remind Frost that they knew each other. She wanted Frost to remember their connection. But Frost wouldn't even make eye contact with her.

As everyone ate, there were hushed remarks from time to time, but hardly anything that Kathryn could make out. After dinner, Miro returned to place her blanket on the ground just behind Kathryn's. She watched Miro. The woman made her uneasy; she was unpredictable and foreign in manner. Kathryn wondered what had happened to bring Miro to this place, for this purpose. Under the grime of no doubt days of travel, she could see that Miro was attractive in her own way, muscled and fit. If Frost was going to forsake her, Kathryn needed to find an ally. Could that be Miro? Was it dangerous to even consider such a thing?

She lay on her side and kept still as Miro tied her ankles together. She grimaced internally each time Miro's fingers touched her skin as she tightened the ropes. Miro, satisfied that Kathryn was properly restrained, leaned over her, braced on outstretched arms. Kathryn refused to look at her. Finally, Miro moved to her blanket.

"Sleep well, Your Highness"

Kathryn lay awake for a long time watching the embers of the fire fade from orange to ash. She felt unskinned, raw, abandoned, but she would not weaken. She would never yield.

CHAPTER FORTY

By late morning the next day, Frost led them through the gates of Windsheer. Kathryn looked with empathy on those who stood in ragged clothing and watched them pass. The whole place reeked of despair. The air was thick with the stench of misery. She felt a knot rise in her throat, but she swallowed it down.

Grooms met them at the castle steps, and one of them helped Kathryn from her horse. She was still tethered to Miro, who lead Kathryn inside and down into the belly of the enormous dark structure.

Miro pulled Kathryn into a small room with no windows. There was a fire in the grate, a washing tub, and a lantern on a small table at the side of a narrow bed. Was this to be her room? She surveyed the space and then turned back to Miro.

"You clean up before you meet Balak. I'll have someone bring water." Miro untied her. Kathryn massaged the chafed skin where the ropes had rubbed her tender wrists. "The door will be locked so there's no need for the rope." Miro turned to leave.

"Thank you." Kathryn's voice sounded small, far away, but she'd forced herself to say something.

Miro turned and regarded Kathryn, and her expression softened just the slightest bit. She said nothing more as she closed the door.

The underground room was damp and cold. Kathryn knelt near the fire and held her hands over it for warmth. She hugged herself and gave the room one more visual sweep. The furnishings were adequate but certainly not designed for comfort. And there was no window so there was no view of the sky. If she were kept in the room for too long, she would easily lose track of what time of day it was.

Kathryn stiffened when she heard the door open.

Frost entered the room with a servant woman. The woman had a towel, what looked like a clean dress, and a large pail of steaming water. She laid the things on the bed and then added the heated water to the already half-full tub. The servant backed quietly out of the room, leaving Frost and Kathryn to face each other.

The urge to run at Frost and pummel her with her fists was almost overpowering. Frost looked at her for the first time since they'd left Olmstead, with an expression that was hard to read. Was she gloating? Was she feeling smug? Kathryn waited for Frost to say something.

"You should bathe and dress. Someone will come retrieve you for the evening meal." Frost stood erect, as usual, with her hands clasped behind her back. The thought of eating anything made Kathryn's stomach sour.

"Frost, why are you doing this?"

"Why am I doing this?" Frost's nostrils flared. Was that anger or simply impatience? Kathryn found Frost's lack of emotional range infuriating.

"I thought you cared about Olmstead."

"I do care, but only as a means to an end."

"What end?"

"Did you know my parents?"

Kathryn searched her memory.

"No?" Frost took slow steps a she began to circle Kathryn. "Probably because they died in the Arranth mines when I was a child."

"I'm sorry. I had no idea."

"You have no idea about many things, Kathryn. I blame your father. Like every king who came before him and will no doubt come after, his primary motivation was greed—"

"That's not true."

Frost lunged at her but didn't strike her. "Don't interrupt me again." Then the circling resumed. "As I was saying, your father didn't care how many lost their lives in those mines. He only cared about the harvest of jewels."

"And you think Balak cares about the people working in the mines?" Kathryn couldn't stop herself from asking the obvious question.

"No, but it doesn't matter."

"Don't do this, Frost. I'm very sorry for your loss, but doing this won't bring your parents back."

"No, it won't. But it might just repay what I've suffered from the loss. Do you know what it's like to be a young girl, alone, unprotected, in a mining camp?"

Frost looked at Kathryn and, for a moment, allowed her to see the hurt on her face before the cold façade returned.

"Frost, I'm so sorry." She truly was. She couldn't imagine what Frost had endured as a young girl. Even trying to imagine it made her shudder.

"To avenge my parents I've given my life to Olmstead. I've forsaken any hope of having a family of my own. I've seen comrades die by the sword. I've watched as others have risen above me. While those who are simply lucky by birth ascend to the throne." Frost glared at Kathryn. She was seeing a side of Frost she'd never witnessed before, revenge and fierce ambition.

"Frost, I had no idea—"

"Of course you had no idea. You're just like your father. You only ever saw me as a soldier. Someone to fight your battles for you, guard your lands, and nothing more." Frost stepped very close to Kathryn, and for a moment, Kathryn thought she might strike her, but she didn't.

"This doesn't have to happen this way. Now that I know, things can be different."

"It's too late, Kathryn." Frost walked away from her then turned just before she reached the door. "I'll be assuming the throne in Olmstead within a fortnight, with Balak's blessing, provided Aiden shows up to claim you."

Frost had been quietly plotting against her father for years. This was the *why* she'd been struggling to uncover.

"If all you are after is control of the mines then leave Aiden out of this."

"Balak wants Aiden. My part of the deal was delivering what Balak wants, a missing heir in return for Olmstead's throne. It seems like a fair trade."

"So if this is all just an elaborate trap, why feed me dinner?"

"Balak wants you at the table. I suggest you don't disappoint him."

Frost closed the door behind her, and Kathryn heard the unmistakable sound of a bolt sliding through a lock.

CHAPTER FORTY-ONE

Darkness greeted Aiden's return to Windsheer Castle. This time they did not enter through the central gateway, but instead from the south, through one of the gates on the harbor side, used primarily for cargo. They disguised their gear-laden horses with ragged blankets and then donned cloaks, so they looked like merchants carrying goods. No one was at the gate to stop them anyway, which surprised them a little. Balak probably assumed they'd come in a blaze of glory, making a big entrance, but Aiden's plan was exactly opposite.

As they traversed the area outside the keep, Aiden could see an increased number of guards at the main gate, which confirmed Venn's theory as to what Balak would expect. But the solitary guard at this secondary entrance had obviously not seen them as a threatening pair. He'd simply waved them through.

Aiden followed Venn. It was beginning to rain so the damp cloth clung to their bodies as the blanket did to the horse tethered between them. Their pace was slow despite the fact that adrenaline pulsed through Aiden's every fiber. She was desperate to find Kathryn, but she knew if they appeared anxious it would cause them to stand out among the downtrodden villagers. It would also not serve the element of surprise.

Venn turned into a narrow alley before they reached the wide stone steps at the front of the castle. Several soldiers were stationed there also. They were clustered under the decorative eaves to avoid the rain. Aiden followed Venn as they wound through dark, narrow passages. Venn signaled a stop near a small guard station along the southeast wall. They tied the horses and pulled weapons from under the blanket.

Light was visible in the single window of the small cube-shaped building.

"Give me a minute. Then follow."

Aiden nodded and watched Venn approach the soldier standing near the open door. All Aiden could see was the subtle, swift movement of Venn's arm, and in the next instant, the man fell against her. Aiden moved to Venn's side and helped drag the body inside. His throat had been cut. Venn propped him on a bench, facing away from the door, so that if anyone passed by it looked as if he were taking a nap on duty.

Aiden stared at the man's vacant, lifeless eyes. Venn reached to close them.

"Aiden, listen to me."

She looked up from the bloodied corpse. Things felt as if they were moving in some surreal slow motion.

Venn put her hands on Aiden's arms and faced her fully. "Once we enter the castle we must move silently and quickly. There will be no room for doubt. There will be no time for sentimentality. Anyone we encounter would be willing to kill Kathryn at Balak's command. Remember that. If one of us falls, the other must keep moving." Venn put her hand on Aiden's cheek. "Aiden, your father was Edward, King of Belstaff. Your mother was Isla, Queen of Belstaff, and you…you are the rightful heir. Your ancestors stand with you tonight and so do I."

Venn pulled Aiden into a tight embrace. They held each other.

"Thank you, Venn." Aiden didn't know what else to say. There was too much to say and no words large enough to capture all that she was feeling.

One floor above the guard station roof was a terrace. That was to be their entry point. Venn tossed the grappling hook up and tugged the rope until it caught. She handed the line to Aiden.

Aiden looked at the line disappearing over the ledge above her and quoted a line from the warrior poet, Amairgrin. *"I am the spearpoint that gives battle."*

"What did you say?"

"Now we fight."

Venn put her hand on Aiden's shoulder. "Yes, now we fight."

Aiden nodded and placed her hand over Venn's.

"Stay low until I join you. One foot at a time, and make sure each foothold is secure before you climb farther."

Aiden nodded as she braced her right foot against the stone wall. It was fully dark, clouds hid the moon, and the rain was coming down in a steady cadence. It was as if the elements themselves had arrived to offer cover. Aiden adjusted the dagger at her belt one more time and then began to climb.

She was over the ledge and kneeling on the terrace in a matter of minutes. She sat as still as a stone while she waited for Venn to join her. She had no real experience with close combat. She tried to settle herself for what was to come. For Kathryn's sake, she would not weaken.

Venn dropped to one knee beside her and pulled a short blade free from her belt. "Quiet. Do everything quietly. Get close; go for the throat. Remember, do not hesitate. Hesitation will get you killed."

Aiden also freed her blade and looked at Venn. Rivulets of water ran down Aiden's face. She wiped at her eyes to clear her vision. The cloak she wore was hooded, but it was so soaked it could absorb no more water.

She started to stand but felt Venn's hand on her arm.

"Walk at a normal pace. Haste will only attract attention. Surprise is our ally." Venn stood and walked toward the door leading from the terrace to the interior.

The first room they entered was empty and dark. Venn stopped at the threshold and then signaled for Aiden to follow her. It was near the dinner hour so they reasoned any nobles on the premises would be in the great hall. That room was their target.

Aiden saw a man approach. He looked up, but before he could sound an alarm, Venn punched the short blade through his neck.

She covered his mouth and eased him to the floor, then retracted the blade and kept walking. Venn took out another man as they rounded the corner, stepping behind him, covering his mouth, and dragging him backward into the shadows as she sank her dagger in a sweeping motion across his esophagus.

They hadn't gone far when two men approached. So far, Venn had done all the work. They would have to strike almost in unison or risk exposure. Aiden waited for Venn to move and then she mirrored her. When the flesh and cartilage of the man's neck offered resistance against the thrust of the blade, Aiden leaned into it. The man collapsed and pulled her with him. She untangled herself and kept moving.

Venn paused and whispered to Aiden. "Now it gets tricky. The closer we move to the great hall the more opposition we're likely to encounter. Don't flinch. Don't withdraw. Be the sword."

"I'm ready."

As Aiden followed Venn down the wide corridor toward the great hall, the last lines of the poem came to her with searing clarity:

Who tells the ages of the moon, if not I?
Who shows the place where the sun goes to rest, if not I?
Who is she that fashions enchantments—
The enchantment of battle and the wind of change?

Aiden pulled her sword free as she strode with purpose. *I am the wind.*

CHAPTER FORTY-TWO

K athryn cringed as Balak ordered one of the servants to bring more wine. The boy couldn't have been more than fourteen. He cowered when Balak bellowed at him. Balak spoke to the boy as if he were part of some inferior race.

Balak was everything she'd heard he was and worse. Bitter and pathetic, he approached the world with childish contempt.

Kathryn couldn't decide which she loathed more, Frost for her duplicitous treachery or Balak for his insatiable greed for power.

The room was populated by others, but it was impossible to know their role in Balak's court. Some were dressed as noblemen, fat with wine and food. Some, apparently, only for the entertainment of others, like the small groupings of women who flirted with any man in the room who showed them attention. In the back of the hall at the last table, she spotted Miro and some of the men who'd been with Frost when they brought her from Olmstead. There were a few people seated at the head table who did nothing but flatter Balak and stroke his ego.

Frost sat at the end of the table near Kathryn, eating quietly and watching the room, as if she were waiting for something.

A sentry approached and whispered in Frost's ear. Frost rose and followed the sentry to the door.

Kathryn had been focused on a carving knife temptingly close to her plate. With Frost away from the table and Balak distracted, she took a sip of wine and at the same time, with her other hand, slid the knife off the carving block and up inside the sleeve of her dress. No one noticed. She was simply bait, so obviously no one considered her a threat, otherwise they would not have left sharp objects so easily within her reach.

Balak came over and took Frost's vacant seat. He casually took a chicken leg from Frost's half-eaten plate. His build was stocky, his hair gray at the temples, and his face scarred as if he'd suffered some burn on his left cheek. He leaned forward as he pulled meat from the bone with his teeth. He studied Kathryn, saying nothing, and she offered nothing.

She'd bathed, put on the dress Frost had provided, and she'd sat through Balak's wretched tirades during dinner. Since she'd arrived at Windsheer, she'd been scarcely conscious of her own misery because of her fear for Aiden. As she watched Balak chew, she fingered the cool edge of the knife inside her sleeve and visualized thrusting it through the fine fabric of his dinner attire, into his chest.

"So do think my niece will arrive soon?" He wiped his greasy thick fingers at the edge of the starched white tablecloth.

Kathryn didn't respond.

"It doesn't matter what you tell me or what you don't tell me. Your fate has been sealed and so has Aiden's." He leaned closer. "Who knows, maybe I'll keep you for a little while after I've dispatched Aiden, as a pet. You're very pretty. It's a shame to squander that when it's right under my own roof." He smiled, but it was the sort of smile that offered no comfort.

"What is to become of Olmstead?" Kathryn tried to keep her tone neutral, when what she really wanted to do was scream.

"Haven't you heard? Frost will assume control on my behalf. Second to the king, is that what you'd call it?"

Kathryn hadn't believed that Balak would relinquish even a small part of control to anyone, but Frost had apparently told her the truth.

The young servant who'd been sent to fetch wine returned. His hand shook as he refilled Balak's raised glass, spilling some. The deep red of the liquid ran down Balak's wrist to the cuff of his shirt. Balak exploded with rage. He struck the boy so hard that he fell to the floor and the earthen carafe of wine with him. The carafe broke apart, and the wine pooled on the stone tile like blood.

He struck the servant in the face with his fist and then kicked him across the floor as the boy tried to scuttle away from the blows. The people still seated for dinner laughed, talked, and continued eating. They showed no indication that they'd witnessed Balak's violent outburst or that it continued as the boy cried out. It was as if they purposefully looked anywhere but at the scene unfolding near the head table. The experience was surreal and desolate for Kathryn. She could no longer bear witness to the boy's abuse and had to look away.

CHAPTER FORTY-THREE

Venn had been right. They'd met with more resistance and were no longer able to quietly move through the castle. A sword fight with three men had ended with three dead and Aiden with blood on her shirt and face, but both she and Venn were unharmed. When they reached the outer vestibule of the great hall, Frost was waiting. Eerily, she stood alone, facing them. She pulled her broadsword free. Blood from Venn's sword dripped onto the floor as she faced off with Frost.

"Aiden, you get Kathryn. I'll take care of this." Venn pulled the axe she'd brought so that her sword was in one hand and the small axe in the other. Frost pulled a dagger from her belt with her free hand.

"I'll be with you in a minute, Aiden." Frost's lips cinched into a thin smile.

Venn moved between Aiden and Frost giving Aiden access to the large double doors of the great hall. She placed her hand against the rough wood of the heavy door. This was the moment of reckoning. She closed her eyes for just a second and whispered, *"I am the wind."*

As she pushed the door open, she heard Venn, calm and confident. "Let's dance, Frost."

The celebratory scene on the other side of the closed door was surreal. Outside, a battle raged. Inside, feasting, women, and song. At first, no one took notice of Aiden. She realized she was still wearing the dark cloak. She shucked it off her shoulders and let it fall in a heap to the floor. Still no one noticed her. Was she invisible or was everyone in Balak's court simply mad?

A woman walked past her and flirtatiously smiled and brushed her shoulder with her fingers as she passed. She wasn't invisible to everyone. She scanned the room for Kathryn and finally spotted her at the table on the raised platform at the front of the hall. And then she saw Balak at a seat very near Kathryn's.

She stood for a moment, tightening her grip on the sword handle. Despite the clamor of the room, a sense of calm washed over her. She felt something against her leg. When she looked down, she saw that she was not alone. The wolf had come. It looked around and snarled. Emboldened, Aiden took long strides toward the front of the hall. As she walked, she dragged the tip of her sword across the stone floor. The screeching sound silenced the revelers who turned to watch her. The wolf shadowed her, lunging and snarling at anyone who didn't step out of her path. As she got closer, she could see Kathryn, regarding her with wide eyes.

Aiden wanted to run to Kathryn, but instead she turned to face the crowd. She held her sword aloft and shouted.

"I am Aiden Roth, daughter of Edward Roth. I am the true heir to Belstaff, and I am here to claim my throne." Aiden's words echoed across the now silent room. The great white wolf circled her, pushing the crowd back. This time, others could clearly see the wolf because they were quick to move out of the animal's way each time it circled to expand the open space around where Aiden stood.

Someone slowly began to clap behind her. She turned to see that it was Balak. He stood and walked around the table. He took a sword from one of his guards as he passed by him. The other guards stationed around the head table edged closer. Aiden stood her ground.

One of the guards rushed at her, but the wolf intercepted him before he could reach Aiden. There were a few minutes of agonizing cries, and then the wolf backed away from the man's unmoving body, its white fur smeared with red.

At the sight of their comrade's mauled body, the other guards eased back a few steps. Aiden pointed her sword at them. "My quarrel is not with you. Stand down."

First one guard and then the other two dropped their swords and moved aside. Balak's face reddened with rage. "Get over here. Do your jobs!" He shouted at them, but they didn't move. He swung his sword wildly, skewering one of the men through the gut. When he turned back to face Aiden, his sword glistened red.

Aiden moved sideways up the steps of the raised platform. She wanted to put herself between Balak and Kathryn, who was now standing behind the table. Aiden reached for Kathryn's hand and pulled her away from the table. "Stay behind me."

"Oh, Aiden, you shouldn't have come."

"I will always come for you." Relief that Kathryn was unharmed gave Aiden the steadiness she required to focus on what she needed to do now—face Balak.

Balak must have realized that no one was going to come to his aid. This was a fight he would have to win by himself. His guests were huddled together as the wolf continued to pace back and forth, keeping anyone from approaching the stage. Aiden, Balak, and Kathryn were the only ones still standing on the raised platform.

"So, Aiden Roth has come home at last." He swung his sword, slicing it through the air a few times, and then leveled it at Aiden. "Too bad your visit will be so short."

She didn't respond to his taunts. Venn's admonishments to stay focused echoed in her head. *He will try to make you angry. Don't let him. You are in control, not Balak.*

They slowly circled each other. Balak lunged first, reaching across the space between them. Aiden dodged and then answered his thrust with a downward strike. He blocked the blow and they volleyed. Balak's attack was swift and aggressive. Aiden shifted behind one of the thick marble columns; he struck the rock and sparks flew. He cursed and threw a chair aside.

In a flurry, he went after her, finally backing her against the wall. She stilled his sword using the handle guard of hers, but he pressed close to her chest and spoke to her in a quiet voice.

"How dare you come here and proclaim to be the rightful heir. I will end you." She shoved him off and sidestepped. He was breathing hard. His age and poor physical condition was beginning to show.

Aiden glared at him through damp tendrils of hair that fell across her eyes. She would not let his words shake her. She would stay focused.

"It was so easy to poison her. She never suspected. So stupid, so naïve."

Aiden stopped moving and looked at him, her heart pounding in her chest.

"Oh, didn't you know?" He twirled his sword as if he were playfully pointing. "I poisoned your mother. Too bad I didn't think of it while you were still in her womb."

Something inside Aiden snapped. She rushed him. In a furious frenzy of arced strikes, she pushed Balak back until he stumbled over the chair he'd tossed aside earlier. He dropped to one knee then shoved the chair between them in an attempt to halt her advance. Aiden kicked the chair aside and swung downward. He caught her sword against the handle guard of his sword and then from his lower position pulled a small blade free and swung at her midsection.

She saw the smaller blade in his hand a fraction of a second before he tried to cut her in half with it. Aiden bowed outward as the razor sharp blade sliced the front of her shirt. She stepped back and looked down. A thin line of red seeped across the tear in her shirt. He'd just grazed the surface, but she'd felt it nonetheless. The pain was like a streak of lighting, scorching and precise. White-hot fury filled her senses. He'd drawn her close to kill her with a blade she didn't even know he had. He was still on one knee. She kicked his arm so hard that he dropped the knife and it skidded across the floor.

Balak was on his feet again, now with a sly grin spread across his face. It was too late when she realized what he was doing. He angled close to Kathryn and pulled her in front of his chest. His sword was in one hand and her throat in his other.

The wolf turned toward Balak, growled, and lowered its head as if it were about to attack. Aiden held her open palm toward the animal and eased forward with an intense focus on Balak. Every muscle in her body was coiled to launch onto him if he hurt Kathryn.

Miraculously, Kathryn produced a knife from her sleeve. It was only a carving knife, but when she sliced it across his wrist, he released her with a yowl, blood gushing from his arm.

"You bitch!" The unexpected attack unbalanced him.

Aiden sprang forward with a burst of quick strokes, and he tried to deflect the blows as he scuttled backward. He stumbled to a stop when his back hit the wall and, with one huge thrust, she drove her broadsword into his chest. Time suspended as he lowered his sword and grasped the blade protruding from his chest with his bloodied arm. His hand fell away and he sank to his knees. His mouth was open as if he wanted to cast one last barb, but his last utterance was nothing more than a sputtering raspy gasp.

His body thumped to the tile floor, unmoving, lifeless.

Kathryn looked around the room, prepared for someone to rush Aiden to avenge Balak, but no one moved. The room was cast in hushed silence. Kathryn ran to Aiden and held her close. "Oh, Aiden." She finally allowed the tears to come.

Aiden refocused her gaze as if she were slowly coming out of some fevered trance. Her eyes regained their focus, and she kissed Kathryn despite her tears. She touched Kathryn's face, rubbed her arms, and then kissed her again. "You're okay? You're not hurt?"

"No, but you are." Kathryn tugged at Aiden's torn and bloody shirt.

"It's not serious. It looks worse than it is."

"Spoken like a seasoned warrior." Venn climbed the steps toward them, her shirt was bloodied and torn also, but she appeared to be without serious injury.

Kathryn heard the sound of excited voices at the back of the room and looked up just as a sea of blue uniforms spilled into the great hall. A battalion of Olmstead troops had just arrived.

Kathryn looked from Venn to Aiden. "How did—"

"Rowan sent for them the morning you were taken." Aiden kissed Kathryn's temple.

And then something miraculous began to happen. The wolf sat on the floor near Aiden, and as they watched, light began to spread from every part of the wolf's fur, the wolf began to transform into a figure. But the light became so intense that Kathryn was forced to shield her eyes. Slowly, the light receded to a glow.

Aiden recognized the figure hallowed by soft white light. The figure was her mother. Isla smiled at Aiden and reached to touch her face.

"Mother." Aiden released Kathryn, and for the first time, embraced her mother. A feeling of warmth flowed through her body as her mother held her gently.

"I'm so proud of you, Aiden." Her mother's voice sounded like lyrical velvet. She turned to Kathryn and brushed her cheek with her fingers. "And you are Kathryn. I'm so happy that my Aiden has you in her life. Thank you for all that you have done for her."

Kathryn was speechless.

Then Isla turned to Venn, who was awestruck. Tears began to well up and run down her cheeks. Isla took Venn's face in her hands and kissed her on the lips. It was a sweet kiss, a lingering kiss, a good-bye kiss.

"Venn, you saved me, in ways that you cannot even know." Isla began to cry also. "I want you to be happy. I want you to allow yourself to love again."

Venn nodded mutely.

Isla took Venn's hand and Aiden's hand. Standing between them, the outline of her figure began to dim. The light ebbed. "I am going now, but remember, I am always with you."

Once the light was gone, the cavernous space seemed dark. Everyone present had witnessed the vision of Aiden's mother, and the wonder of it was evident on every face.

Someone in the crowd raised a cheer. "Long live, Aiden Roth! Long live, Aiden Roth! Long live, Aiden Roth!"

Aiden turned and pulled Kathryn into a hug as cheers and a cacophony of cheerful noise erupted around them. Encircled in Kathryn's embrace, Aiden felt insulated from it all. The room slipped away, her only focus the beautiful woman in her arms.

"Kathryn, I love you with all my heart."

Kathryn smiled up at her, the paths of tears glistening on her face. She held Aiden's face in her hands and kissed her tenderly. "Aiden Roth, I love you. I am yours."

She hugged Kathryn close, vowing silently to never let go.

EPILOGUE

Aiden stared out over the assembled crowd. Nobles from Olmstead and Belstaff gathered, along with commoners from both kingdoms so that the great hall at Windsheer was filled to capacity, standing room only.

Three months had passed since she'd entered the great hall, sword in hand, to claim what was hers by birth. She had been concerned that the residents of Belstaff wouldn't accept her as their monarch, but they'd rejoiced at Balak's demise and welcomed her with open arms. Of course, certain nobles loyal to Balak and a few members of the royal guard had been routed and exiled. But the average citizen of Belstaff celebrated Aiden's ascension to the throne.

The first month had been spent feeding and caring for the needy that had suffered as a result of Balak's greed and heavy taxation. Kathryn had generously opened the stores of food and grain in Olmstead to the needy in Belstaff.

Once basic needs were addressed, Aiden searched for the child of the man she'd seen beaten by Balak during her first visit to Belstaff. She'd been haunted by the scene. She still carried the regret of knowing she could have stopped what happened. The least she could do was care for the child, orphaned by the hand of Balak, as she had once been. The little girl's name was Renan. Aiden smiled at the child who stood near the front of the crowd with Nilah and Gareth. Gareth still had a scar on his lip, but otherwise he was back to good health. It would be a while before his wounded arm returned to full strength, but as he wrapped that arm around Nilah, a smile spread across his face. Aiden thought Gareth would never forgive her for falling in love with Kathryn, but maybe he was coming to terms with it. It seemed Nilah was helping him adjust.

Today, all who were present had come to Belstaff to celebrate her union with Kathryn. Their kingdoms would be joined in an alliance based on love. It had been decades since a royal wedding had been held in Windsheer Castle. This was a place in serious need of celebration.

Venn, wearing the crimson wool uniform of Belstaff's royal guard, stood at Aiden's left, watching the back of the great hall with her. Aiden's nervousness increased with each moment that delayed Kathryn's arrival. Finally, Brother Francis appeared in the entryway to the hall. He began to walk toward the raised podium at the front where Aiden and Venn waited. His slender bearded face seemed to hold nothing but pride and affection for Aiden on this day. Around his neck he wore a draped green sash that contrasted against his long dark robe.

A moment later, Rowan followed and began to walk slowly along the dark burgundy runner that stretched the length of the immense stone room. She wore a gown of blue silk, the color of Olmstead, and carried a small bouquet of fresh cut flowers. Rowan smiled at Aiden and Venn as she took her place across from Aiden, leaving room for Kathryn.

A hushed gasp of awe issued from the audience, and Aiden felt her own breath sucked from her lungs as Kathryn stepped into the great hall. She looked exquisite in a flowing white gown that trailed behind her as she walked slowly forward. Stringed instruments played some tune, but Aiden could hardly hear it for the blood pounding in her ears. She had to remind herself to breathe as Kathryn climbed the carpeted steps to take her hand. Kathryn looked to Rowan as she handed her flowers over so that she could hold Aiden's hands.

Kathryn could feel how nervous Aiden was as she entwined their fingers. She was nervous also, but at the same time at peace.

This seemed so incredibly right. Aiden was gorgeous in the crimson jacket Kathryn's tailor had made for her the night of the solstice celebration. For today's ceremony, a red sash bearing the Roth family crest was draped over her shoulder and across her chest. Aiden had tried to tame her wild dark hair, but errant curls hung loosely at her temple.

Their eyes met and held, the intensity of Aiden's gaze piercing her chest with a longing for them to be alone together, away from the crowd. The past week had been a blur of activity in preparation for the royal wedding, and she'd been in Olmstead making ready. She was craving Aiden's touch, her scent, and her lips.

Brother Francis began to speak, calling Kathryn's attention away from Aiden's handsome face.

"Please take each other's right hand." He paused for a moment while Kathryn adjusted and let her left hand fall to her side. "Kathryn and Aiden have chosen to seal their union with a traditional handfasting ceremony. This symbolic binding of the hands is intended as a sign of their commitment to one another." Kathryn looked down as Brother Francis draped a braided cord of blue and crimson around their joined hands. "The cords are not permanent but perishable as a reminder that all things of the material world eventually return to the earth, unlike the bond and the connection of love, which is eternal."

Kathryn looked at Aiden. Her eyes were glistening as she squeezed Kathryn's hand lightly.

"This is the hand of your best friend, strong and full of love for you. This hand holds yours on your wedding day, as you promise to love each other today, tomorrow, and forever." Brother Francis smiled warmly. "Kathryn and Aiden, look into each other's eyes. Will you honor and respect one another and seek to never break that honor?"

"We will," Kathryn and Aiden responded in unison.

"And so the first binding is made." He wrapped the first strand of the cord around their joined hands.

"Will you share each other's pain and seek to ease it?"

"We will."

"And so the second binding is made." The second strand was draped around their clasped hands.

"Will you share the burdens of each so that your spirits may grow in this union?"

"We will."

"And so the third binding is made." He wrapped the cord around once more. "Kathryn and Aiden, as your hands are bound together now, so your lives and spirits are joined in a union of love and trust. Above you are the stars and below you is the earth. Like the stars, your love should be a constant source of light, and like the earth, a firm foundation from which to grow."

Aiden's heart felt huge in her chest. It pressed against her lungs as she struggled to take slow, even breaths.

A tear trailed down her cheek as she listened to Brother Francis. "These are the hands that will work alongside yours as you build your future together. These are the hands that will hold you when fear or grief weigh upon your mind. These are the hands that will countless times wipe the tears from your eyes, tears of sorrow and tears of joy."

Aiden couldn't help smiling as Kathryn wiped the tear away gently with the thumb of her free hand.

"These are the hands that will give you strength when you need it, support and encouragement to pursue your dreams. And lastly, these are the hands that even when wrinkled with age will still be reaching for yours, still giving you the same unspoken tenderness with just a touch."

Brother Francis placed his hand over theirs, entwined with the braided cord. "May pure be the joys that surround you. May true be the hearts that love you." He squeezed their hands as he looked at Aiden. "You may kiss your bride."

Aiden regarded Kathryn with a sense of wonder. This magical, beautiful woman was her wife, her queen. She pressed her lips softly to Kathryn's and lingered there, time suspended, the air around them charged with electric particles of desire. As they separated, a cheer went up from the crowd. Aiden couldn't stop smiling.

Venn clapped Aiden on the back. "Well done. I'm so happy for both of you."

Rowan embraced Kathryn. She held the braided cord loosely, along with her bouquet. The music started up again, and food and wine were set on long tables for the wedding feast. The room was filled with joyful noise and chatter.

Aiden could hardly believe how much her life had changed since she'd left the safety of the monastery. She'd been rescued by Kathryn and then rescued Kathryn back. She'd discovered her heritage, met her mother, and claimed a birthright she hadn't even known was hers. But most importantly, she'd found love. True love. And that had changed her world more than anything else. A sense of belonging, a sense of being known, these were the things she felt enriched her life the most. Yes, she'd gained a kingdom, but the real treasure was Kathryn's love. She smiled and reached for Kathryn's hand.

"What are you smiling about?" asked Kathryn.

"About how Gareth used to call me the Prince of Nothing."

"You knew about that?"

"I overheard him say it more than once."

"Well, you are the prince of my heart now, which makes you the prince of everything." She kissed Aiden's cheek.

"I love you, Kathryn." She pulled Kathryn into a fierce kiss. Ignoring the fact that they had quite an audience who cheered and clanged glasses as Aiden felt her cheeks flame.

"This is just the beginning of the celebration, which won't last long if you kiss me like that again. I have plans for you for later, my love." Kathryn's eyes twinkled with a mischievous glint.

A woman that Aiden recognized from Olmstead touched Kathryn's arm, pulling her attention away. Aiden watched as Kathryn graciously chatted and held the woman's hand in hers.

It took all of Aiden's strength not steal Kathryn away to their private quarters. She would eat and drink and share the joy of this day with those who had gathered to honor their union, but it would be difficult not to rush the day's end. Aiden sipped wine and watched those around her as they took seats at the long table and servers delivered steaming plates of food.

How strange was the world, changed and new.

When she'd least expected it, destiny had found her. Fate had guided her to this place, to this day. She was happy, truly happy. Kathryn touched her shoulder lightly as she stood to greet someone else, and warmth spread down Aiden's arm and straight to her heart. This was what love felt like and she wanted to feel nothing else.

Aiden lifted her head finally and regarded the great hall. It was a microcosm of her kingdom, her birthright, changed as it was into something new, something different, the beginning of something beautiful. Something enchanted.

I am the wind.

About the Author

Missouri Vaun spent a large part of her childhood in southern Mississippi, before attending high school in North Carolina and college in Tennessee. Strong connections to her roots in the rural south have been a grounding force throughout her life. Vaun spent twelve years finding her voice working as a journalist in places as disparate as Chicago, Atlanta, and Jackson, Mississippi, all along filing away characters and their stories. Her novels are heartfelt, earthy, and speak of loyalty and our responsibility to others. She and her wife currently live in northern California. Vaun can be reached via email at: Missouri.Vaun@icloud.com

Books Available from Bold Strokes Books

Amounting to Nothing by Karis Walsh. When mounted police officer Billie Mitchell steps in to save beautiful murder witness Merissa Karr, worlds collide on the rough city streets of Tacoma, Washington. (978-1-62639-728-6)

Becoming You by Michelle Grubb. Airlie Porter has a secret. A deep, dark, destructive secret that threatens to engulf her if she can't find the courage to face who she really is and who she really wants to be with. (978-1-62639-811-5)

Birthright by Missouri Vaun. When spies bring news that a swordswoman imprisoned in a neighboring kingdom bears the Royal mark, Princess Kathryn sets out to rescue Aiden, true heir to the Belstaff throne. (978-1-62639-485-8)

Crescent City Confidential by Aurora Rey. When romance and danger are in the air, writer Sam Torres learns the Big Easy is anything but. (978-1-62639-764-4)

Love Down Under by MJ Williamz. Wylie loves Amarina, but if Amarina isn't out, can their relationship last? (978-1-62639-726-2)

Privacy Glass by Missouri Vaun. Things heat up when Nash Wiley commandeers a limo and her best friend for a late drive out to the beach: Champagne on ice, seat belts optional, and privacy glass a must. (978-1-62639-705-7)

The Impasse by Franci McMahon. A horse packing excursion into the Montana Wilderness becomes an adventure of terrifying proportions for Miles and ten women on an outfitter led trip. (978-1-62639-781-1)

The Right Kind of Wrong by PJ Trebelhorn. Bartender Quinn Burke is happy with her life as a playgirl until she realizes she can't fight her feelings any longer for her best friend, bookstore owner Grace Everett. (978-1-62639-771-2)

Wishing on a Dream by Julie Cannon. Can two women change everything for the chance at love? (978-1-62639-762-0)

A Quiet Death by Cari Hunter. When the body of a young Pakistani girl is found out on the moors, the investigation leaves Detective Sanne Jensen facing an ordeal she may not survive. (978-1-62639-815-3)

Buried Heart by Laydin Michaels. When Drew Chambliss meets Cicely Jones, her buried past finds its way to the surface—will they survive its discovery or will their chance at love turn to dust? (978-1-62639-801-6)

Escape: Exodus Book Three by Gun Brooke. Aboard the Exodus ship *Pathfinder*, President Thea Tylio still holds Caya Lindemay, a clairvoyant changer, in protective custody, which has devastating consequences endangering their relationship and the entire Exodus mission. (978-1-62639-635-7)

Genuine Gold by Ann Aptaker. New York, 1952. Outlaw Cantor Gold is thrown back into her honky-tonk Coney Island past, where crime and passion simmer in a neon glare. (978-1-62639-730-9)

Into Thin Air by Jeannie Levig. When her girlfriend disappears, Hannah Lewis discovers her world isn't as orderly as she thought it was. (978-1-62639-722-4)

Night Voice by CF Frizzell. When talk show host Sable finally acknowledges her risqué radio relationship with a mysterious caller, she welcomes a *real* relationship with local tradeswoman Riley Burke. (978-1-62639-813-9)

Raging at the Stars by Lesley Davis. When the unbelievable theories start revealing themselves as truths, can you trust in the ones who have conspired against you from the start? (978-1-62639-720-0)

She Wolf by Sheri Lewis Wohl. When the hunter becomes the hunted, more than love might be lost. (978-1-62639-741-5)

Smothered and Covered by Missouri Vaun. The last person Nash Wiley expects to bump into over a two a.m. breakfast at Waffle House is her college crush, decked out in a curve-hugging law enforcement uniform. (978-1-62639-704-0)

The Butterfly Whisperer by Lisa Moreau. Reunited after ten years, can Jordan and Sophie heal the past and rediscover love or will differing desires keep them apart? (978-1-62639-791-0)

The Devil's Due by Ali Vali. Cain and Emma Casey are awaiting the birth of their third child, but as always in Cain's world, there are new and old enemies to face in post Katrina-ravaged New Orleans. (978-1-62639-591-6)

Widows of the Sun-Moon by Barbara Ann Wright. With immortality now out of their grasp, the gods of Calamity fight amongst themselves, egged on by the mad goddess they thought they'd left behind. (978-1-62639-777-4)

18 Months by Samantha Boyette. Alissa Reeves has only had two girlfriends and they've both gone missing. Now it's up to her to find out why. (978-1-62639-804-7)

Arrested Hearts by Holly Stratimore. A reckless cop with a secret death wish and a health nut who is afraid to die might be a perfect combination for love. (978-1-62639-809-2)

Capturing Jessica by Jane Hardee. Hyperrealist sculptor Michael tries desperately to conceal the love she holds for best friend, Jess, unaware Jess's feelings for her are changing. (978-1-62639-836-8)

Counting to Zero by AJ Quinn. NSA agent Emma Thorpe and computer hacker Paxton James must learn to trust each other as they work to stop a threat clock that's rapidly counting down to zero. (978-1-62639-783-5)

Courageous Love by KC Richardson. Two women fight a devastating disease, and their own demons, while trying to fall in love. (978-1-62639-797-2)

Pathogen by Jessica L. Webb. Can Dr. Kate Morrison navigate a deadly virus and the threat of bioterrorism, as well as her new relationship with Sergeant Andy Wyles and her own troubled past? (978-1-62639-833-7)

Rainbow Gap by Lee Lynch. Jaudon Vickers and Berry Garland, polar opposites, dream and love in this tale of lesbian lives set in Central Florida against the tapestry of societal change and the Vietnam War. (978-1-62639-799-6)

Steel and Promise by Alexa Black. Lady Nivrai's cruel desires and modified body make most of the galaxy fear her, but courtesan Cailyn Derys soon discovers the real monsters are the ones without the claws. (978-1-62639-805-4)

Swelter by D. Jackson Leigh. Teal Giovanni's mistake shines an unwanted spotlight on a small Texas ranch where August Reese is secluded until she can testify against a powerful drug kingpin. (978-1-62639-795-8)

Without Justice by Carsen Taite. Cade Kelly and Emily Sinclair must battle each other in the pursuit of justice, but can they fight their undeniable attraction outside the walls of the courtroom? (978-1-62639-560-2)

21 Questions by Mason Dixon. To find love, start by asking the right questions. (978-1-62639-724-8)

A Palette for Love by Charlotte Greene. When newly minted Ph.D. Chloé Devereaux returns to New Orleans, she doesn't expect her new job, and her powerful employer—Amelia Winters—to be so appealing. (978-1-62639-758-3)

By the Dark of Her Eyes by Cameron MacElvee. When Brenna Taylor inherits a decrepit property haunted by tormented ghosts, Alejandra Santana must not only restore Brenna's house and property but also save her soul. (978-1-62639-834-4)

Cash Braddock by Ashley Bartlett. Cash Braddock just wants to hang with her cat, fall in love, and deal drugs. What's the problem with that? (978-1-62639-706-4)

Lightning Source UK Ltd.
Milton Keynes UK
UKOW03f1412090317
296246UK00001B/111/P